Francena Hallett's Heart

A Novel of Romances and Revenge

Robert W. Spencer

To my late father, Robert Wilson Spencer, Sr., a lifelong gardener, who taught me how plants grow and how to use a shovel.

Acknowledgments

Once again I am so grateful to my initial editing team: Doreen, Kay and Geraldine, my love. To Nancy Marcotte and other members of the Waterford Historical Society for their history books and archives. To the staff at Maine Authors Publishing, especially Nikki, Dan, Genie and Michelle for making this beautiful book.

1: Prologue

Aphia Stevens is bored to distraction. In seven months confined to the Maine State Prison in Thomaston, she has been forced to mend blankets, a task she hates. All day, a matron armed with a sawed-off broom handle keeps track of her and the five other inmates who sit at a large table using darning eggs and needles to repair holes worn by prisoners in rough woolen blankets. Aphia's fingers are worn and calloused, her hands often twisted in muscle spasms. Occasionally another woman would throw her work on the table and stand up to stretch. Unless it is time for everyone to rest, something only allowed every two hours, the guard bangs the violator's chair with the club and forces her back into place.

I bet these holes are made by the *men*, Aphia thinks. They are such animals. No woman would let herself get so dirty as to use a blanket smelling of piss and sweat.

Her eyes ache all the time. Two dim lights hang from the ceiling so high above her head that she can barely make out the directions of her cross stitches. Little light comes through the windows, which are covered by outside shutters or hoods so that male prisoners in the exercise yard would not be able to look in and see the women. If a man were bold or drunk enough to stand outside a window and shout lewd comments, the women might try to ignore him. One time, a tall girl no more than seventeen or eighteen had screamed back obscenities only to be slapped across the face by the bully matron and led out of the room in handcuffs. She had yet to return.

Each morning before going to the workroom, the five women are led in single file from their cold cells in the oldest part of the eighty-year-old institution. In a musty kitchen, they get weak coffee and hard biscuits for breakfast. At the end of each ten-hour day, they are marched back to that same room for a supper of soup or watery stew and slices of stale bread. After months of such an existence, they are all as thin as fence posts.

"Stevens," bellows the matron, "pick up the pace there! You have been working on that same blanket for two days. Can't be that badly damaged. If you don't do your part here, we can always send you to the laundry room."

Go to hell, Aphia thinks. The change might do me some good.

The woman next to her whispers, "You don't want to go down there, darlin'. Especially with summer coming. Hot as hell there in the summer."

Aphia smiles at the guard through tightly clenched teeth and forces her hands to move faster. She wants so badly to do something else. Perhaps working in the kitchen would be better. She has plenty of time to figure out where it would be best to work. After all, she is here for the rest of her life, thanks to Lizzie Millett and her goddamn family. If those meddlers had only paid attention to their own lives instead of ruining hers, she wouldn't be in prison. But her being behind bars wouldn't keep them safe from her revenge.

2

Maeve Cain hurried along the foot path which led past Mr. Pride's granite quarry toward Lizzie Millett's large raised cape. Her crimson curls bobbed around her shoulders as she ran. Seeing her dear friend sitting on the front porch, she shouted out with joy.

"Lizzie, dear! My sister Mary is coming home. Can you believe it? After all these years."

She leaped the four steps to the porch in two strides.

"Maeve, girl, don't hurt yourself. Slow down a bit and sit with me," cautioned her friend.

"Mary is coming back from Ireland! How exciting!" said Maeve. "This is the best news I've had since my Will was killed. She wants to live with me and the kids. As God is my witness. Here, read the letter. It came just minutes ago. I had to share the news with you."

Putting on her reading glasses, Lizzie attempted to read the letter.

"Maeve, I can't make out the writing. You know how my eyes are failing. Please read it to me."

"I shall. I surely shall. She mentions you so many times. And how much she has missed us both."

Dearest Maeve,

My darling Sister. Many's the time I have thought we would never be together again on God's good Earth. The ten years since I waved farewell to you and sweet Lizzie on the train platform in Portland seem a lifetime. Now that Dad has left us for a better world, the thought of being alone in Lis-

3

doonvarna for the rest of my life makes me sad. Brother Patrick and his wife are moving into this little house. There is no room for me, although they say there is. I might take a room in town, but then I would just molder away.

I so wish to feel your and Lizzie's arms wrapped around me. You are the dearest people in the world. Memories of you both have made my days here happy and filled my dreams at night. Sister, you have told me in your letters how sad life is without your darling Will. There never was a better man. And Liz has lost her dear husband. Perhaps there is room in your lives for me.

A new ocean liner, the RMS *Adriatic*, sails from Liverpool on 5 July. I have booked a small cabin. Surely the accommodations will be much more luxurious than the bunk I had on that scow out of Boston a decade ago. The brochure says they have a swimming pool and Turkish bath. My nose will be so high in the air when I arrive in Westbrook! The crossing to New York takes 5–8 days, depending on weather. I will wire you the day we sail and again when I arrive in the USA.

I have so much love for you and for Lizzie.

Best Regards,
Your Mary

"I must share this news with the children," laughed Maeve. "Only Faith and Janey are old enough to have clear memories of their aunt. Perhaps Owen, but he was only a toddler."

As Maeve left, Lizzie wiped tears from her eyes and sat back in her chair.

My dear, dear Mary, she thought. I pray for your safe passage back.

3

Aphia lay awake on the cot in her cell. A wild dream woke her, a dream which some would consider a nightmare.

Potter, the miner who lives in her farmhouse, sits at a desk in a mine head house checking record books. On the floor beside him, a young boy, perhaps his son, plays in the center of a circle of empty wooden buckets turned upside down. The boy is throwing small stones at each bucket. When a stone lands and stays on top of a bucket, he claps, runs to the bucket and turns it right side up. It is a dream she has had at least once before. Perhaps more than once. The last time, there was a fire at the end.

This time the end is different. As the child continues to play his game, he throws larger and larger stones until one as large as his head lands on a bucket, crushing it. Suddenly the building begins to shake and rattle as if an earthquake has hit. The miner, fearing that his son is causing the commotion, stands and strikes the boy across the face, knocking him into a wall. The wall collapses and the roof falls on the miner's head. Just as the entire building falls in on the man, the boy crawls out of the building and escapes. The miner is trapped and dies.

A smile came to Aphia Stevens's face as she stared at the dim light bulb hanging from the ceiling. She knew that something good had happened. Though she couldn't be sure what it was, it was something which pleased her.

4

Lottie Adelaide Potter set sandwiches for her two boys in brown clay plates on their large kitchen table. Five-year-old Con drank deeply from his milk glass, then grabbed the bread and blueberry preserves with both hands. Two-year-old Francis sat in the mahogany highchair her late father, John, had given to the family. The little one pulled the sandwich apart, rubbing preserves all over his face. As she wiped the mess off his face, sunlight streaming through the large southern window over her soapstone sink lit his face. He was the spitting image of her husband, Clarence.

Clarence had gone to Canada five months before to pursue one more get-rich-quick scheme, one more of his hare-brained fantasies that a fortune might be dug out of the bowels of the earth with very little effort. After all the failures, mine closings, moves from town to town to follow the dream, she had put her foot down. If he left her to find silver in Ontario, she would never forgive him. He went anyway, saying that he would let her know of his success. She had heard nothing. The baby moved in her belly, and she reached under her shift to feel it kick. In two months' time there would be a third mouth to feed.

There was a knock at the door and, when she opened it, she saw her husband's friend, Dr. Hiram Francis Abbott. He wore a three-piece riding suit of worsted wool fabric, despite the warm weather, and carried a short riding crop. When he removed his hat, dust rose into the air around his head.

"Dr. Abbott, you look a mess. Have you been riding hard?"

"Yes, my dear. I have news for you. I'm afraid it isn't good."

She knew already what his news would be.

"It's about Clarence, isn't it?"

"Please step outside with me, Mrs. Potter, away from the children."

"You can tell me whatever it is in front of the whole family."

He hesitated for a moment, drew a handkerchief from his vest pocket and blew his nose before starting.

"I have heard from a business acquaintance, Mr. Albert Warren in Ohio, that your Clarence was killed in a mine tram accident nearly five months ago. Warren used to be his employer before you moved down here to Maine. He has kept in contact with him over the years and was informed of the accident by an associate who operates a silver mine in Ontario."

Lottie said nothing. She showed little reaction, only turned to the boys to make sure they were eating. When she turned back to him, tears were running down both cheeks and her face was red.

"I thank you, Dr. Abbott, for delivering this news to me. It brings to conclusion the uncertainty I have been feeling. Has he been buried already?"

"Yes, ma'am. Apparently, when his body was discovered, he had been dead for a few days and was buried immediately. I am sorry to bring such ghastly news to you."

"Not really so ghastly. It was expected. He had left me forever. I knew it was permanent."

"My dear, please accept this payment from sale of the Beech Hill mica mine. It is Clarence's and now your share. It should be enough to help with the children." Handing her an envelope, he noticed her abdomen. "Are you expecting another?"

"Yes, in September." She pushed the unopened envelope into her apron pocket. "Thank you. I'm sure it will help. Now, would you be so kind as to leave us alone. I want to explain this to my boys."

5

Next day, Lottie hitched her small carriage to a quarter horse borrowed from her neighbor John Kimball, secured the boys into the seat beside her with rope, and ventured out to visit her friends, the Halletts in Bridgton. She didn't know if anyone would be home, but she was willing to wait until someone arrived. She wanted to share news of her predicament.

The road to North Waterford was a washboard from recent downpours, making progress slow. Once on Valley Road, conditions improved somewhat, and she was able to reach Bridgton in three hours. Pulling up to the big house on South High Street, she saw that the barn door was open, a sign that someone was there.

Nathan and Hattie's son Nate stood at the door with a shovel in his hands. He wore blue jeans and a shirt soaked with sweat. In the year since she had last seen him, he had become a handsome young man.

"Lottie Adelaide," he greeted her as he approached the wagon. Seeing that she had some difficulty maneuvering herself from the seat, he gave her a hand down. "What a surprise to see you."

She untied Francis and carried him up onto a large porch which wrapped around the house. Nate lifted Con, placed him on the ground and led him by the hand to join his brother.

"My mom and dad are not here right now. They went to visit Franny at Aunt Liz's in Westbrook. Should be home any time now. Is there anything I can get you or the boys?"

"Nate, would you be so kind as to get the boys some water? Then we can all sit here in the sun to rest. It was a long trip."

Lottie sat with the boys on the long porch swing while Nate leaned against the wood railing.

"Nate, my Clarence has died. He was killed in an Ontario mining accident. Crushed under a mine tram." She spoke slowly and calmly, as if the news had little to do with her.

"No! Oh, I am so sorry for your loss." He reached for her hand, but then held back as she continued.

"Thank you. Yes, it is a loss. Not really a surprise. I knew he would never be coming back."

Not knowing what to say, the young man stood and began to rock nervously from side to side still holding the railing. He wasn't sure he wanted to get into any further particulars with his sister Franny's best friend.

"Lottie, please rest here in the warm sun while I finish my chores in the barn. My parents should be returning very soon."

"Yes, yes. Of course. You have been so kind to help me."

Returning to the barn, Nate stared back at the Potters. Lottie picked up the younger boy and held him to her chest just above the belly which held her third child. How sad, he thought. She will be raising her children alone, just like Maeve. How does a single mother handle all that?

6

By the time Hattie and Nathan Hallett returned, the afternoon sun had moved to the west, casting a shadow on the front porch. Their visitors had moved into the parlor, where both boys slept on a plush red Victorian sofa while their mother read a fashion magazine. Nate had moved Lottie's wagon and horse into the barn and was sitting on the porch.

"Mom, Lottie and her boys are here. Clarence had a terrible accident. He is dead."

Not believing her ears at first, Hattie looked at him with a questioning expression. "What did you say?"

Lottie came to the open door and said quite loudly, "Yes, Hattie, Clarence is dead. He died in Canada. I told him not to go. He wouldn't listen."

Hattie rushed up the stairs and took the younger woman in her arms. She hugged her gently, so as not to press too hard on her belly.

"My dear, how sad! I am so sorry to hear this. Please come inside and sit down."

"No, I want to let the boys sleep. They don't need to hear all that I have to say. Clarence ran off to find buried treasure once again, even after I warned him something would happen and he might never return. I told him that Aphia would make something happen to him. She has powers that we do not understand, and I feared for his safety."

Nathan entered the room. "What type of accident was it?"

"A mine tram tipped over on him. Then a shack collapsed, crushing him to death. The mine owner found him a few days later. Had to bury him up there." As she told the story tears came to her eyes.

"What a tragedy. How did you find out?"

"Dr. Abbott rode down from Bethel to tell me."

"Dear, please sit here on the swing next to me," said Hattie, taking her hand. "You need to get off your feet. They must be swelling. Mine always did when I was pregnant."

Through her tears, Lottie continued. "He wouldn't listen. I told him that witch would hurt us all again. She killed her husband. Killed Maeve's Will. Now she has taken my Clarry. She has cursed us all."

"Please sit with Hattie for a while, until you are able to calm yourself," said Nathan. "I daresay his death was more his own doing, rather than the deed of an imprisoned woman, no matter how evil she might be."

7

Seamstress Lizzie Millett sat on a tall stool at her drawing table working on a design for a custom-ordered wedding dress. Above her head hung a three-foot-square work light, yet she still had to squint at the lines drawn on bright white draft paper. Scattered on the floor around her lay crumpled scraps of the same paper.

"Darn," she whispered to herself. "I'm only forty-five. Why can't I see the lines? Have to get more light."

Years of close work making the dresses and other garments for which Millett's American Designs was known had left her with failing eyesight. She recalled how clear her vision had been when she first worked in the Pepperell mill in Biddeford a quarter century before. It was only in the last couple of years that she had begun to use a magnifying glass. Recently, most of the detail work had been given over to her niece, Francena Hallett, who was becoming a better craftsperson than she herself had ever been.

A loud ringing sounded from the second-floor apartment. It was so loud that she dropped the pencil and stood up suddenly.

Oh, she thought as she sat back down, I can't get used to that telephone machine. After two months, you would think it wouldn't shock me so to hear that alarming sound.

Her niece shouted down from the apartment. "Auntie, it's Daddy. He wants to speak with you."

Leaving the table and climbing the stairs, Lizzie walked across an oriental rug, took the earpiece from Franny, and held it to her ear. She leaned against the back of a green velvet winged sofa.

"Nathan. Hello to you, too. I guess you got home all right. How was the road?"

"Oh, fine for springtime. Liz, I am afraid I have some bad news. I didn't tell Franny because I am afraid it will severely depress her to hear it. Please keep this to yourself for now."

"Hold on a minute, Nathan, while I have a word with your daughter."

"Franny, would you kindly do me the favor of taking a look at that design on the table. I can't seem to put the waist in the right place. It's my darn eyes. I'll be down in a moment."

Once Franny disappeared into the workshop, Liz returned to the conversation. "What is the news, Nathan?"

"Clarence Potter has died. Lottie has just come here to tell us. She thought that Franny might be here to console her."

"How horrible," Liz said in a quiet voice, so as not to be overheard. "How did it happen?"

"He was crushed to death in a mining accident in Canada. Lottie would like to come see you both and tell you personally. Please let her share the news with Franny. It would be better that way. You know how sensitive my daughter can be about such things."

"You have my promise on that. When will she come?"

"I will have her there for dinner tomorrow. She and her two boys. She drove a wagon here herself, but she looks to be nearly ready to deliver the third. I will drop her off."

"So, I will see you tomorrow. Goodbye, dear Nathan."

When she returned to the dress shop, Franny was hard at work completing the drawing. When asked what Nathan had to say, Lizzie said only that Lottie and the boys were coming for a visit, which made her niece very happy.

8

The dreary day dawned with heavy windswept rain, the trees swaying into each other. All morning, water drained off the Forest Avenue pavement, turning the drainage gullies on either side into turbulent rills. Francena could hardly wait to see her best friend again after so many months, but rather than wait on the damp porch, she stayed in the front parlor, reading *The Virginian*, a novel Lizzie had recently given her. As she read about the adventures of a tall, dark-haired, handsome cowboy who worked on a ranch in Wyoming, she nearly forgot about her friend. The hero, whose name is never revealed in the book, falls in love with Molly Stark Wood, a schoolteacher from Vermont. The hero was arguing with a poker player across the table from him when the sound of a carriage entering the driveway jarred Franny back into reality.

Dropping the book face down on the sofa, she hurried to the door. Before she could open it, Lottie threw it back and rushed into the room to grab her young friend in a bear hug.

"Franny girl, I couldn't wait to hug you and give you the biggest kiss. How long it has been! So much has happened. You can't believe it."

"Lottie, please let me go. Let me look at you. You are more beautiful than the last time we were together. And look how big the baby is! Please, come sit down on the sofa. You must be exhausted."

Nathan entered the room, cradling young Francis in one arm and leading Con by the hand. Franny took the young one from him and kissed her dad on the cheek.

"Dad, sit for a spell. You must be tired, driving in weather like this."

"It's not too bad. The sun has broken through just now. I told your mother I'd be home tonight. I must away. Please come out and get their bags."

As father and daughter went back to the carriage, he said in a soft voice, "Be as understanding as possible with her. I know that you had some serious problems with her marriage to Clarence,

12

but don't let that keep you from consoling her. It's what she needs now."

"What happened, Dad? Has he left her for good?"

"She has come all this way to tell you the story. You'll know soon enough. Now, call me when she is ready to return. I'll be working at home for the next few days."

Before Francena could press him for more information, he passed three satchels down to her, leaped onto the carriage seat, and waved goodbye. She turned in a huff and climbed the steps carrying the heavy bags up the stairs.

"What is going on?" Franny demanded. "What is such a secret that Dad wouldn't speak of it?"

Lottie knew by the look on her friend's face that the story needed to be told immediately. "Hush, Franny. Don't disturb the boys. Come into the next room where we can talk in private," she said as she walked into the office and closed the door behind them.

"It's Clarence, isn't it? Something has happened to him. Has he left you?"

"Yes, left me for good. He has died."

"What? How?"

"He was crushed to death in a mine train accident at a silver mine up in Ontario. Happened a few months ago. I only heard about it the day before yesterday."

"My God! How could he do this to you? You have the two boys. A third on the way. What will we do?"

Lottie sat on a tall stool behind Lizzie's drawing table. She was not crying. Placing the palms of both hands on her belly she spoke calmly.

"You know I didn't tell him about the new one. I left it to him to decide whether he wanted to be with me without any guilt he might feel about my pregnancy. If he decided to stay for that reason only, then he would have left sometime in the future. Better that he made the decision than have it hanging over our heads. What difference does it make whether I have two or three children?"

Franny paced back and forth in front of a floor-to-ceiling window, her shadow changing length as she moved. Finally, she stopped and stood close enough to her friend that their faces nearly touched.

"I warned you years ago, didn't I? Before you married him. Warned you about his character. He has always been out for his own good. You believed he was honest and loyal."

"I know you did. And now I see that I was blind to his weaknesses. If only I had listened to you. When you told me that he stole gems from the mine in Bethel and gold from his employer in Nova Scotia, I didn't believe you. Thought he was out to help me and his other children from the first marriage up in Canada."

"He was only out to prove that he was smarter than every-one else. That he could get rich quicker than anyone else. Had nothing to do with charity."

By now both friends were standing at the window, staring out at the front lawn and the traffic on Forest Avenue. Their shadows merged on the floor behind them. Neither was crying or speaking a word.

9

After dinner, Francena and Lizzie sat on the porch. The three Potters were already in bed. It had been a very long day for them.

"Auntie, I hate to leave you for even the shortest of times," said Franny, "but Lottie needs some help right now. She can't be alone with a baby about to come."

"My dear, you must go, though your help here in the shop will be missed. Take as much time as you need. Once the dresses for the Falmouth wedding party are completed, there is very little else to do. If new orders come in, I will ask your mother to help. Or perhaps Mary Flaherty when she arrives."

"Thank you for being so understanding. I'll make a phone call to Dad and arrange for him to bring the bigger carriage to carry me back to Waterford along with the others. Nate can return her wagon at some point."

They were startled by a noise coming from the second-floor apartment. A window over the porch slammed open and Lottie's head appeared.

"Please, come quick! Help me! My water has broken. I'm about to have my baby."

Both women jumped from the seat and headed for the door. Lizzie took charge of the situation, knowing that her niece was likely to panic.

"Francena, run over to see if Maeve is at home. She has five kids. She must know something about giving birth. Take the two boys with you. Her daughter Janey will take care of them. I'll go upstairs and tend to Lottie. When I have her settled, I'll call Dr. Rowan to see if he can come."

As Liz climbed the stairs, she thought back to a time in South Waterford more than been thirty-five years before. Following a blizzard, she was trapped in her father's farmhouse with her pregnant stepmother, Rose. How was it that she had helped deliver her stepsister? She remembered following instructions shouted out by Rose. If only she could remember how it went. Well, Maeve would know.

"Lizzie, please do something!" hollered Lottie, who had come out into the hallway. Her dress was soaked. She stood in a puddle of her own fluids.

"Girl, get back in the room and lie down on the bed. Take off that dress right now."

"On the bed? I'll make such a mess of it."

"Get out of that dress and lie down on the bed. Do it right now!"

Following orders, Lottie stripped off her dress and slip before sitting on the bed. She was unable to lift her legs, so Liz lifted her feet and swung them over. There was a circle of blood on the quilt where she had been sitting.

Liz could think of nothing to do but draw a pot of water and heat it to boiling. That was one thing she remembered from that first time. On the way to the kitchen, she grabbed the telephone and rang the operator.

"Linda, hello. I have an emergency here. A girl is having a baby in my bedroom. I need you to ring Dr. Rowan. He must come quickly. Can you do that for me?"

Maeve and Franny rushed up the stairway and into the kitchen.

"Maeve, please help me do something. Poor Lottie is in such pain. Something must be wrong to have the baby come this early. I've asked for the doctor to come, but he may be too late. Can we birth the child?"

The three women ran to the bedroom with Maeve in the lead. She turned to Franny. "Make some clean rags. Cut up a clean sheet into strips. When the water boils, bring me the rags and water. Also, I will need a very sharp carving knife. No, better to bring a pair of those large sharp shears you use for dressmaking. Those will work."

"Are we going to deliver the baby by ourselves?" said Franny.

"I'm not sure. Just in case, we need to prepare."

They heard a loud cry. And then a second. The three of them looked at each other in fright. Franny began to cry and run toward the bedroom.

"No, dear," said Liz. "You have your orders. We two will see to your friend."

Maeve knelt on the floor beside the bed and took firm hold of Lottie's hand.

"Lottie, listen carefully to me. Liz has asked the doctor to come. Until then, we will do our best. You must start to breathe deeply over and over. I know your contractions are painful. Remember, I have been through this a few times. There is no way to stop the pain. You must concentrate on breathing deeply in between each one."

"Oh, no," groaned Lottie through gritted teeth. "The contractions are coming one after another. I think the baby is coming— *now*. I know it. Please help."

Again, she cried out, but this time not as loudly. She squeezed Maeve's hand so hard that she cried out. Then Lottie started to breathe deeply.

"That's the way, girl. In and out, over and over. It will help," said Maeve as she rubbed Lottie's stomach. Something was wrong. It felt to her that the baby's head was in the wrong place, in the top of the womb instead of down toward the birth canal. She turned to Liz and gestured for the two of them to step into the hall.

"There's a problem," she whispered. "I think she is having a breech birth, where the baby is upside down. It never happened to me, thank God. But it can be pretty serious."

"What can we do? If the doctor doesn't show up soon, you and I are going to have to do this. Can we, without risking her life? Or the baby's?"

"Lizzie, we have no choice. She's releasing the baby right now. It's up to us."

Liz shouted down the stairs. "Francena Hallett, where are you with the rags and water? What is taking so long?"

"Auntie, the doctor is here!" Franny hollered from the bottom of the stairs.

Both Maeve and Liz breathed a deep sigh of relief. They moved to either side of the bed, each holding onto one of Lottie's hands.

"Dear, the doctor is here. Keep breathing deeply and push when the pain starts," instructed Maeve. She got no answer from the patient who only rolled her eyes. When Dr. Rowan entered the room, his nurse, Virginia Regan, was with him. Maeve met them at the door.

"Sir, I believe she has a breech baby. You can feel the head at the top. She is contracting every two or three minutes."

The doctor nodded in understanding. "Nurse Regan, please sanitize the forceps. This may be quite difficult. The baby is not in vertex position. Administer laudanum immediately."

Gently, he spread Lottie's legs and felt the opening of the birth canal. The baby's bottom was beginning to push through. "It is a frank breech. Thank God," he said. "We must move quickly."

Franny was in shock, standing there with her hands on either side of her head. She moaned and rocked back and forth. Lizzie grabbed her about the waist and led her out of the room.

Maeve watched for several more moments before joining them in the hallway.

"Auntie, birth isn't always like this, is it?" Franny asked "She is in such pain!"

It was Maeve who answered. "No. My deliveries have all been much easier. There has been discomfort, but nothing approaching this. When I was a toddler in Clare, I remember my aunt having a breech birth. It is a rare thing, thanks be to God." She made the sign of the cross. "Do not let this discourage you from having children, Francena. My children are a blessing to me, worth a moment of pain."

After a few minutes, Nurse Regan came to the three women. "Ladies, I am sorry to say that we have lost the baby girl. Her umbilical cord was twisted and prolapsed, cutting off her oxygen supply. Mother is fine. Somewhat worse for wear, but she'll recover in a few days with proper care."

"Oh, no," sighed Franny. "How sad."

"It's for the best," said Regan. "If the baby had survived, she would never have been quite right."

All three women slumped against the walls, then slipped down to sit on the floor, totally exhausted. "Francena," said Lizzie, "you will have your work cut out for you for a few days. Your dear friend will need a lot of care"

10

Lizzie had grown accustomed to the quiet of her big house. In the two years since the Potter family, after staying with her temporarily, had moved out of the third-floor apartment into their own home in Waterford, she and Francena had lived by themselves. There had been several visits from sister Hattie. Maeve and her wonderful children were around on occasion. Nathan was also a regular visitor for short stops on his way to and from business appointments.

How suddenly things had changed. Lottie was laid up after

her trauma, having to stay in bed for an unknown length of time, with Franny serving as her nurse. The two boys had become Lizzie's responsibility. This morning, Con was running in circles around the parlor, while Francis sat on the floor cheering him on. It was all she could do to keep them from jumping up and down on the furniture, but it did make her feel good to have others share her space once again.

In several days, her old friend Mary Flaherty would be returning to live with Maeve and the children. Memories of wonderful times spent with both Flaherty sisters over the many years of their friendship came back to her as she sat in the sunny parlor. Maeve was surely a good friend, and Mary had always been a favorite. The thought that they would be able to spend many hours together once again brought a smile to her lips.

"Auntie," called Franny from the second floor landing, "Lottie is so much better today. She has asked for the boys to visit. Is that okay?"

"Of course. Come on, boys. Your mother wants to see you."

Con stopped running and looked up at her. "Auntie Liz, is Mommy all better?" He took his younger brother by the hand.

"Not all better yet, Con. But soon she'll be taking you home. Not too many more days."

"Will Daddy be there at home?"

"You will have to ask your mother about that, Con."

11

Mary Flaherty stepped off the B&M Express onto the Union Station platform, which was deserted except for two men painting the exterior walls of the station office. As she waited for her bags to be unloaded from the freight car, she walked up to the closed ticket window. Though she had expected the train station in a city like Portland to be teeming with travelers, it was as empty as a bus stop in the village of Gort, County Galway near where she had been living for ten years.

"Pardon me, fellas," she said to the painters. "Is there anyone about who might help tote me bags to the tarmac out front?"

They looked at her with questioning smiles and said nothing. She was clearly a foreigner, and by her accent, they guessed she was Irish. The heavy tweed of her long coat was rough, like the homespun material not seen by them in many years. Her red tresses, streaked with gray, hung loose beneath an old-fashioned pale-blue bonnet tied beneath her chin with a green ribbon.

"Miss, there might be a porter inside the office. Why don't you tap on the ticket window to see? The sign says closed, but I know someone is in there," said the taller of the two men.

The shorter one, with a full beard and hair nearly as long as hers, only grunted and turned his face away.

"What's with you, Amos?" said the first man. "Ain't you ever seen a Mick woman before? I'm told they are very flirtatious."

"Listen, lady," the other began. "We have enough of your people around here. More than enough, if you ask me. Why don't you just stay on the platform with your stuff and catch the next train to Canada. They like your kind up there."

Mary stared in shock at his words, although the sentiments were not foreign to her. She had heard them many times when she and Maeve had first come to America. When they worked in Biddeford at the Pepperell Mill, male supervisors had berated them and the other factory girls who came from foreign countries. Even some factory workers from Maine abused her verbally, calling her all sorts of names, usually behind her back. That had been nearly thirty years ago.

She turned away and tapped on the ticket window. A tall man in a dark-blue uniform slid the window aside. "Yes, ma'am. What can I do for you?"

"Sure, I would be lookin' for someone to help with a cart to get me trunk and bags to the street. Me sister is to be at the curb in front."

"Well, you can just get your sister to help you, colleen," said the man as he slammed the window in her face.

Upon arrival in the port of Boston, she had been so confused by the bustle and crowds that she was unsure how to get from Commonwealth Pier to North Station to catch her train. People had been so helpful. She had expected that the people in Maine would be just as kind. In Boston, a policeman had hailed her a wagon to get from the harbor to the train. The wagon driver had politely assisted with her luggage, especially the heavy trunk, and when she offered him a tip, he refused. He said that he himself had once been an immigrant.

Mary decided to ignore the animosity of the painters as much as possible. She piled her smaller bags on top of the trunk and began to push it across the platform to a door marked EXIT. When her hat fell off, she picked it up and tucked it into her satchel. Then she decided it might be easier to pull the trunk toward the door by its leather handle. That worked much better, so that soon she had backed up to the door.

The long-haired man turned toward her and laughed. "Don't let the door hit your ass on the way out, missy."

When she reached the curbside, beads of sweat covered her forehead. Off came the warm coat. She tried to straighten the hat, then decided it looked so bad that it could stay in her satchel. If only Maeve would show up soon.

Maeve and Liz traveled in Will's old buckboard to meet Mary's train. Both were so exhilarated by her return that they had chattered every minute along the twelve-mile route from Westbrook. It was a hot day, but as they approached the city, a sea breeze brought with it the refreshing coolness of the harbor at high tide.

When they reached the big station on St. John Street, Mary was the only passenger standing on the sidewalk in front. Her luggage was piled in a haphazard jumble. She held her hat in one hand and a large satchel in the other. Her friends were dismayed at her appearance, but still, they were overjoyed.

Maeve jumped from the bench seat, ran across the pavement, and threw her arms around her sister, knocking the satchel to the ground. Liz joined them, after tying the horse to a hitching post. The three ladies embraced each other, laughing and crying with joy.

Liz was the first to step back from the embrace and speak. "Mary, I have missed you so. You're as lovely to look at as you were when you left. Ireland must have suited you well."

"Sure, it did, lovey. Sure, it did. Yet t'would have been more suitable if you had been with me. And look at you, dear Maeve. You've not lost the fire in your eyes." She grabbed both sides of her sister's face and pulled it toward her before giving her a big kiss on the mouth.

"Mary, whatever happened to you? Why are you out here on the sidewalk and not in the station waiting room?" asked Maeve.

"I wasn't going to wait with those arrogant blokes inside. Must have been me accent or style of dress. No one would help me, so I dragged the fuckin' stuff on my own."

"I will go find them and give them a piece of my mind," said Lizzie. "We've come a long way since the 'No Irish Need Apply' days, haven't we?"

"No, dearie. Don't get into any trouble on her behalf," said Maeve. "Being Irish is fine with most people. But there are some. They may be a blasted Presbyterian or even Scots Baptist. They're the worst, you know."

"Liz," said Mary, "one of the things we two liked about you from the very beginning when we roomed together down in Saco was that you accepted us as we were. You always was respectful. That's why we stayed with you for so long. Why we are still your friends after all this time."

Liz took her hand and stood with her face almost touching Mary's. "You are one of the dearest people I have ever met. I will love you both forever."

12

A week to the day after the stillbirth, Lottie was finally able to get out of bed and walk around the bedroom. At first, she held on to Franny's arm for support, but after a few wobbly steps, she gained confidence to walk alone. Con and Francis sat on the bed, cheering her on.

"Why don't you sit in the easy chair and rest a spell," said Franny, who had been a nearly constant companion for the week. "You're doing so well. The doctor says you should be strong enough to return home next week."

"I want so to return. The place must be a dusty mess. But I don't trust that I will be able to take care of the boys and the house, too. And there's garden work to do now that it's late May. Would you be able to come for a visit to help me?"

"Yes. That is my plan. Auntie said that she could handle the work without me for a while. We have already made the arrangements."

Lottie shook her head. "I am so grateful. Not sure what I would do without your help. You are my angel."

"You know I won't be able to stay with you forever. Just until you're back to full health. Is there a farmer who might be able to lend a hand with the outside work?"

"I suppose you think I'll need another man. After the last one, I'm not so sure about that."

"Oh, there will be another one. Don't worry about that. Hopefully, he will be like my cowboy in *The Virginian*. So handsome and kind. So brave." She pulled the novel from her pocket. "Have you read this novel? I'll lend it to you when I finish. Auntie said it might give me ideas about the world outside of Westbrook."

"I'll not be looking in a novel for a husband, if I decide to find another. Real men are not like those made up to fit a story by some writer of fantasy. You know that Clarence was handsome. I thought he was kind and considerate of me and his family. Perhaps I was the one living in a fantasy world."

"Well, I can dream about meeting the Virginian, can't I? Someone who would sweep me off my feet like that cowboy does with Molly Wood. Grab me up with his strong arms and place me on the horse just behind him. With my arms around his waist." She had her eyes closed as she spoke.

"Okay, I will read that book, though not with the same passion you seem to have for it. I've known a real man. Seen his weaknesses as well as his strengths. You've not had the pain."

"Or the pleasure," said Franny with a big smile on her face.

Lottie gave her friend a gentle slap on the knee. "One thing I want to speak about with you before you come to live with me in on Beech Hill is how dangerous it might be there. After we moved into the Aphia Stevens' old house, Clarence always said that I was foolish to believe that woman was causing us all sorts of problems in order to get us out of it. But I think she has powers we do not understand."

"Hang on, girl. Are you telling me you think she is a witch?"

"Something like that. Remember, she made all those potions with her herbs, and she poisoned two men. Clarence told me a story about a day she drove her carriage wildly through the village of North Waterford. When she was forced to stop, she threw a white powder into peoples' faces, making them blind."

"She was an herbalist, not a witch. I would have to agree with Clarence on this."

"Then there was the fire at the mica mine head house when Clarence and Con were there. They could have been burned to death. That had nothing to do with herbs and potions, if you ask me. Now Clarence is dead."

"You think she killed your husband? Come on, Lottie. You're giving that woman too much credit. Keep doing that and you will bring all sorts of bad things into your life."

"That's just what he said to me all the time. 'Don't give her more power,' he always said. Well, he is gone now, and I can't help believing that it was more than a random accident. That's why I'm telling you this before you get to Beech Hill. You will be a blessing to me and the boys, but I don't want you to be unaware of what could happen."

Franny put her forefinger to her mouth. "Shhh. Hush. We don't want to scare Con and Francis, do we? Thanks for your warning. I am brave enough to go with you."

13

Franny was grateful for how supportive her family was about the plan to move to Beech Hill Farm and help her friend through a very rough time. She thought her mom would criticize the decision to leave Aunt Liz alone, but Hattie was in total agreement. On the day she was to leave, Nathan, Hattie, and even Nate volunteered to help. There were so many people involved that they needed two wagons.

"I didn't think this was going to be such a big project," said Franny as the wagons were being loaded. "After all, there are only four of us passengers and I'm not taking many of my things. It's only going to be for a couple of weeks."

Nate secured his sister's trunk on the rear of the larger wagon, the one that he would drive. "This trunk is pretty heavy for only a few things, Sis. What did you pack, a sewing machine or something?"

"I did not! And I only packed a few books. Your muscles must be getting weak."

He growled at her with a smile on his face.

Lottie led both boys down the steps. "Did you bring that novel about the cowboy? The one you are in love with?"

"Hush about that! I am not in love with him. I just like the story. I know you want to read it after me."

Nathan, Hattie, and Lizzie stood on the porch watching all the preparation and trying to decide how much help to provide in the form of money and provisions.

Hattie told Lizzie, "Nathan and I will stop at our house

on the way to Waterford and load the box of supplies we have already packed. In our icebox are some perishables we purchased just for them."

"You two are so wonderful to help," Lizzie replied. "And I have given Francena fifty dollars to take care of their needs for a while."

Hattie gave her sister a big hug. "We will drop in on them every few days. Not the journey it is for you to get there."

As they spoke, Nate walked past Lottie and lifted both boys, placing them up on his wagon. Then he climbed up and secured them with cords. Both Con and Francis laughed and poked him in the arm and stomach. Nate spoke to them calmly as he jumped to the ground, where Lottie patted him on the shoulder for helping.

Liz watched this exchange, then turned to Hattie and whispered, "Those two have been very friendly lately. Nate has been so helpful and she so appreciative. Perhaps he'll be a regular visitor to Beech Hill Farm. She will need a man to handle chores and things."

Hattie peered over her glasses for a moment and said, "What do you mean by 'chores and things'?"

14

"It's not only you who have been so wonderful to me. Your whole family has accepted me like I was a sister," said Lottie.

Lottie and Franny sat across the oak kitchen table after dinner. The boys were in bed and the two friends shared a bottle of ale left them by Nathan a few days before. A day-bright super full moon hung above the pasture like a giant lantern. Franny sliced two pieces of cheese from a quarter round she had picked up at Nason's store in the village.

"My dear, from the day we first met all those years ago in South Waterford, you have felt like a sister. My family loves you. Especially my aunt. You can do no wrong in her eyes. She was willing to offer you the upstairs apartment once again. I told her you wanted to be in your own home. My dad wanted to keep you three in our house for a while until you were fully recovered."

"That's what I mean. Even though my real parents are dead, I feel that I have family. What have I done to deserve such treatment?"

Taking a sip on the bottle before passing it to her friend, Franny peered out at the tall grass, illuminated in moonlight, waving in a breeze. A cool evening had brought an end to a warm day. Blue jays made a din in a stand of tall maples that lined Greene Road.

"My family is always ready to help others. Always been that way. Dad says he is good at business mainly because he likes people and wants to make his clients successful. Mom and Liz learned as small girls that being greedy and hateful to others can ruin one's life. Even Nate, who still has much to learn about life, is willing to forego his own needs when others' needs are greater. I have been fortunate to be a member of such a family."

Lottie sipped the beer and rose to check on the sleeping children. When she returned Franny was standing at the back door.

"Let's go out into the moonlight and share the hammock. It's so bright that everything is throwing shadows. Look at the long tree shadows along the pasture edge."

"I'll need a shawl. I'll get another for you. Don't be fooled into thinking that you can't catch a cold in the summer. Summer colds are the hardest to cure."

They walked hand in hand to a large canvas hammock spread between two ancient maples and lay down with their heads and feet at opposite ends. Franny reached her left foot down to the ground and rocked them back and forth.

"Clarry and I used to sit here on evenings like this," Lottie said. "You know, for all his faults, there are times like this that I miss him terribly."

"I am sure you do. Our friendship is wonderful, but it must have been hard to lose the love of your man."

"Lovey, you have been such a wonderful companion these last few weeks and for many years. Those first two years when

Clarence and I struggled to get to know each other up in the back woods of Ontario, it was you I turned to for consolation in our letters to one another. Still, he fathered my children. He was good to them and mostly good to me."

"But I'm sure you will find someone. You need a man's hand around the place. There will be another."

"Well, perhaps a cowboy will come along." She winked and squeezed Franny's knee.

15

The Halletts were regular weekend visitors to Lottie's little farm, taking a room in the village so they could spend time with her and Franny. They always arrived loaded down with provisions. Hattie would take over the kitchen, and with Franny's help, create meals that were much more complicated and delicious than the farm's usual fare.

One weekend, Nate accompanied his parents so that he and Nathan could split firewood for the coming winter. When the three arrived, Con and Francis, who were playing outside, met them at the gate. As usual, Hattie gave each a hug and a bag of candy. She was a favorite, almost like a grandmother.

"Con, you remember Nate, don't you?" asked Nathan.

The boy held out his hand for Nate to shake, while his little brother hid behind him.

"Francis. Don't be so shy," said Con. "You like Franny, don't you? Nate is just like her."

Francis stepped forward and held out his own little hand. When Nate grabbed the tiny fingers, they disappeared in his grasp.

"Well, I'm not *exactly* like my sister. She's a lot smarter and prettier. Don't you think so, Conny?"

Overhearing the conversation outside, Lottie came to the door and watched her sons interact with the Halletts. They both had such good manners, she thought. Their father would have been so pleased with the way she was raising them.

"Hey, Nate," she said loudly. "I think you *are* pretty smart. Don't sell yourself short."

Hattie agreed. "Yes, Nate. You are smart in a different way from your sister. And you are quite a handsome young man. Lottie, don't you agree that he is a handsome young man?"

She didn't get an answer to her question. Instead, both Lottie and Nate blushed as they looked at each other. Franny came around the corner of the house carrying a wicker basket full of eggs she had gathered. She ran to her family, giving her parents big hugs before handing the basket to Nate and kissing his cheek. Noticing that he was embarrassed about something, she touched his hot forehead.

"You're not feeling ill, are you?" Then, looking up at Lottie, who was still on the porch, she noticed that she too was red-faced. "I hope you and Nate don't have the same illness. Hell of a way to start a weekend."

"No, no," said her dad. "Neither of them is ill. It's just that Nate here isn't used to being with so many pretty women. He doesn't know how to act."

At that the adults burst into laughter. The two little boys looked confused at first, but they finally joined in.

16

Later that day, after a delicious dinner of roast beef, boiled potatoes, and fresh greens which the Halletts had brought with them, Lottie put her boys to bed and then joined Hattie and Nathan on the rear porch. The sun filled the western sky with high clouds of red, yellow, and orange. In the stillness of dusk, the repeated call of a whippoorwill could be heard.

"I'm afraid we have to leave this little paradise until morning," said Hattie. "We have a room at the Alpine again."

"You're regulars there, now," commented Lottie. "I'm sorry we don't have enough room for you to stay with us."

"Hush, dear. They give us the same lovely room each time.

They hold it for us from weekend to weekend. There will be an extra bed this time for Nate."

"Where is Nate?" asked Nathan.

"Dear, he and Franny are out walking in the pasture. She wanted to show him the old mine site at the top of Beech Hill."

"Well, they better return soon, or we will be driving to the village in the dark."

The siblings had left immediately after dinner, thinking that there would be plenty of daylight left for their hike. They had spent little time together for the past few weeks, and there were many things to be discussed. In particular, Franny had some concerns about what she perceived to be a liking he had taken to her best friend.

"Bet you'll miss the peace of this place when you finally have to leave," said Nate.

"I have to say it is a little slice of heaven. Yet sometimes the isolation grates on me. I read quite a bit. There are always chores to do, and the boys keep me busy. But I do miss the energy and social life back in Westbrook."

Nate thought for a moment. "The town is so close to Portland that it's always so busy. I prefer to be a bit out of the way, like we are in Bridgton. Or definitely like Lottie is here."

"Nate, tell me in private. Do you like Lottie? Have you started to think of her as more than just my friend?"

"Hell, I must not be doing a good job hiding my feelings. Dad asked me the same thing the other night. What if I *am* attracted to her? Isn't she beautiful and smart? Don't forget that I have known her as long as you have."

"Don't get so hot under the collar. No question she is a good woman. Nate, have you considered that she is five years older than you and has two kids already? We're not talking about courting a cute neighborhood girl. Lottie has been through some of life's difficulties, and you have only just begun."

"Sis, I'm not a teenager anymore. Or haven't you noticed?" He had stopped in his tracks and pointed to himself with both hands.

"Nate, please calm down. Yes, I'm sure you would be a great help to Lottie and her sons, but she needs a man to share her life. Con and Francis need a good father. I'm concerned that you might not know what you would be getting yourself into."

"Franny, that is really up to me, now, isn't it? You, Dad, Mom, and anyone else who has questions will have to go along with what I decide to do with my life. Won't you?"

There was no use talking further on the matter, so she put her arm around his waist and waited for him to calm down and start walking toward the house again. When they reached the others, the three visitors wished Lottie and Franny a good night and departed.

"We'll be back quite early tomorrow," said Nate to Lottie. "Dad and I want to get your winter wood stacked before we leave."

She smiled and waved at him. Franny thought her friend almost blew a kiss in his direction.

"You're such a good friend, Nate," Lottie called out as they drove away.

17

Lottie was not able to get a vegetable garden planted for the short growing season. Weeds reclaimed the open soil that had been cultivated the year before. Francena suggested that they get a few chickens from Farmer Kimball and enclose them within the garden space with a wire fence. At least the space would be productive.

Recovery from the miscarriage was taking much longer than the doctor said it would. Lottie was unable to stand for long periods or bend deeply. Her biggest disappointment was not being able to do much work around the house. She was also worried that damage done to her uterus might make it impossible to have another baby. Dr. Rowan assured her that she would heal with time. Something about the stomach pains she felt when getting out of bed each morning made her suspect that he might only be trying to make her feel better.

Having Franny to help during the healing was a godsend. She was a nurse to Lottie and a second mother to Con and Francis.

"Con, honey, please go get me two eggs from the coop," Franny said one morning. "Remember, do not disturb the hens who are sitting on their nests."

At the age of six, the boy enjoyed helping out around the place. He took a small basket lined with hay from her and walked out to the chicken yard. When he returned, he presented her with six eggs instead of two.

"Franny, I took them from the empty nests. Maybe you can use the others later."

"What a good boy. Of course we will. You're getting very smart, planning ahead like that."

As he handed the basket back to her it slipped and one of the eggs fell against his leg and smashed onto the floor.

"Oh, no!" Con cried out. "That witch has made me drop one. Just like Mommy says."

He burst into tears and ran from the room. She chased after, finding him on the sofa with his head pressed hard to a pillow.

"Con, dear, don't be so upset. It is just a broken egg. Remember I only need two and you brought me six. Let's go back to the kitchen and clean it up."

"Don't tell Mommy. She'll be angry at me. And it ain't even my fault. It's that woman in jail who made me do it."

She didn't know how to calm him. Lottie had spoken so often of Aphia's powers to wreak havoc on their lives that now Con was afraid, too. A child should not be living in fear. She said nothing as she sat next to him and straightened his hair with her hand. Eventually his crying stopped. She led him back to the broken egg to clean it up together.

"There, Con. It's like nothing ever happened. Only a small accident."

"Franny, please promise not to tell Mommy. She wants me to be good all the time."

"Okay. It will be our little secret. And you know what, you *are* a good boy all the time."

18

The village of North Waterford was no longer the devastated ruins left behind by the Great Fire five years before. A new hotel, the Alpine, occupied one entire side of the four corners intersection across from Tim Nason's brand-new store. His general store, which had occupied the same spot since the early 1800s, had been destroyed. The new one was a modern two-story structure with an apartment for rent on the second floor. New houses lined both sides of Valley Road as far as Francena could see. Large elm trees, their pale green foliage waving in a southerly breeze, gave a speckled shade to both sides of the main street. It was nearly noon, so a group of workmen from nearby Crooked River Mill were clustered in front of the Alpine's café.

As Franny stepped down from the carriage and hitched her horse to a post at Nason's, a conversation among several of the workers caught her ear. They were commenting on her appearance and wondering why her husband had let her come to town alone. She suspected such old-fashioned ignorance was still common here in the hill towns. She ignored the comments and entered the store.

"Good day, ma'am," said a tall young man behind the dry goods counter. "'Tis a pleasant day to be out and about, I'd say."

"And you'd be quite right to say that. Indeed, you would."

The man looked her up and down before returning to his work of stacking blankets on a deep wooden shelf.

"Is Mr. Nason here today?" she asked. "It's the first of the month and I want to settle accounts."

"Oh, I can handle that for you, miss. What is the name on the account? I'll check in the ledger for you."

"Well, it's in the name of Potter, Mrs. Clarence Potter."

"Oh, yes. I have it here. Are you a friend of Mrs. Potter's? Please tell her I am very sorry to hear of Mr. Potter's death."

"Yes. I'm a friend staying with the family for a while. Lottie Potter asked me to settle on her behalf. I'm Francena Hallett. My family lives in Bridgton Center. Perhaps you know my father, Nathan Hallett."

Franny smiled at the clerk and held out her hand. He didn't seem to know how to respond to her offer of a friendly shake. He was not used to women acting like men. After a couple of seconds, however, he reached out and shook her hand as he blushed.

"No. Afraid not, Miss Francena Hallett." He whispered her name several times as if trying to memorize it. "My name is Ethan."

Once the account was paid, she presented him a list of needed provisions. As he moved about the store gathering her goods, she noticed how handsome he was and how tall. His full head of black hair was longer than most men's, but not messy by any means. He wore a short-sleeved shirt, and when he reached for a bag of flour from a high shelf, she noticed the well-formed muscles in his bare arms.

"Would you be needing a firkin of butter? We just got a delivery from South Waterford Creamery this morning. Real fresh. Their butter has gotten awards at the Fryeburg Fair."

"Yes, I know about their butter. Please add that to the list. You're quite the salesman, aren't you?"

Again, Ethan blushed as he turned away to get a firkin from the ice chest behind him. "Anything else I might do for you, miss?"

"No. You've been very helpful. Thank you."

"Don't mention it. Thank you for your business. Here is the invoice. I'll put it on your, ah, I mean on the Potter account. Allow me take the goods to your carriage."

Mounting to the seat, she reached down to him. This time there was no hesitation. He shook the offered hand vigorously. "Miss Hallett, I'm very pleased to have been able to assist you today. Hope to see more of you here in the future."

On the way out of town, she thought about his final words. A smile came across her face as she thought of the Virginian.

19

She had been with the Potter family now for nearly a month, much longer than planned. It was not only Lottie's body that needed to heal, but also her mind. Con and Francis were their mother's pride and joy most of the time, but there were periods when she wanted nothing to do with them. Depression at the loss of the baby and the death of Clarence often alienated her from the boys, leaving their care in Franny's hands.

As those periods lessened, Lottie began to be a parent once again and to take more care of the house. Franny had more time on her own to reflect on what a wonderful place Beech Hill was. This very morning, she had walked up to the old mica mine site where she was able to view large herds of dairy cows dotting the flanks of Rice Hill to the east.

Returning from her walk, Franny lay across the hammock, watching the sun set over the top of Beech Hill. A pair of large birds soared on thermals rising from the pasture, pivoting around each other in a smooth double spiral. She identified them as red-shouldered hawks by their widely fanned, black-and-white striped tails. A few other large birds, likely crows, were perched high up on a towering dead pine tree at the top of the ridge. They were so far away that she could not make out how many of them there were.

She pulled *The Virginian* from her apron pocket and in the fading light thumbed through its pages to find the corner she had folded to mark her progress. She had been reading about a hanging when she was last interrupted. The hero was hanging Stevie, a range hand who had been his friend, because the man had rustled cattle from their employer, Judge Henry. As cruel as prairie justice was, she respected how loyal the Virginian was to the judge.

"Come in for dinner, Francena," Lottie shouted out from the kitchen screen door. "Your plate will be cold if you don't come in now."

The family was already seated when she came in. While washing her hands at the sink, she was surprised to see a bouquet of roses on the center of the table. A sweet scent filled the room.

"Lottie, what a beautiful thing to see. Where did you find those?"

"A young man from the village brought them to the door while you were hiking on the mountain. His name is Ethan. He worked with Clarence on a couple of projects."

"How sweet is that?" said Franny. "Did he come to call on you?"

"No. No, he is quite young. Maybe twenty or so. He was being a friendly neighbor, but he did ask to be remembered to *you*."

"That must be the boy I met in the village last week. Long black hair? Very tall?"

"That would be the one. You must have made quite an impression."

"Lottie, stop smiling like that. He is little more than a boy. Twenty would be quite generous, if you ask me."

"Well, as far as I am concerned, these blooms were meant for you. And now you're leaving. It will break the lad's heart."

Franny sat down, pulled her chair forward, grabbed her napkin, rolled it into a ball and threw it at her friend. They both laughed so hard that little Francis began to cry.

"Stop that, Fran," said Con. "They ain't mad. It's a joke." He laughed and then so did Francis.

20

In the two years since her husband, Will, had lost his life at the hand of Aphia Stevens, Maeve Cain had devoted most of her time to raising her five children with plenty of assistance from her two oldest daughters, twenty-year-old Faith and seventeen-year-old Janey. The carpentry business left behind by Will generated a decent amount of income for her at first. When she sold it to one of the carpenters, she lost her regular income, but gained a good profit.

Sister Mary Flaherty's return from Ireland brought a welcome change to Maeve's life. Mary was treated like royalty by the children. Faith, who had been ten when her aunt left, loved her accent and the way she dressed—as did Janey. Owen and James both claimed that they were also Irish and wanted to hear about what kinds of sports were played by boys in the "old country." Willie, the youngest at eight, was shy at first, thinking that having a foreign lady in their home might cause embarrassment for him at school.

"Mom," asked Owen one morning, "did you and Dad ever go to Ireland before Faith was born? I think I would like to live there. Seems a bit like Maine from what Aunt Mary says."

Maeve looked across the kitchen table at her sister. "Don't you be believin' half of what your aunt tells you. Life has never been very easy over there. Yes, winters are better than here. And summers last longer. But it rains most of the time. You don't want to live where it's damp all the time, do you?"

"If it rains all the time," said Willie, "there must be a lot of rivers. Plenty of fishing. That would be good."

"Children, please don't bother yourself about going to Ireland," said Aunt Mary. "You have such a wonderful life here in Westbrook. Why do you think I was wantin' to return? Although Ireland is fine, you wouldn't have as much play time as you enjoy here. Everyone must work to put food on the table. Even the littlest ones."

By this time everyone was sitting at the big table as Faith and Janey served a breakfast of fresh-picked peaches, toast, and milk. As they ate, Lizzie entered through the rear door.

"Sorry to disturb you, Maeve, but Mary told me I might be able to speak with you both this morning."

"Oh, my dear. I completely forgot," said Mary.

"Please come in, Lizzie. You're very welcome to join us for breakfast on this lovely morning," said Maeve. "Janey, please set a place for our friend."

"You ladies are so fortunate to have so many helpers," said Liz as she sipped her cup of tea. "Having Franny with me these last few years has been a blessing. Now that she has left to help Lottie, I miss the companionship. Maeve, these children must be a solace to you."

"Lizzie dear, there is not a day since Will has been gone that I haven't thanked God in heaven for the family my husband and I made together."

Mary poured herself another cup and reached across the table to touch Liz's hand.

"What was it you wanted to talk with us about this morning?"

"It can wait. I don't want to disturb your family breakfast."

"Children," said Maeve, "we three ladies could use a little privacy. Please finish your meal and then clean up. We women can retire to the parlor for a chat."

As soon as the three entered the sunny eastern room, Maeve sat down in her favorite stuffed chair and pulled her knitting kit from behind it. Mary and Lizzie sat on the velvet love seat and stared out at a flock of robins pecking in the garden.

"Maeve, you're still knitting," said Liz. "You've always been so talented with making clothes for your family. I remember how quick you were with the machines when we worked together to make so many wonderful dresses."

"I still use my small Singer 27 machine sometimes. It's not as powerful as the ones you have in the shop. Are you still using them?"

Lizzie pulled a card from her dress pocket and studied the notes she had made for this meeting. "We use them some. Not as much as I would like. First, there is only so much business right now. Second, with my eye problems, it takes longer to get the work done. Francena has been doing more and more of my work. Actually, that is one of the things I came over to talk about today. I'm wondering if either or both of you might be looking for work."

Maeve set her knitting down in her lap.

"You aren't thinking I would be able to take that girl's place, are you? There is so much to do here at home that I can't work for you. Perhaps some time in the future."

"I know you have your own household to run, but if Mary had time to work, we might think about reuniting the three-woman shop we had back at the start of Millett's American Designs."

Mary said nothing, continuing to watch the robins.

"Lizzie dear, let me see if I understand what you're saying. You're thinking that we two old ladies might be able to keep your business afloat. How would that work exactly?"

Looking at her notes again, Liz answered. "Well, first of all, there's not a big load of work right now. So, the projects could be shared. We all know how to run the machines. Mary, you used to be the best."

Mary laughed. "'Used to be the best' is a good way of saying it. We'd have to see if I remember how to work at the table again. I've not used one of those Singers for a decade. I'd probably sew my fingers together."

"It may take a bit of time to test this plan, but it has some merit," said Maeve. "And what would you be having me do, if I joined you later on?"

"There has never been one so good at design as you. I'm not saying it won't take some time to warm up your skills. That's okay. We needn't be in a big hurry."

Mary walked to Liz's side and put her arm around her shoulders. "You are very resourceful, my friend. You have always been able to set your mind on a goal and organize around it to reach success. I have great respect for that ability. You mentioned that business may improve in the future. Perhaps I can make a suggestion in that direction. My cousin Timothy works with a weaver in Galway who makes linen of superior quality. What would you think of my reaching out to him about selling us some fine Irish linen that we could use in your designs? Wouldn't that give us a leg up in the marketplace?"

Both other women applauded her for the idea.

"What a great idea!" exclaimed Lizzie "Irish linen! There's nothing like that anywhere here in Maine. My dear, it is a pleasure to have you back at home."

21

Lottie's condition continued to improve, and both friends knew that it was only a matter of days before Franny would be able to return home to Westbrook. One morning, they sat at the breakfast table watching Con and Francis running in the pasture.

"I don't know what I shall do without you, but you must return to your regular life. Will you return to live with your auntie?"

"Yes, I'm excited to return to her house. I may spend a few days in Bridgton, just to visit with my parents."

"They've been here so often, and I hope they will continue to visit us. They have almost become my own family."

"Oh, I'm sure you'll see them occasionally, especially my brother. He fits right in here. It's his type of place," said Franny with a big grin.

After staring in silence for a moment at her smiling friend, Lottie said, "What are you grinning at?"

"My dear friend, it is as clear as daylight that you and Nate have an affection for each other. Do you think no one notices? You are mooning over each other at every opportunity."

"Mooning, is it? Well, he has been very helpful to me. And he is so good with the boys."

"But he is six years younger than you. Mightn't that be a problem? He has lived a much quieter life than you. He has hardly ever dated any of the local girls. You've got a lot more experience in life than he does."

"That means I have a lot to teach him about life, doesn't it? Don't you see that? You may be looking for your handsome dark-haired cowboy to ride in on his steed and carry you off. I have already had that happen. What I want is different now."

The smile on Franny's face turned into a frown as she listened.

"You certainly had your adventures with Clarence. I know he hurt you when he tricked you into believing that he would make your life better if you eloped with him. All he did was force you to grow up too quickly and support his desire for success, regardless of what was best for you. Nate has had a more normal pace of growing up. He is such a dear boy, not a man yet."

"You sell your brother short. I see more maturity in him than you do. You have been living in Westbrook for so long that you may be out of touch with what a good man he really is."

"Wait, dearie. He is surely a good man. More honest than most and wise in many ways. Maybe I'm being overly protective. I am also concerned for you. I only want both of you to make wise decisions about each other."

"Francena, please don't fear that I will make the same mistakes I made the last time around. Any decision to be with another man will be made to make both parties happy. But I will make that decision soon, so that my sons have a good man as a role model. You are so precious for feeling the way you do about both Nate and me. I love you for that."

22

"Francena's coming home!" Lizzie shouted down the stairs to Mary, who was working in the shop. "Nathan just phoned and said that we will see her tomorrow morning. We've got to have a welcome home party for her."

In the long weeks her niece had been away, the only communication with her had been an occasional letter. As the pace of business began to pick up due to the addition of Irish linen to her materials, it had been difficult to get away. Even the weekends were busy with customers who came in by appointment to see the new designs. Mary picked up right where she had left off on the sewing machine, and besides making women's dresses and skirts, she made men's shirts with the new Irish material.

"How wonderful," said Mary, jumping up from the Singer. "I'll ask Maeve to make us one of her fancy tortes. The children will be so excited."

As she left the shop, Liz descended the stairs and sat down at her desk. When Franny had first departed, the thought of living in such a big house all alone made her feel so old, so isolated from the rest of the family. One needed to have companionship in order to live a full and pleasant life. Living singly was not what she had in mind for the second half of her life. Surely, at some point, her niece would find a husband and move away again, this time permanently, but at least for now there would be a full-time companion with which to share her life once again.

Maeve's Janey stuck her head in the door.

"Lizzie, Mom says we should have the party at our house. She'll take care of everything. It will be so elegant. She has a turkey to roast. Says it will be like Thanksgiving."

At seventeen, the girl had blossomed into a red-haired beauty, tall like her late dad. Freckles dotted her cheeks and forehead, and just like her mom, she had wonderful dimples in her cheeks when she smiled. Liz beckoned her to come in.

"Are you back in school yet?"

"Oh, yes. I'm a sophomore this year. Only two more years and I can go to college. Mom says I might be able to go to Bates in Lewiston. They let women go there, you know."

Janey quickly switched back to the party plans.

"So, what do you think about an early Thanksgiving at our house tomorrow? I can help make a chocolate cake for Franny. She likes chocolate a lot."

"Tell your mom I love the idea. And let's keep it a secret from Franny. A surprise Thanksgiving. That will give me time to clean up this place and make a special gift."

The girl turned on her heel and bounded back through the door, just stopping long enough to keep it from slamming. Lizzie watched her and thought how proud old friend Will Cain would be of that young lady, if he were still alive.

23

Aphia had been perplexed by her dreams her entire life. Sometimes it seemed to her that she lived completely in a dream world where there was little or no difference between her sleeping and waking states. Thinking back to her childhood, before she left her family at age fourteen to marry Henry Greene, she couldn't remember any repeated dreams. Then, after he had been poisoned and died, he started to appear in her nightmares. She was glad he was dead because he had mistreated her and deserved to perish. Yet there he was night after night. Sometimes he appeared in his own wicked form. Other nights he took on shapes of demonic animals that threatened her.

Later, when she poisoned a vagrant farmhand and buried him in the pasture next to Henry's body, the two men began to haunt her as a team. Then, after mistakenly shooting Will Cain, she began to see the three together as a vengeful gang who cursed and laughed at her each night. They might show up as a pack of rabid mastiffs. They would run in circles around the house, falling all over each other trying to get at her. She realized that they would be with her forever. Though she had ended their lives, their spirits could not be destroyed.

"Prisoner Stevens, stop talking to yourself and get back to work," shouted the guard. "I'll not stand for your laziness much longer. I warn you!" She tapped on the back of Aphia's chair with her baton.

"Was I talking to myself? I thought you said something to me." She smiled through grinding teeth. As the woman walked away, her shape morphed into that of the cursed Canadian miner. What was his name? Porter? Potter? Yes, that is it. What is he doing here? Has he joined with the others to haunt me? Why? I didn't have anything to do with his death. She had seen him in a dream, crushed under the collapse of a building. I saw it. But I had nothing to do with it. Begone, you bastard miner.

"Did you say something, Stevens?"

"No, just thinking to myself."

"No thinking allowed. This ain't a school, you know."

24

Hattie was surprised at how her daughter had changed. Franny had devoted so much energy to caring for Lottie and her family that she seemed to have aged, become more introspective, almost withdrawn. It was clear from the moment she hugged her daughter that something bothered her.

"Franny, dear. You seem to have lost some weight. Have you been feeling all right? You didn't catch anything from the boys, did you? Young children are always getting ill."

"I don't think so. Maybe I've grown a little taller, that's all. The boys have been fine. I have come to love them. Won't it be nice when I have children of my own someday?"

Hattie looked at her for a second before speaking very carefully, studying each word before opening her mouth.

"Can't do it by yourself, darling daughter. Do you have anyone in mind to help you?"

"No, no. Don't be so silly. But it will happen someday." Franny began to giggle. She held her hands up to her face.

"There. That's better. Now I see the smiling face I know so well. Welcome back, baby," she said as she touched her daughter's hair.

Nate entered the room, sat down next to his sister on the sofa and touched her shoulder with affection. They had not spoken since their hike to the top of Beech Hill several weeks before.

"Franny, it's wonderful to have you here for a visit so that we can stay home for a change. I have missed being with my own friends."

"Oh, I thought you were making a new friend for yourself in North Waterford. Or am I wrong?"

"You are correct, but Lottie is a girl, not really a friend."

A laugh exploded so loudly from Hattie's lips that her children were shocked. Franny, too, then began to laugh. Nate rose from his seat and nearly ran to the front door before turning to say, "You both are so cruel. Don't tease me so!"

His mother calmed herself. "Lottie is certainly not a girl. She is a twenty-six-year-old widow who has two children and a small farm to run. A girl is that Virginia Todd you used to visit over on Church Street. Or the Smith girl whose father owns the sawmill. Lottie Potter will have to find herself a man to help raise those boys as soon as possible. Those others have a few years to go before they have to make any big decisions."

Nate was embarrassed at the route this conversation had taken. He left the house and headed toward Highland Lake. When he was gone the two women continued to discuss Lottie.

"She has already told me she wants to get married again right away. She is looking already."

Again, Hattie carefully chose her words.

"I'm sure. You know your dad and I have been concerned that one of the men she is considering might be our Nate. Did you know that?"

Franny nodded. "I share your concern. He also has got a bit of a crush on her."

She didn't mention her conversation with Nate about his being so much younger than Lottie.

Hattie continued. "It isn't so much the age difference that bothers us. It's that she is so experienced in life, while he has only begun to learn about love and relationships. My God, he would go from being a boy to becoming a father of two. We don't think he's ready for that."

"I'm sure he knows what he would be giving up," said Franny. "But he has always liked her as a friend. They hit it off from the very first meeting at Bear Mountain House in Waterford so many years ago."

"He told your father and me that same thing when we spoke about her last week. He said he feels that she needs someone to help her in life. We really don't know what to do."

"What can any of us do? After all, it's his decision to make. I love both of them and don't want to see them hurt. Maybe we're wrong. Maybe they would make a wonderful team."

25

E ugene Bailey had lived in Westbrook his entire life of thirty-two years. He hardly ever went anywhere else for longer than a short visit. Portland was the only city he knew, and he hardly ever went there any longer than it took to buy supplies for the family store, which he'd inherited from his uncle Hiram. The store stood at the four corners where Brook Street and Bridgton Road met, at what most people recognized to be the center of Prides Corner. A sign in his store window said *Westbrook is down the road. This is Prides Corner.*

He was not a tall man, but not as short as some. Only a couple of girls in town thought of him as handsome. That might have been because he was such an affluent eligible bachelor. Standing behind the cash register, he was the very image of commercial confidence, wrapped in a long white apron to protect his tweed waistcoat, white cotton shirt, and four-in-hand tie. When the store was closed, he often felt ill at ease. Any leisure activity—reading, gardening, walking down to the Presumpscot River by himself—caused him to recognize how lonely he was. His parents were dead, and his brothers had moved away to make better lives for themselves. He often thought he needed a companion, a partner, a wife. Yet he had not met the right woman. Or perhaps the women he met were looking for a different type of man.

Lizzie Millet and Mary Flaherty were regular customers at Bailey's Store. They often came in together, both to purchase household needs and to deliver their Irish table linens. Lizzie had been coming in for years, and when her husband, Moses, passed away, she had become a person of romantic interest. Such interest lasted only a few months as he began to see that she was much too confident and independent to be a promising mate. However, Mary had good potential. She had been away in Ireland for a few years and returned with a wonderful accent and an alluring sense of humor.

One chilly and damp autumn day, Mary came in by herself. She was carrying a large basket.

"Good day, Miss Flaherty," he greeted her.

"Top o' the marnin', Mr. Bailey. How you keepin' today?"

"Fine. And yourself, miss?

"Bit of a chill in the air today. Back home they would say the fog rising from the river would be a fine soft mist. Here it is nothing but a cold cloud."

He loved the way she talked. "And how is Miss Millett doing? Haven't seen her in a while. Mary, do you mind if I use your given name?"

"No, Mister Bailey, go right ahead. It is my name, after all. Lizzie is doing quite well, thank you."

"Well, Mary, please call me Eugene. How can I help you today? We have fresh eggs, just delivered this morning."

"I didn't come to shop today, but you being such a good sales-man will likely convince me you have something I need."

"Always here to serve you, Mary."

She pulled the cover off her basket and placed it on the counter in front of him.

"Today it is I who have come to sell something to you. Lizzie and I are making lovely men's shirts of Irish linen."

She set one on the counter. He picked it up and opened it wide.

"This is wonderful! I've never seen such a finished cloth in a shirt."

"Irish linen. It's linen we buy direct from Ireland. Isn't it delightful?"

He rubbed the cloth between his hands and held the shirt up against his chest.

"This is a bit large for me. Do you have other sizes? Depending upon the cost, I might want one for myself."

"'Tis not so dear as you might think. We have made three sizes. Here, try this one. It is a medium size. It may fit you. Why don't you try it on?"

"My dear lady," he began, "I am not accustomed to changing my clothes in the presence of others." He was embarrassed that she had even made such a suggestion. "What is the cost of this medium? It looks to be the correct size."

"All sizes cost the same, seventy-five cents."

"So much? Why, this fine cotton shirt I am wearing is only fifty cents."

"But yours is made of cotton. This one is so much more stylish than the usual country style."

Bailey turned taciturn at her comments. Was she criticizing his style of fashion? Perhaps in Ireland men were used to such a high price, but it was doubtful. From what he knew of the rural character of that country, it was highly unlikely a farmer over there would have anywhere near the amount of money he himself had to spend on clothes. The woman must be pulling his leg.

"Miss Flaherty," he said, returning to a more formal tone. "I am afraid that such a high price tag will not be popular here in Westbrook, nor especially in Portland, where so many fine clothes are available."

Mary looked the man up and down and then peered right into his eyes.

"I am sure you are correct. You know your business. However, I cannot let these go for less than what it cost us to make them, now can I?"

As she began to pack the two shirts back in her basket, he turned away and looked at himself in a full-length mirror behind the counter. He adjusted his tie and straightened the waistcoat before returning to the conversation.

"Miss, perhaps you might allow me to purchase that medium from you for fifty cents. I will wear it for a day or two to see if it would be worth the extra. Let me be your model and show your shirt off to my other customers."

"You've got yourself a deal! One-half dollar it is."

She handed the folded shirt back to him.

"Eugene, if your customers will pay you seventy-five for such a beautiful handmade linen garment, Liz and I will make your price fifty. Then you will have a better shirt than the cotton for the same price."

Once again he felt that she was insulting his manner of dress. How impudent this foreign woman was. Still the cloth was very beautiful. He would let her opinions pass and give one shirt a try.

26

Lizzie met her niece on the front porch before the young lady had a chance to knock on the door. She had been sitting at her desk pretending to work on the shop's ledger, keeping her attention focused on the driveway for the arrival of Nathan's chaise.

"Francena Hallett, you are a sight for sore eyes."

After giving her a big welcoming hug, Liz held the girl at arm's length.

"You look thinner than when you left. Have you not been eating?"

"Auntie dear, don't worry about me. I have been eating very well. With the meals Lottie and I have been preparing, I have become quite the cook. You'll see. I have been very active with hiking and chasing those little boys all over."

"I know what it is that makes you look different. It's your hair. You've let it grow so long. So beautiful. That is the length your grandmother Francena used to grow her hair, but she would usually have it stuffed up in a bun."

She stroked Franny's hair, then hugged her again.

Nathan and Hattie stepped up behind their daughter, carrying her luggage.

"Come on, girls," said Nathan. "You can continue your embraces, but please let the porters through. These bags are quite heavy."

Dropping two bags on the floor next to the stairs, Hattie walked to the two women and wrapped an arm around each. "Doesn't my girl look different, sister dear? She looks a bit older than when she left. Or perhaps I should say that she looks more mature. And you, Mrs. Webber, you look much younger than I recall from our last visit."

Liz smiled and curtsied to her sister.

"It must be the booming business I'm running here that makes me look that way. For so long, there was little to do here in the shop. Ask Franny. When she left, there was not much for her to do. Since Mary has returned, we've taken on new customers and the old ones have been returning."

"Auntie, do you have enough work for me? That would be fantastic. I didn't know what I was going to do."

"There's plenty to do now that we've started using the Irish linen that Mary found for us. You will love working with it. With you home, I'll be able to get two machines going, one for you, one for Mary. Despite my weak eyes, I have been back to doing some designs."

Hattie sat down at the drawing table.

"Sis, you may find yourself with nothing to do but the bookkeeping."

"Or I might just leave the place to these ladies and come visit you for a while. I haven't seen Nate for so long. He must have grown taller than the last time he was here."

Hattie suddenly became very serious.

"Nate is not around most of the time. You'd get to see him some during the workweek, but on weekends he is with a new friend quite a bit."

"Friend?" asked Liz.

Nathan entered with another piece of luggage.

"Your young nephew has a woman friend. I would say girlfriend, but in this case, she is a woman. He has been spending time with Lottie at her farm. They are becoming quite the item."

"Item? What do you mean?"

The Halletts did not want to make her worry, but Lizzie could easily see from their tones of voice that all three were unhappy with what was happening on Beech Hill Farm. She wanted to know the entire story.

"Auntie, he is apparently head over heels in love with Lottie. And he loves her two boys. Wants to be with them all the time. I tried to talk him into being cautious about a May–October relationship. She is so much older and more experienced than he. We are all afraid he will get hurt."

"I didn't know you had discussed your fears directly with him," said Hattie. "When did that happen?"

"Why didn't you tell us? What did he say to you?" Nathan was upset about both children keeping such a secret from their parents.

"It happened that day when he and I went for a walk up the mountain, while you waited with Lottie. I also spoke with her about my doubts."

"Francena, it's hard for me to believe you've known so much about this affair much longer than us and never told us," said Hattie waving her index finger in her daughter's face. "You've left us to guess what is going on. Very disappointing!"

"Well, he is my brother, for God's sake. We do have some confidences between us." Franny began to cry.

Lizzie put her arm around the girl's shoulders before speaking. "Please don't let this disagreement ruin the joy of your return. Which of you is to say that Lottie might not be a good match for the boy? I imagine she is looking for a good man to help with the children and the farm. He certainly is that because of the way he has been raised. And he couldn't find a more intelligent and beautiful companion."

"Liz," said Hattie, "as you just said, he is still a boy. I am concerned a match of these two will lead to pain for both."

27

"I'm not going to miss another gardening season next spring," Lottie told Nate, who had come from Bridgton to spend the day. "It was a good idea to raise chickens, but we need more vegetables put aside for next winter."

The two of them stood on the rear porch, looking out at the patch of weeds where hens pecked at bare patches of earth. Three blue jays perched atop the chicken coop roof, while in the distance crows circled over the line of pines bordering the old mine site.

"I can help you with that when the time comes. Conny is probably old enough to help us, too."

"Won't he look funny using a spading fork?"

"We won't work the garden with hand work. Much too difficult. I bet your neighbor, Mr. Kimball, would plow and harrow a large enough plot for us to keep you and the boys from going hungry."

She patted him on the back before returning to the house to check on her boys, who were playing in their room. By the time the three of them returned, Nate was sitting at the kitchen table sketching a garden plan on a sheet of paper in the fading light coming through the big window.

"Nate, you are such a good friend to put your energy into feeding my family. Perhaps I'll share some of what we grow with your family. After all, they have been so supportive of me during the last year. Without help from you Halletts, I likely would be homeless or dead."

"Don't be so melancholy. Things have never even come close to either of those outcomes. I'm sure Mom and Dad would be grateful to receive your extras. But they would want you to take care of your own needs first."

She turned to face him directly and touched his shoulder, where her hand lingered for a moment.

"Clarence always laughed at the idea of my being a gardener. He thought I would fail and wanted nothing to do with it. You are considerate for someone so young."

This was his turn to touch her. He reached for her hand and held it firmly.

"You know, I am not as young as you think. No matter what my parents say, I am mature enough to live my own life and make my own decisions."

"I didn't mean to make a joke, Nate. You often show wisdom beyond your years. The six years I have on you have not made me half as wise in some ways."

Con and Francis grew bored with the garden planning and asked to go back to their play. After they left, Lottie pulled another chair up close to Nate and looked at what he was drawing.

"Lottie, you know that my parents and Franny are concerned that we like each other too much. All three of them have spoken to me about it."

He took hold of both her hands.

"I know very well. Franny got angry with me about something she sees going on between us. Until she did, I really hadn't paid much attention to it."

"When we met in South Waterford eight years ago, I took a shine to you. Do you remember how I splashed you while you watched Franny and me swimming in Bear Pond?"

"You did, and when you pushed me into the water, I grabbed you and pulled you in right behind me. My mother was so upset about my soaked dress."

They both burst into laughter, thinking of that day so long ago.

"I think I've had a crush on you since then. You were the first girl I ever had that much fun with, besides Franny. I never realized how I felt about you until years later. Really not until you were so sick last year."

"I didn't have any idea. You see how oblivious I can be to things that are staring me in the face?"

"Do you think we can ignore all the concerns my family has and try to make our lives different from now on? Will you marry me?"

"Whoa! Let's slow down a bit. I've been through a lot more experiences than you in the last few years. You might even say

I'm damaged goods, and I've only been a widow for a short time. There is still a little sadness and grief when I think of Clarence. And you know I'm not sure I will ever be able to have another child. You probably want to have your own children, don't you?"

"Yes, of course. I'm sure you will heal, and even if you don't, we would always have two wonderful boys."

Nate dropped her hands. He stood and stared out the window at the future garden space. Neither said a word for the longest time until Lottie rose from her seat and walked up behind him. Putting her arms around his waist, she whispered in his ear.

"Nate, I think I am beginning to fall in love with you."

He turned and placed a tender kiss on her lips. "I can wait for you if you need more time to answer my question. We can get to know each other better working on the garden. That will be fun."

Looking into his dark-brown eyes, she smiled and said, "Hey, we don't have to make a big decision to get married right away. We could always practice."

28

The joy that Francena felt at moving back to Westbrook was short-lived. At first, Aunt Liz told her to relax for a few days before going back to work, so she took advantage of warmer than normal November weather to revisit her favorite spots— the riverbank near Forest Avenue Bridge, her path along the edge of Prides Quarry. She even ventured out to spend an afternoon walking the wooded trail across the river in Riverton Park. Then, as the weather turned cold, she was unable to stay outdoors and spent most of the time alone in her room trying to read. She found it difficult to concentrate because of the melancholy which had come over her since her return. When she tried to read, her mind would fill with thoughts about how lonely she felt even among family.

She kept thinking that she was almost twenty-six years old. Would she ever be able to strike out on her own? Find a good man for herself?

Liz had originally thought it a good idea to give her niece a couple of weeks of leisure to recover from the long, hard weeks of effort caring for the Potters. After a few days, she realized that something was wrong with Franny and giving her something to do might make her happier.

"Franny, while you were away, Mary and I came up with new designs using that beautiful Irish linen. Business has picked up, and we both have been working long hours. Do you think you're ready to help on production? You are so skilled."

"You're only complimenting me to make me feel better, aren't you? When I first came to live here, you were so fast on the machine that I was embarrassed at my own pace."

"Yes, that was before my eyes became so weak. Now I'm so slow that Mary sometimes takes over my machine to complete the work for me."

"Perhaps I could start in again. Why don't I start working for you on Monday?"

"Okay. Monday it is. Could you do me a favor today?"

"Of course."

"I know it's a bit chilly today, but would you be so kind as to bundle up and walk over to Bailey's Store? Mr. Bailey is offering our men's shirts to his customers, and we need to see if he wants to reorder. He's even serving as our mannequin, wearing our shirt in the store."

Franny felt better walking to Brook Street. She had something to do to keep her mind off her worries, and she would be returning to work. Neighbors whom she had not seen in a while waved to her as she passed. It was good to be at home again. At the Brook Street corner, a young man who had just left the store tipped his cap to her and smiled.

Eugene stood in the open door of his establishment as Franny approached. He looked much older than she remembered. He couldn't have changed that much in only a few weeks. Perhaps it was the way he was dressed or a new type of haircut. She didn't recall that he ever dressed so formally, with a waistcoat and a wide silk tie atop a lovely creamy-white linen shirt.

"Miss Hallett, so wonderful to see you again. You've been away quite a while. It was very charitable of you to be caring for that friend of yours. How is she? And her boys?"

"Mr. Bailey, how kind of you to ask after them. Lottie has completely recovered, or at least enough to take care of her family."

"It must have been a lot of work for you, with the two young ones and all. Thankfully, that part of Oxford County is beautiful. Must have made the time away easier on you."

"Yes, it is lovely there in Waterford, but the winter can be more difficult than it is here in Westbrook. They get even more snow on Beech Hill than we get at my family's home in Bridgton. Glad I got to leave before December. How have you been, Mr. Bailey?"

He smiled at her, then turned to enter the store. What a beautiful young girl, he thought. She appeared to have matured quite a bit. Must be the experience of dealing with her friend's illness that had given her a more charming allure. She had always been quite fetching, but now she was truly beautiful.

"Please call me Eugene. You will hopefully be a regular visitor here at the store. No need to be so formal. How can I help you today?"

There was something in the way he stared that bothered her. He was a decent man with a good reputation, and she had no reason to think that he had changed. He certainly had always been friendly and courteous to her.

"Yes, Eugene, I'm likely to be a regular visitor. Especially because you are carrying Aunt Lizzie's men's shirts. That one you are wearing looks quite elegant."

"Why, thank you, Miss Francena. If I may use your given name."

"Please feel free. As you said, no need to stand on formality."

He was beginning to appreciate the girl's familiarity. He straightened his tie and turned to look at himself in the mirror.

The shirt did look nice, and the off-white color of the linen complemented his ruddy complexion.

"Francena," he said, dropping the Miss. "What can I do for
you today? I am at your service."

He bowed slightly with his left arm at his waist. She smiled
at the gesture.

"Eugene, my aunt asked me to check with you about your
inventory of our linen shirts."

"Well, let's count them. I've sold several recently. In fact, one
gent actually purchased two. Said he hardly ever finds shirts that
fit him. His wife bought one for him as a gift, and he ran right
over to get another."

Joining him at the section of shelves where menswear was
displayed, she began to count the shirts he had by size. As she
pulled each shirt off the shelf, he saw that her hands were strong
but delicate. Her long hair was lovely.

"I believe you need to restock the small size. The others will
last you for a while. I will likely be making those myself when I
get back to work next week."

"Yes, my dear. Please take an order for three that size and
perhaps one each of the medium and large sizes."

"Are you sure?"

"Oh, yes. Now that I know you will be making them, I will
surely sell more. Just to get you to visit more often."

She curtsied and took the shirts from his arms, replacing
them on the shelf before turning to leave. There on the counter
near his register she noticed a magazine she had never seen
before, *Western Home.*

"Oh, do you subscribe?" she asked, picking it up to look at
the cover.

"No. That really is not to my taste. I like the news magazines
and *Retail News.* That sort of thing. My vendor convinced me to
add that to my selections. I believe there is a second edition over
on the rack there."

"The western parts of our country fascinate me. So different
from what we have here in New England. I'll take both editions."

"Shall I put that on your aunt's account?"

"No. I'll pay for them myself. No need to use credit for such trivialities."

What a responsible young lady, he thought. He walked behind her as she left and smiled as she headed up Forest Avenue.

"Be careful now, Francena!" he called after her. "There are many drivers along this busy highway who might not notice you on the side of the road. I don't want to hear of anything bad happening to such a beautiful woman."

By the time she reached her driveway, she felt much better about her prospects. At least there was one good man who might take an interest in her.

29

"Mother, I am nearly twenty-two," said Nate. "It's time for me to begin making my own decisions."

Nate sat at the kitchen table across from both his parents. Dinner had been done for half an hour, but the dirty dishes were still in front of them. Hattie rose from her seat and stood for the longest time staring out a window at light snow falling in the garden. Nathan stared directly at Nate. He had not said a word since the heated discussion began.

"Son," he began. "Neither of us have tried to keep you from making your own decisions. You are a grown man."

Hattie interrupted. "Yes, and we are proud of the man you've become."

"Yes, indeed," said Nathan, "very proud. We want to make sure you understand the importance of this particular decision. You're not talking about going out on a date with the woman. Marriage is a permanent commitment. You must consider the effects your choice will have not only on you, but on Lottie and her two sons."

"You think I haven't considered that, Dad? I've been going over this for months. I love Lottie. She is the best woman I have ever met. She loves me, too. We have both been sorting out all the factors, trying to make sure our relationship will work for Con and Francis as well as ourselves. I didn't make this decision quickly."

Hattie put her hands to her face before speaking, as if fighting back tears.

"Nate, we don't want to keep you from her. She is a wonderful woman. You might be just the person to help her get back on her feet and give those boys a good father. We're worried you might be hurting yourself in the long run."

"I understand your worries, Mom, but you have to understand how happy Lottie makes me. How much in love I am with all three of them. It takes most men years to find a beautiful, intelligent woman and to make a family with her. My family is all ready for me."

His parents stared at each other for a moment. Then Nathan rose from his chair, slid it under the table and stood with hands propped on its back.

"Thank you for hearing us out, Son. We want you to have as happy a life with your mate as we have had together. That's why we are so concerned. If you're going to be with her, why are you not getting married? Marriage by common law is not a sign of true commitment."

Nate rose from his chair and walked to Nathan's side. He put his arm around his father's shoulder.

"Dad, we thought practicing would give the boys time to adjust to my replacing Clarence in their lives. If it makes you and Mom happier, I will speak with Lottie about a wedding."

30

"Hello? Hello! Is anyone home?"

Lottie was surprised to hear someone knocking and shouting at the front door on such a snowy afternoon. Ethan Blaine stood at the door, long black hair hanging to his shoulders. She hadn't seen him since he had dropped off a bouquet of flowers for Franny.

"Ethan, what brings you to my door today?" she asked.

"Good day, Mrs. Potter. I'm looking for Miss Francena. Is she here?"

"No, she has returned to her home in Westbrook. Is there anything I can do for you?"

"Well, I did want to speak with her directly. She and I had several conversations, and since I was riding out this way making a delivery, I thought I would stop by to renew her acquaintance."

"I can tell her you dropped by next time I see her."

"I'd be much obliged if you did. Tell her that I remember her fondly and would like to see her again."

"I'm sure she will be happy to hear that. Perhaps she can come by the store next time she's visiting."

"Will she be coming soon?" he asked, his voice louder with excitement.

"I'm not sure. With winter coming on, I doubt we will see her until spring."

"Let's hope it's a short winter."

She watched the man saunter back to his horse and climb up into the saddle. He was certainly handsome. As he rode off, his long hair blew in the wind.

31

In the two years since Will Cain's death, Maeve had never thought of returning to work, but when her sister returned, she began to have more time. Having five kids to raise had always kept her busy. Mary was so good with the kids, almost like a second parent. Maeve would often say that they obeyed their aunt more than they did their own mother. She decided there might be time to work with Lizzie and Mary. As daughters Faith and Janey cleared the table after dinner one night, Maeve asked them both what they thought of the idea.

"Girls, you help me so much about the house. Sometimes

I think that family life could go on even if I were not here all the time."

"Whatever do you mean?" asked Faith. "Have you some news?"

"Nothing new, really. You have heard Mary and me discussing her job with Lizzie. Well, I am thinking of working, too. Only a couple days a week. And not full days. I don't *have* to work, but it might be fun. What do you think?"

"Mom, if you were only away a few hours, it could be fine. What does Owen think?" asked Janey.

Brother Owen, fifteen, was considered the man of the house. He was the oldest boy, eight years ahead of Willie, only one year older than James.

"Do you think he will give me permission?" Maeve asked with a grin.

Faith, who had continued to clear the table without saying a word, smiled and said, "Mom, I really think you need to have a family meeting on this. After all, we will all be affected."

"Okay, then. Let's call everyone together tomorrow after school and discuss the matter. Shall we invite Aunt Mary?"

"Oh, yes, Auntie is sure to share an opinion. She always does," said Janey.

"Jane Cain, you sound quite harsh about your loving aunt. She always wants the best for us all, doesn't she?"

"Janey is right," said Faith. "Sometimes Mary is very demanding. It's almost like she's our father."

Maeve was surprised. She had never realized that her children, at least two of them, didn't love her sister as she herself did.

"Then perhaps we might hold the meeting when Aunt Mary is at work. Would that suit the two of you? If that's what you want, I must say it makes me disappointed. I thought you accepted her as part of the family."

Faith stopped and sat in the chair next to her mom.

"When Auntie returned, I was fascinated with her. It was like she brought Ireland back with her. We all got to learn so much about your childhood home. As time has passed, though, there have been times when she has told us to behave in ways that are different from what you want. Different from what Dad wanted."

"You know she means well," said Maeve. "It might just be that ten years in the Emerald Isle have made her see things a little different. Children over there are raised in a different way."

"But, Mom, we are Americans."

"Thanks be to God, we are. I can understand some of what you're saying, but I know she loves you all dearly, as if you are her own. It would be inconsiderate not to have her involved in the discussion."

When Maeve told the other children about the family meeting to take place the next afternoon, she didn't open the door to any further discussion. She was afraid that the others might harbor similar reservations. When she questioned Owen, he answered in his usual tone of juvenile wisdom.

"Mom, Auntie Mary should definitely be considered part of our family. I'm aware of complaints about her from my sisters, who don't like how she tells them to live their lives. She loves us all, so it doesn't bother me."

32

After two years in Thomaston Prison, Aphia still believed that there was a way she might reduce her sentence on some technicality and be able to return to her little farm on Beech Hill. She learned that prisoners who exhibited good behavior could be rewarded with free time to to study in the institution's small library. While not a model prisoner, she was able to control herself for several months and gain access to the library's law books.

Twice each week, she was able to comb through a meager collection of books and pamphlets of Maine laws pertaining to murder versus self-defense and accidental homicide. She came upon mention of what was called "the slayer rule." Such a rule, often called "no profit theory," was based on ancient English common laws which denied the right of a person who killed their spouse from inheriting the victim's property. This had been the basis for Oxford County's taking of her property. Since the land had been in her husband's name and she had murdered him, the court had denied her title to the land.

If only she could prove that Henry's death had been accidental, the farm might be hers once again. There were, of course, the matters of the other two deaths at her hands: Maeve's husband, Will, who had been shot, and the poisoning of that curious young farmer. She could not forget them, but getting back ownership of the farm in Waterford would be a first step toward being set free. She wanted to find more books on that law.

"Excuse me, ma'am," she said to the woman who oversaw the library. "Do you know if you have any books here about English common law?"

The plump librarian who sat with her back to Aphia turned around and flashed a toothless smile. "Can't thay, really." Half of what she had to say was unintelligible. "Whath sat?"

"Might there be law books available from other libraries?"

"Yesh, th'orden hath more bookth in his offith. Ya haf to athk a guard abouf it."

What an idiot, Aphia said to herself. How could this woman get a job, even a menial one? It was going to take more time than she had coming to her this day to get permission to access the warden's private library. When she left the library as mealtime approached, a notice on a bulletin board caught her eye. It was an announcement that a local law firm was offering its entry-level clerks to provide legal advice for prisoners free of charge. She took down the notice, folded it, and slipped it into the waistband of her uniform.

That night she dreamed again about flying.

She discovers that someone has forgotten to lock the cell door. Once in the corridor, it is easy for her to sneak past a napping guard and into the exercise yard. She wills herself to jump off the ground and into the starlit sky above the prison.

Over the empty streets and darkened houses of Thomaston she moves, like a stealthy bird, not making a noise. Soon the town turns to farmland, and the scene below begins to look familiar as she rises ever higher. In only a moment, her farmhouse and barn are below, and she hovers for a moment. There is no one about the place, but she senses that a family sleeps inside. She senses that they are people she has met. Three young boys sleep in a new room added just off the kitchen where her herb beds used to be.

"I know this family is related to that seamstress. They must be. She doesn't relent in trying to ruin me. Damn her to hell."

At her curse, the dream ends, and she lies wide awake in her bed once more.

"I will have that place back as mine," she mutters, "if it is the last thing I do on this earth."

33

"Nate, I had a weird dream again last night," said Lottie as he made their morning coffee. "That witch Stevens was here with us, watching us sleep."

He looked at her for a moment with a crooked smile. "Was she on a broomstick?"

"Are you mocking me? You don't believe that the woman has some sort of power to affect our lives, even from behind bars. Clarence didn't believe me, either."

"No, I'm not mocking you. The feelings you have about that woman are valid. She's a murderer. She lived in this very house for years. You are sensitive to her vibrations that are still here."

"Nate, we've never talked about my fears. It's common knowledge that she is responsible for the murders of three men, and I think she was also responsible for Clarence's death."

"How could that be? She was in jail before he left you. She couldn't have arranged for his demise."

She rubbed her hands together, as if they were cold.

"Yes. Yes, you're right. Perhaps I am being foolish. But from the time Clarence and I moved into this house, weird things happened. Not just dreams. Once, he and Con were nearly burned to death in the head house at the mica mine. They barely escaped."

"You told me about that fire. It may have been as Clarence told you, just a simple failure on his part to check for a dirty chimney."

"Of course, that's a rational explanation. Even when he explained the cause to me, I felt there was something eerie about it. I have always felt she was involved in that fire. Clarry always told me that I was foolish to be afraid of her."

Nate went to the kitchen door, opened it, and stared out at the snowdrifts covering their garden.

"I know your premonitions must feel very real. I can't doubt the reality of what you feel. Clarence must have also had similar feelings. I remember that first day when you moved here from Lizzie's. He was determined to get rid of every remnant of her herb garden. He had me whacking away at every root to make the space safe for the kids."

"He even built the boys' room on top of that garden. As if the structure's weight would crush and wipe out her memories."

As they talked, Con entered the room rubbing the sleep from his eyes. He went to his mother and grabbed the fabric of her apron.

"Mommy, I had a dream last night. There was a woman flying around in the sky. Can that really happen?"

"No, Conny. People don't fly. Birds fly. You know that."

She looked at Nate and shrugged her shoulders.

34

That night, Nate and Lottie sat on the sofa in front of a crackling fire in their Franklin stove, which was open so they could watch the flames. They listened to the sound of ice pellets against the windows and knew that another storm was approaching from the west. At each gust of wind, the flames would roar, and embers would fly against the fire screen. The day had been filled with hard work of carrying split firewood from the barn into the woodshed between the barn and house.

"Do we have enough wood for the season?" he asked. "I've not been here for an entire winter, so I can't judge."

"Eight cords should do it. There might even be a little left over if the winter is not unusually long."

"We likely would be able to get more from Kimball or even my dad, if we run low, but being self-sufficient is good."

He hadn't mentioned the conversation with his parents about a wedding. They had offered to have the ceremony at their own house and were anxious to have a date set.

"Mom and Dad think we best get married. In fact, they are wholeheartedly behind the idea of us being a regular family. It surprised me."

"Weren't we going to wait? Try to see how we get along? Test the relationship?"

"Well, that was the idea originally. Now that I see they are in favor of our marriage, it might be time to reconsider. What do you think?"

"I'm not sure, Nate. I love you. No question. It's just that I still have some demons in my mind because of the way Clarence deserted me and the boys."

"As I've said before, I love you and am ready to give you my life. The date when I can do that is totally up to you."

She reached for his hand and held it to her lips. He put his other arm around her waist, pulling her close. She could feel the beat of his heart against her breast as she lifted her mouth to his and kissed him with such passion that she accidentally bit his lip. He pulled away for a moment before dropping his head to her chest and kissing first one breast and then the other through the fabric of her bodice. She had not felt like this with him before. Now she wanted him to take her, be inside her, make her feel the way she did in the early days with Clarence.

"I want to make love to you," he whispered in her ear.

"I'm not sure we can, Nate. Not yet."

"I don't want to hurt you. It may be too early. Can't we lie in each other's arms?"

He had been sleeping on a narrow bed in the boys' small room. Both he and Lottie would often doze off on the sofa after holding hands and kissing. They knew sleeping together might lead to lovemaking, something each of them desired.

Lottie rose and took his hand.

"Yes, my love. It is time. Let's go to my bedroom. There are things we can do to show our love for each other without having intercourse."

They lay naked in bed, caressing each other until both surrendered to sleep.

Suddenly, Nate heard a great noise and jumped from under the quilt. He hurried to the window and watched great bolts of lightning strike across the sky like cracks in plate glass. Each bolt was followed by an immediate clap of thunder so loud that he knew the storm was directly on them. Lottie continued to sleep amidst such cacophony. As he watched, one mighty shaft struck the barn roof, shattering the building's windows. The large door burst into flames.

"Wake up, Lottie! The barn's afire!" he shouted as he put on his trousers and rushed out of the house. Snow had turned to heavy rain, which quickly soaked him to the skin. Running to the pump, he filled two buckets and ran toward the small blaze, hoping to douse it before more timbers might ignite. Lottie donned a heavy slicker and joined him, filling two more buckets so that he could pour water on the fire more quickly. Con and Francis came to the door. The young one was wailing and waving his arms about.

"Go back inside, both of you!" she yelled. "We will keep you safe."

Soon the intense rain falling on the fire enabled them to control the flames. As the storm and fire abated, the couple held each other to keep from falling with exhaustion. Lottie called the boys out to see what had happened.

Con held on to Nate's hand as he stared at the charred barn door. "Did that flying lady land on the barn? Did she light a fire to stay warm?"

35

Bert Learned's life had been hard on him, left him a weary vestige of a man who looked to be a generation older than his real age. For many decades, he had been a friend of Will Cain, Lizzie Millett, and her sister, Hattie Hallett, but had not recently been in contact with them. He grew up in Waterford with Henry Greene. He parted ways with the man when his friend threw aside fiancée Lizzie to marry a younger, more attractive woman. He lost his wife and infant son in a house fire, then spent years in drunkenness to quell his grief. When he returned to his hometown a sober man, he fell in love with Greene's mysterious widow Aphia Stevens, only to find that she had killed his former friend and buried him in the pasture near her house. In shame for his foolishness and in fear that his lover might do the same to him, he disappeared once more into the confines of a whiskey bottle.

Returning to Waterford after again finding the salvation of sobriety, he found that Aphia had taken the life of Will Cain, his dear friend, leaving Maeve with five children to raise on her own. Anger drove him to visit the sheriff of Oxford County and reveal for the first time what he knew about Henry Greene's death and show where the body was buried. Once the murderess was behind bars, Bert visited her one more time before heading back to an isolated cabin in Chatham, New Hampshire.

At the age of sixty, he felt that his years were nearly gone, so he decided to visit his old hometown one last time. He couldn't be sure he knew anyone who might still be living there, except for that young couple who had taken up residence in Aphia's old farmhouse, the one he himself had shared with her for a year or so. He remembered the place occasionally, how beautiful the location was up on the top of Beech Hill. On a warm April day, he rode his swayback nag south to North Waterford village and then up Greene Road. Neither he nor the horse was used to traveling up such a hill. They approached the Potter house very slowly.

Con was the first to notice the man approach. He ran into the kitchen where Lottie sat reading. "Mommy, Mommy! There's a man walking up the road. He looks like a farmer's scarecrow. His horse is nearly falling down."

With Nate away for a couple of days, she was reluctant to have anything to do with a vagabond. When she spied the spindle of a man in his worn overalls, ragged straw hat, and stubbly face, she felt relieved. It was that man who witnessed against Aphia. He had made it possible for Clarence to get this house for her and the kids.

She recalled his name. "Bert, Bert Learned. Please come and sit by the fire. It's such a chilly day to be out."

"Yes, downright cold. Indeed it is. Especially on an old man like me. It was much warmer when I left my home this morning." He mounted the steps with a great deal of effort, stopping several times to rest on the way up. When he reached the porch, he stopped to rest, holding the porch railing and inspecting the front of the place.

"Seems you and your man have done a good job keeping this place up. I remember how ragged it looked before you moved in. You know, I lived here once, many years ago. Believe me, I know there's a lot of work in running an old house like this."

She offered him a glass of water. While she went to get it, Con and Francis approached Bert and stared up at him. He reminded them of the scarecrow in a book Nate had been reading to them,

The Wonderful Wizard of Oz. Francis went up to him and peeked into his sleeve cuff to see if there was any straw in there.

"Boys, don't pester the man. He traveled a long distance to be here. Go back to your playing and let us visit."

Lottie led her visitor into the kitchen, setting a chair for him close to the range. She gave Bert his water and sat watching as he emptied the glass without taking a breath. It had been two years since he had dropped by to warn her and Clarence about Aphia's strange powers.

"Young lady, how is that wonderful Canadian husband of yours? Is he around today? I would like to give him my regards."

"Bert, I'm no longer with Clarence. He died last spring in a mining accident up in Ontario."

"So sorry to hear that, my dear. Very sad indeed. How are you keeping since then?"

"Oh, doing well, really. After a few rough months. I have a new man. His name is Nate Hallett. I believe you know his mother, Hattie."

"Hattie? Not Hattie Millett, is it? Oh, my God. Such a small world. Yes, we are old friends. I've known the Millett sisters since the eighties when we all lived with their grandparents. Nate must be an upstanding young man."

"Yes, he is a blessing to this family. Tell me, Bert, when you were here before, you mentioned that Aphia Stevens possessed strange powers that you did not understand. Do you still believe that?"

"I lived in this house with that woman for most of two years. At first, I thought her the most beautiful and intelligent woman I'd ever met. We were planning on being married, you know. Then, as time went on, her darker side was revealed to me, aspects that I had missed completely. In spring, when most people like to see sun and warmth return, a horde of flies would invade the place. She cursed them, blamed her grandad, who had buried some number of dead horses in a pit next to the barn. She put me to covering the spot with load after load of dirt. Had to do it to prove my love."

"Nathan Hallett has told me about that. We haven't had any problem with flies."

"Good. Perhaps my grading worked. Or the horse flesh may have rotted into earth."

Lottie tried to change the subject, but he went on. "She came up with the idea of raising herbs and making soaps and potions to earn some money. Seemed like a good idea, but her garden produced so many herbs that she turned the house into a factory. Drying herbs hanging in bunches from the ceiling, cauldrons always boiling on the stove. Some of the smells made me ill."

"It was because of your warning that Clarence demanded that all the herb beds be torn up before we could move in."

"Yes indeed, I am sure some plants were poisonous. She sold certain potions to farmers for killing rats. I left her that second spring. The fumes were beginning to give me strange dreams. She could have killed me, as well as the rats."

"You warned us about her powers as well as the herbs. Why did you say that? Was it just speculation?"

"My dear miss, I didn't have to be too smart to put two and two together. She told me about accidentally poisoning her husband with an herb. She was fooling around with herbs that were giving me strange dreams and headaches. She was obviously having the same problems as me. Then she started to paint devilish symbols on the doors and windows. And telling me she could predict the weather."

Bert was speaking with such fervor that Lottie decided it best to stop this discussion.

"Bert, where are you staying tonight?"

"Sorry to get so carried away. My memories of that woman stir my ire each time she comes to mind."

He took two deep breaths and then saw by the kitchen clock that he had been ranting for over an hour. "Forgive me. I didn't realize the time is gettin' on. I was plannin' on a visit with the Halletts. It's a bit late for that."

"No. No, Bert, we can make a place here for you for the night. And you can eat with us, also."

"Much obliged. Don't want to put you out, though. All I need is a tick on the floor. You see, I'm so tall that most beds don't fit me."

He spotted the hammock strung between two maples next to the muddy garden.

"As long as that hammock is not near to the place where the horses are buried, I can fit right there real good. Just need a warm blanket."

"No. I will not have a guest sleeping outside when we can make a space in the boys' bedroom."

"You'd likely have to put two beds end to end for me to fit. I will be fine out there." He pointed to the hammock. "At home, I'm pretty well sleeping outside even when I'm inside. My life is very simple, you know."

She had no choice but to accept the man's wishes. So, after supper, Bert wrapped himself in a wool blanket and slept in the hammock fully clothed.

As he slept, a breeze from the top of Beech Hill rocked the hammock slowly back and forth. His slumber was as deep as that of a contented baby in its cradle. As dawn light began to gather, he awoke with a start.

Six lovely black horses race each other through the nearby pasture. One rears up on its hind legs and shakes its forelegs in Bert's direction. Watching them gallop round and round each other, he barely notices a figure dressed in black who walks up behind him and points toward the barn in silence. The barn bursts into flames while the figure laughs hysterically. He jumps from the hammock and starts for the well pump when a loud voice cries out, "You fool, Bert Learned, you old fool! You dare return to meddle in things that no longer affect you. I lost this house because of you, but I will get it back. There is no fire now. It is all in a dream. But the future is in my control."

He knows the voice is Aphia's and that she wants revenge.

"Damn you, Aphia! Damn you to hell! I stopped you before. I will stop you again."

Lottie saw her guest waving both fists in the air and yelling so loudly that he was sure to wake the children. He certainly was a strange sort. A good man at heart, to be sure, but one who had been sorely damaged by a very difficult life.

36

On the way home, Nate stopped at Nason's to purchase goods on a list Lottie had given him. He was greeted by Ethan, who sat on a barrel near the door wearing a long canvas grocer's apron.

"Mr. Hallett," the lad said. "Nice to see you again. How can I help you this fine day?"

"Ethan, I've been here enough to be called Nate, haven't I?"

"Yes, sir. Nate it is, then. What can I do for you?"

"Here's a list of goods Lottie asked me to get for the family. Can you put everything together while I check at the post office?"

By the time he returned, two wooden crates, heavy with household goods, had already been loaded into his wagon.

"You're a good man to tote those boxes for me. I could have done that myself, you know."

"Sir—I mean Nate." He seemed perplexed for some reason. "Nate, do you have a sister who lived with your wife for a while last year? I think her name was Hallett also."

"Oh, you mean my sister Francena. She cared for Lottie when she was ill. So, you met her?"

"Yes, several times. But then she left. We were only introduced and then she was gone. I was sorry to learn that she left so quickly."

"I will tell her she made you sad."

"No, don't do that. Tell her that she made me *happy* when she came to the store. That would be a better message, wouldn't it?"

"Why haven't you told her that yourself? You can write, can't you? She loves to get letters. She writes a great letter herself. I'm sure she would respond to yours with a prompt reply."

Nate initialed the store ledger and turned to leave.

"Nate, can you give me Miss Francena's address? I may not be as good at writing as she is, but I would like to find out how she is doing." He opened a blank page to Nate, who entered the requested information on its back.

"Can you tell me if she is seeing someone? You know, has a boyfriend."

"We don't talk about everything she does. She's sure to be back soon to visit Lottie. You might ask her yourself."

"Please don't mention this conversation. It would be so embarrassing if your sister learned that I was asking for her and she already had someone special."

"My friend, your interest will be known only to the two of us. My lips are sealed."

On his way home, Nate smiled at the fact that he knew something about a stranger's interest in his sister that was unknown to her. Several times he laughed out loud. When he saw Lottie, he mentioned what had happened.

"Did you know the clerk at Nason's has a crush on Franny? He asked me for her address so he could write her a letter."

"He's such a nice boy. He dropped off a bouquet for her the day after she left. Said it was a gift from Mr. Nason to me as a good customer, but I knew different. When she was visiting, she lost herself each day in the western novel, *The Virginian*. I think Ethan might be her cowboy, the one who sweeps her off her feet. Like in the story, the two of them might mount a set of ponies and ride into the sunset."

Nate looked at her for a moment. "I really have no idea in the world what you're talking about. It must be something that only a woman would understand."

37

Millett's American Designs dress shop was abuzz with activity. Both Mary and Francena sat at the Singers making so much noise that Lizzie had trouble concentrating at the design table. Maeve was ready to return to work on the first of the month. Liz was piecing together a pattern for a new garment, a cotton skirt with a broad belt that would complement blouses made from Irish linen.

"Franny, can you help me here a second?" Liz had to shout to be heard above the din. "I need your eyes to help me line up the seams on this pattern."

"Of course, Auntie. It will give my hands a chance to rest. They hurt from being held in one position for so long."

She moved in close to her aunt, lined up two pieces of pattern paper, and affixed them with common pins pulled from a roll of a hundred.

"Even with your eyes not being as strong as they once were, you certainly haven't lost your ability to make a great design. Look at all the stitchery you've used. Please assign me to work on that one."

"Both of you will be busy with this design. We have an order from R.H. White department store in Boston for twenty of these if the buyer approves the first one."

"Well, let me make the prototype for the buyer. It will be perfect."

Overhearing the conversation, Mary stepped up to join them at the table.

"My cousin's cloth helps make all these garments look like a million dollars. Do you think that explains why we have so much work all of a sudden?"

"That, yes. Along with the Hallett family sales team I have working for me. Franny has such a winning smile that all the store owners in Cumberland County want to buy. When they call to order more pieces, it isn't me they ask for, but 'that sharp young woman.' Several of the men buyers ask to have her deliver the goods personally."

Franny smiled at the praise but was embarrassed.

"I don't do anything special to get the orders, just show them the apparel and smile."

"Perhaps you wink a little?" asked Mary. "Just a bit of flirtation?"

"But Dad's the one bringing in all the big orders from large stores. Do you think he uses flirtation to land the business?"

"Dearie, pay me no mind," said Mary. "It is only me Irish humor kickin' in. Like Nathan, you are very good at sales. Must be in the blood."

"I like that humor. Don't give it up. Now, I better get back to my sewing before my aunt lets me go."

When the two older women were left alone at the table, Mary leaned down so very close to Liz that she almost was sitting in her lap. Although the Singer made enough noise to drown out regular conversation, the two whispered.

"You know, my dear," Mary began, "when I first went to Bailey's's Store, the man hardly gave me the time of day after I failed to respond to his interests. The only way he would take one of our shirts was if I nearly *gave* him one to wear. Because of Francena's smile and sunny disposition, he has created an entire rack for our line."

"Yes, and he is one who asks for her directly. From his tone, I take it he has some interest in a relationship with her more personal than commercial."

"I hope she's not being too friendly with the man. He really wasn't my style, kind of supercilious, if you ask me."

Liz pinched her friend's arm. "*Supercilious*, is it? Been studying Webster's, have we?"

"No, stop joking. I'm only thinkin' that a man like him might not have the girl's best interests at heart."

"Not sure what you mean. She's unmarried, and from what I can tell, is interested in finding a good man."

"Perhaps I'm worryin' too much. After all, I've never been with a man. I get suspicious that they're only out for their own well-being. And it usually has something to do with sex."

"Doesn't everything between a man and woman have sex involved? Birds and bees, you know."

Mary looked deeply into Liz's eyes with a grin. Neither of them looked away, until Mary finally said, "Birds and bees, is it? You know, my dear, it might be the same between birds and birds."

"Or bees and bees," whispered Liz.

They both laughed.

38

"What is that racket?"

Nathan stood at the kitchen window peering out toward the hedge of low, yellow-leafed False Cypress along busy South High Street.

"I heard it early this morning, and there it is again."

"Oh, that. It's a silly downy woodpecker drumming away on Mrs. Smith's tin bird feeder." Hattie had all she could do to keep from breaking into laughter. "He started doing that the other day while you were in Boston. Makes me laugh. The bird must get a headache."

"Sounds like a snare drummer in the Fourth of July parade. Or a hydraulic jackhammer like they use in Oxford County mines. I hope he doesn't drum at night."

As they listened again for the rat-a-tat-tatting, another strange noise drew their attention. A man with a very high-pitched voice was complaining about something out on the street. At first, they couldn't make out what he was saying, but as his voice grew louder, they heard every word.

"Git up! Git up, you lazy old nag! Don't lay down in the street. You can't be that tired. You haven't had to carry me for hours. Git up or I'll just leave you here to die. Or to become somebody else's problem."

The couple continued to watch and saw the head of an old man with long white hair hanging down from beneath a straw hat so twisted and ragged that it looked like he had a bird nest on his head. He was tall enough to be visible above their hedge. When he turned to face the house, Hattie recognized him as her old friend Bert Learned.

Opening the front door, she hailed him. "Bert! Is that you, Bert Learned?"

"Yes, it is me, Hattie. I set out early this morning for an early visit with you and your husband. But this damned animal has given me trouble since we left Waterford. Now it's late afternoon and I'm only just arriving. Miserable animal!"

Nathan strode down the porch steps and out to the roadway.

"Sir, your horse looks like it needs some cold water and a good rest."

"Or something to put it out of its misery," said Bert with disgust.

"Looks like she needs to rest from a long journey. You'll see how quickly she recovers once we cool her in the barn."

Nathan went back to the house, drew a bucket of cold water from the kitchen sink, and returned to rub the horse's back and head with a damp cold rag. He held the bucket to its head and let it drink a little bit at a time. He took the reins from Bert and coaxed the animal back to its feet. Bert stood on the opposite side of the road until Hattie came to his side and led him to a garden bench next to the house. She brought him a glass of ice water.

"Thank you kindly, Hattie. I could use a couple of these glasses. With that horse refusin' to carry me, I'm parched. When I left your daughter-in-law in Waterford, it was my plan to stop here for a short visit and then continue on to visit dear Lizzie."

"Don't fret, Bert. You've made it here safely. You can stay with us tonight and go to Westbrook tomorrow. We've plenty of beds now with both kids gone. Besides, it will be good to catch up with what you've been doing up in Chatham."

"That'll be a very short conversation, indeed it will. Not much has happened to me since I was among the civilized two years ago. You young people have much more to tell than I do. How is that lovely daughter of yours? She must be fightin' off the young men, now that she's of age."

"She is with Lizzie in that big old house and has become quite a seamstress. Perhaps better than her auntie. It must be in her blood. Came down from her grandmother."

"I never met your mother. She had passed on before I entered the picture. She must have been a remarkable woman to have raised two beautiful and talented women like you and your sister."

"She didn't have too much time to raise us. She died so young. I was six at the time, so I do remember her some. Her loss was worse for Lizzie, who was nine. She mothered me until I married Nathan. Even when we lived with my grandparents."

As they chatted, Nate bounded down the porch stairs carrying his duffel. He stopped for a moment to watch his mother in conversation with a strange-looking old man.

"Oh, Nate," greeted Hattie. "You remember my old friend Bert Learned, don't you? He was the man who lived with your aunt and me in the Westbrook house before I met your dad."

"Hello, sir." He reached out to shake the man's hand.

"Son, I just came from a visit with your beautiful wife and two handsome sons. You are certainly a fortunate man to have such a family."

"Mr. Learned, were the boys well behaved for you?"

"Oh, indeed they were. Lottie told me what happened to the Canadian miner. Such a sorry story. She's fortunate to have landed such an outstanding young man as yourself. And, of course, to have such a lovely place to live on Beech Hill."

Following lunch, Nate explained that he would be leaving that afternoon to return home. Hattie offered the man her son's bedroom. Once again, the man turned down the offer of a comfortable night's sleep.

"No, Mrs. Hallett, I'd not sleep well indoors at this time of year. Not that I want to offend you in any way. No, that is not my way. I am grateful for anything offered by either friend or stranger. T'would be better for me to sleep on a tick in the barn near my horse. It's outdoors I sleep most nights. In my own woodshed most of the time. That's what I'm used to."

"Where you sleep is your own choice. I insist you join Nathan and me for dinner. Nothing too grand. We tend to enjoy light meals when we're alone. And then you can join us for breakfast."

"Ma'am, you say your meal will be simple. I say it likely will fill me up so that breakfast will not be needed." He held up his arm and rolled the gray shirt sleeve up to his elbow. "You see how thin is my arm? I'm like that all around my body. No need for much food to keep me going."

"All right, then. Please rest up in the parlor while I run to town to get few things for the evening meal."

As soon as he sat on the sofa, Bert's eyes closed, and soon the sounds of his snoring echoed through the empty house. Nathan returned from the barn and, seeing their guest sound sleep, decided to work in the garden and let him sleep.

39

Bert had been on the road for five days, much longer than he had planned. He was disappointed not to visit Lizzie, but he might do that later in the year. He wanted to return home before the growing season began in earnest. When he finally reached his rustic cabin, a diseased maple had fallen on his woodshed. A branch blocked the way to the cabin door. As he tugged on the branch to break it, the weight of the tree shifted, and the shed collapsed beneath it.

Opening the door, he was surprised to see that dust had settled over the floor and furniture. Spider webs spread across the single small window from corner to corner and hung down from the bare rafters.

"How quickly nature reclaims her territory," he said to himself. "If I had gone everywhere I planned, there'd be nothing left of my home when I returned."

There was no stall for his Bess with the shed collapsed, so she wandered freely about the clearing he had spent twenty years cutting from the woodland inherited from his father. She never wandered farther than the brook that meandered a few steps beyond the pathway, so he didn't worry about her.

There was much work to be done to get the garden ready, but he would need to wait until the muddy soil dried to plant seeds.

"It's the same every year. All the work gets harder and harder as I grow old. Thankfully, there is no one but myself to feed. And because I eat less and less, there's no need to be in a big hurry. Perhaps in time I will become more like Bess and feed on what grows by itself."

He always spoke aloud, as if someone other than the horse was with him. The sound of his voice helped to fill the emptiness around him.

40

Eugene Bailey seldom wandered very far from the corner of Brook Street and Forest Avenue, where he lived above his store. This very spot was for him the center of the universe, the heart of Prides Corner. There were enough neighbors at the busy intersection and across the avenue on Pride Street to keep him company. Over the last decade, too many people from away had moved into the neighborhood. The development was very good for his business but detrimental to his sense of privacy. There were too many families with young children whom he knew could one day turn into destructive ruffians. He allowed some elderly veterans to while away the hours sitting on the front steps of his store. They hardly spent enough to justify his willingness to let them congregate there.

This fine clear Monday, he broke from his custom and closed the store to walk the mile or so up to the local dressmaker's shop. He had sold all the linen shirts, and after waiting a few days for Francena to return and restock his supply, he decided to take matters into his own hands. Dressed in a pair of tan worsted slacks, a white linen shirt, and a checkered waistcoat, he cut quite a stylish figure as he strolled along the edge of the road with his walking stick in one hand, a small folder in the other. As he approached Lizzie's house and shop, he stopped to wipe the dust from his freshly polished leather boots.

When he knocked at the shop door, Francena opened it, smiled, and reached out to shake his hand. He stood still for a moment before making an awkward bow with both arms swept back behind him. His cane hit the door frame and his folder fell on the threshold. Amused at such an old-style greeting, she picked up the folder and took his elbow, directing him into the showroom.

"My dear Eugene, please come in. What a pleasant surprise to see you today."

"Miss Francena, please forgive my barging in like this with no announcement in advance."

"No apologies necessary. This is, after all, a business establishment. We hardly expect to know that a customer is coming before he shows up. I imagine it is the same at your store."

Her smile was so bright and reassuring that he broke into a wide grin himself.

"So right you are, miss. So very right. I have come to place a new order for the linen shirts you delivered to me some time ago. They have proved very successful. I have sold them all."

"Except for the one you are wearing, I see. You look so handsome in it. No wonder people have been buying them."

Was she complimenting him? He felt ill at ease. Her words of praise were perhaps a bit too personal.

"Miss Francena, if you have the invoice for the original delivery, I will be very happy to settle the balance before placing another order."

She went to Lizzie's big desk and pulled the ledger from the top drawer.

"Yes, here's the record for that transaction. The balance is $20.80."

"Oh, that much?"

"Yes, Eugene. I made the ledger entry myself. Didn't I give you a copy of the invoice for your records?"

"You may have. Oh, I'm sure you did. If you figured what was due by yourself, I will assume you are correct. After all, you're very intelligent for a woman in the ways of business."

He reached into his coat pocket and produced a twenty-dollar bill. Then he reached into his pocket for the change.

Franny didn't know how to take his comment about her being a woman but thought it best not say anything. The customer is always right, she thought. She was sure he meant no harm.

"My dear, are all of Miss Millett's garments bespoken?"

"Most are, but the shirts you stock are made in three standard sizes. Did you want to order all three sizes? If so, I believe we may be able to fill your order in the next couple of days."

"Wonderful. I hate to miss out on any opportunities for a sale. Would you yourself be able to deliver them to me? If so, I would invite you to join me for lunch. I am a very good cook for a bachelor."

"Eugene, I'll be away for a couple of days visiting my brother and his family. When I return, it will be my pleasure to deliver your shirts. Lunch is not necessary."

"Please, I insist. I enjoy your company. Shall we say next Friday?"

41

Nate and Francena rode along Bridgton Road in their father's brougham on the way to Beech Hill Farm. The dress shop had been so busy Franny had not been able to visit her dearest friend Lottie for five months. Now, before the dog days of August arrived, she would spend a few days on Beech Hill. The towering elm trees along Main Street in Bridgton were fully leafed out. When they reached Bear Pond Road in South Waterford, the sight of mature maples and oaks clustered amongst groves of towering hemlocks made them pause more than once.

"You are so fortunate to live in this hidden paradise," said Franny. "The streets of both Westbrook and Bridgton are sometimes so crowded and noisy."

"Westbrook is too much like Portland. I love Bridgton, but I know what you mean. At the farm in winter there are times I feel isolated from civilization. Even then I am grateful for my new home with Lottie."

"You really have changed these last few months, Nate. Two years ago, you would never have been talking like that. Having a good marriage must make life much better than being alone."

"So true. However, it's more than that. Many of my friends are married to good women, yet some of them are still looking for better things. My future looks brighter with each passing day, but my present day is all that I need."

"You are very fortunate. I hope my future will be as bright."

As they approached Beech Hill, a cool breeze shook the trees, sending brown sparrows and golden finches up to the sky. Franny pulled her collar up a little tighter.

"This night may be a cool one. We may need to light a small fire," he said. "The kids love a fire burning in the Franklin, especially Con. He helps me get the flames going. Then he takes full responsibility for making the family warmer. He is such a great son."

Franny shoved her hands into her jacket pockets. Her words came slowly as the carriage turned into the driveway. "Please forgive me for saying this. You cannot forget that Clarence was their real father. The ruination he caused in Lottie's life made it easy for you to have a family."

"I know my loving family is a true gift from a loving universe. No question of that. And I hope that you will have as easy a time finding your true happiness as have I. Please remember that Lottie made her pain and disappointment possible by surrendering to the first prince who crossed her path. He then destroyed her dreams in pursuit of his own selfish goals. I want to live with her long enough to make the hurts she has suffered become faint memories."

"If Clarence was her prince, you are her king. Now, let's go to your queen."

42

Lottie had worked for two days to prepare a supper that would welcome her best friend. Baked potatoes and fresh green beans from her own garden complemented the large ham purchased from Nason's, where it had drawn great attention hanging in the window. She had even baked a blueberry cobbler for dessert. Both boys sat at the table propped up on cushions and ate a bit of most dishes and a lot of the pastry. After the meal, Nate took charge of both children and prepared them for bed. Lottie and Franny cleared the table and washed the dishes.

"You have not graced us with your presence for such a long time, Franny," said Lottie as she washed a plate. "Has your life been so crowded that there was no room for me?"

Franny threw the dish towel over her shoulder and took hold of her friend's wet hand. "You sound perturbed with me. Please don't be. Mary, Liz, and I have been working nearly every day. It is so exciting. We are already working on new designs for spring, and it isn't even winter yet."

"I am only pulling your leg, dear. Don't let it bother you. I am really very excited for you. Have you been able to have any sort of social life? You must take some time for yourself occasionally."

"Oh, yes. I have been to a few Grange dances and church socials. The Prides Corner crowd includes some very interesting people."

"Any boys your age?"

Franny began to dry another plate. "Boys my age? What do you mean? Do you think I don't have a date now and then?"

"Well, is there anyone special?"

"Lottie, you're getting a bit nosy, aren't you?"

"There are more things in life than work. After all, you *are* twenty-six years old. Do you want to always be a spinster?"

Franny burst into laughter and pinched her friend's arm. "You know, my auntie has always called herself a spinster, even when she was married to Uncle Moses. In my grandmother's day, a spinster was a woman of any age, married or unmarried, who made her livelihood by spinning thread and making cloth. So I guess that is what I am."

"That's not what people think the word means today. A spinster is a woman who can't find a man to marry. You know that. That's what I mean."

"I know you want me to be happy, and for you that has always been to be married. I see it a little differently. When I meet a man who makes me feel happy and who wants to be a partner, like my dad is to my mom, I will know it. So far, it hasn't happened. I've had a couple of evenings in the company of a man who owns the general store in Prides Corner. He is some years older than me and a bit set in his ways, but he's nice to me and treats me kindly. I'm not in love with him or anything. We're just getting to know each other."

By now the dishes were put away. The two women went to sit in the parlor, where Nate was lighting a fire in the Franklin. Lottie brought out a bottle of sherry and poured three glasses. When all three were seated, the conversation began on a somewhat different topic.

Lottie turned to her friend. "Ethan Blaine was asking about you when I was in town to buy that delicious ham. He wondered if you might be visiting soon."

Lifting her glass in front of her eyes, Franny looked through the tan liquid at the open flames.

"Is that the young man at Nason's?"

"Yes, the very one who dropped off a bouquet of flowers for you the last time you were here. You've caught his attention."

"He has asked me about you several times," said Nate. "Wanted to know if you were married or engaged. I told him he would have to ask you for himself."

"Brother dear, you know he is a little young for marriage. Wouldn't you agree, Lottie?"

"How much older than you is that storekeeper you've been seeing in Westbrook?" asked Lottie.

"Mr. Bailey is thirty-two. And I have not been *seeing* him, if you please."

"So, he is six years older. Nate, how old do you think Ethan is?"

"Oh, I'd say about twenty-one or -two. He graduated from Bridgton Academy a few years ago."

"So, Franny. If six years isn't too much of a difference for you with an older man, can it be any different with a younger one? Look at your brother and me. He is five years my junior. That didn't keep me from falling for him. A strong younger man can be good for us older ladies."

After a long moment of silence and a few looks back and forth amongst them, the three burst into uproarious laughter.

"Here's to us younger men," said Nate, lifting his tumbler.

That night Nate laid out a bedroll on the floor of the boys' bedroom. He'd offered to sleep there for the time that his sister would be visiting so that she would be comfortable. They had no guest room, so Franny took his place in the bed with Lottie. Into the wee hours, the girlfriends chatted about what they had done since being together months before. It wasn't until the predawn light began to seep into the room that they both slept.

When Lottie woke, the sun was high enough in the sky to overheat the room. She saw that her friend was still asleep, rose quietly, and opened the window to let in fresh, cool air. As she tiptoed toward the door, Franny sat bolt upright, though still asleep, and shouted out, "Stop! Stop! Get away from that window!" Then she lay back down, returning to quiet slumber.

Lottie stopped in her tracks. As she watched, her friend began to stir, opened her eyes, and smiled. "Lottie, what's the matter? You look like you've just seen a ghost."

"Dearie, I was shocked when you hollered at me for opening the window."

"Oh. When did I do that?"

"Just now, silly. It was stuffy in here, so I opened it a bit."

"No. It wasn't you I was speaking to. I thought Aphia Stevens was standing at the window and opening it from the outside. She was trying to get in while we were still sleeping."

Lottie said nothing, went to the window and threw it wide open.

"There is no one outside. I didn't see anyone. It must have been a dream."

"But it was so real. It frightens me even to see that witch in a dream. One time, she showed up at our door in Westbrook, brandishing a revolver. She threatened to shoot Auntie."

"Sometimes I think her spirit still hovers in this place even though she's been in prison for three years. Nate says I'm foolish. Clarence said the same."

Rising from bed, Franny donned her bathrobe and took her friend's hand.

"Her effects on this family have left indelible scars. Curse her to hell."

"Come. Let's go see if the three men have left us anything for breakfast," said Lottie.

43

Liz and Mary were working long days on designs for the new spring line. In order that Mary not have to return home late each night, the two of them decided that she could use Francena's bed while she was away. Many years had passed since the two had spent so much time together when they and Maeve shared a room in Saco while working at the Pepperell mill. Now, at the end of working days, the tired friends ate dinner together and then went to their beds. One night, they sat across from each other at the kitchen table, chatting about old times.

"We were quite a gaggle, we three. Your sister was the cute one. Always had a boy or two hanging around her," said Lizzie.

"Remember that time we rode in a wagon with Will Cain back from his uncle's farm in Biddeford? Maeve had three lads riding along with her in the back. She was always flirting."

"And in Will's case, it became more than an innocent flirtation. It resulted in a house full of children."

"Lizzie, you know the thing that bothered me the most about being a decade in Clare was missing family times with my sister. I was here and able to help out when the first two children were born. The others were strangers to me when I got back. You were fortunate to be here."

"There wasn't anything for me to do except play the doting auntie. Maeve has been so fortunate. She never really had a difficult pregnancy."

"Touch wood. She has always been healthy. Takes after my mom, she does. I don't think the old lady ever had a midwife on her three deliveries. I wonder if I would have been the same."

"Well, I guess we old ladies will never know anything about having babies."

"The other thing that most bothered me about being away for so long was that I missed *you* so much. My heart ached every time I thought about you. When Maeve wrote to tell me that your Moses had died, I cried for days thinking of your grief."

Liz watched as tears ran down her friend's cheek. She reached across the table, took one of Mary's hands in her own and wiped the tears away with her other hand. Mary rose from her seat and crossed to the other side of the table. She touched both sides of Liz's face, drawing her head to her own chest. Both women wept until Liz stood, threw her arms around Mary, and spoke very softly.

"Moses was so kind to me. When he passed on, I knew that I could never be with another man. He was so tender and passionate. Sometimes I felt that I didn't deserve his love. That I couldn't return the love he gave me."

"Lizzie, I'm sure you gave him great love, just as you have always given your love freely to me. You always respected me, treated me as your equal. You listened to me when I needed to give my fears an airing."

"Mary, that's because you and I are so much alike."

44

"Nate, slow down. No need to be in such a hurry to get to the village," said Lottie from the carriage's rear seat. "Franny and I are bouncing around so much that we have to hold onto each other to keep from being thrown off."

"My brother has always been in a rush to get somewhere. I thought he might have slowed down a bit in his old age, but no, he still moves around willy-nilly."

He smiled back at them and slowed the horse to a walk.

"Old age? What do you mean? I suppose when I start to dodder, my pace will slow. For now, I am still a child at heart."

"There, that's better. I want our visitor to take in our views across the valley, not hold on for dear life."

As they proceeded along Greene Road, the view of Valley Road below them opened across fields where drying hay lay in windrows. Albany Mountain to the north poked its rocky face above the forest. Nate brought the carriage to a halt for a few moments so that they could enjoy the panorama. Entering North Waterford, they slowed once again to avoid a crowd of men carrying lunch pails on their way to the mills on Crooked River.

Nate jumped from the wagon and hitched his horse to the fence in front of Nason's General Store. Then he helped his wife and sister step down. Ethan Blaine greeted them from the open door.

"What a wonderful surprise," the clerk said. "It's always good to see you, Nate, and Mrs. Hallett, but to greet Miss Hallett is a great pleasure."

He bowed to Franny and took her hand to lead her up the steps. She had forgotten how handsome he was, or perhaps he had grown more attractive in the time she had been away. His black hair, which had hung down to his shoulders was now neatly trimmed. He had become an interesting-looking young man.

"Mr. Blaine, I'm so pleased that you remember me. It was only those few times that I came to the store to shop for Lottie."

"Yes, but our conversations have stayed with me. Ask Nate—I have asked after you every time he's been in the shop. How has your life been going in the city?"

"I'm not really in Portland, you know. I live and work with my aunt in Westbrook. Though that is nearly a city compared to your town."

"We may be country bumpkins here in North Waterford, but we do appreciate the presence of a beautiful woman."

"Hey, you two, stop flirting for a second," said Lottie with a grin. "We have some shopping to do."

"Mrs. Hallett, please forgive me. Please give me your list. If you three wish to run other errands, I'll fill it for you while you're gone."

Nate excused himself and went off to Kinney's blacksmith shop to see if his chain had been repaired. Lottie and Franny asked for bottles of birch beer and sat on a shady bench out front while the order was filled.

"Franny, why don't we invite your friend to come to dinner with us some night? It might be nice to spend time with someone new."

"Are you trying to play matchmaker? If he has any interest, he will ask to see me. It's not good to appear too forward."

"Yes, I suppose so, but with you being here only for a few days, he mightn't get around to asking until you're gone. Just like the last time. Nate and I will invite him as neighbors would do. Nothing too aggressive about that."

So, they decided to have Nate extend a neighborly invitation to Ethan for dinner the following night at Beech Hill Farm.

45

To the surprise of matrons, guards, and the warden at Thomaston Prison, Aphia Stevens had turned over a new leaf, becoming almost a model prisoner. The only staff member to continue being troubled by her was the elderly librarian, whom she bothered regularly to get law books from other institutions. Aphia was determined to prove herself innocent of her late husband's murder. There had been no witnesses to the death. The only evidence against her was the secondhand account given by her ex-lover Bert Learned, who knew nothing about the crime except what she herself had told him in confidence.

"Mrs. Jameson, were you able to locate the book on self-defense that I requested?"

"No, Prishoner Shtevens. Th'only book I have for you today is *Black'sh Law Dishonary*."

"Well, I guess that will have to do, then. Won't it?" She smiled at the librarian as she took the book. What an old fool, she thought. She probably can't even read.

As she thumbed through the four-hundred-page volume looking for references and definitions that could be used in her case, Warden Lewis entered the room and pulled up a chair across the table from her. She had spoken with the man only once before, the day she was first admitted.

"Prisoner Stevens, it has come to my attention that you are investigating the law pertaining to your incarceration. I'm not sure what it is that you seek to prove. I can assure you the Maine State judicial system will make it impossible for you to get out of your concurrent life sentences. A jury of your peers has found you responsible for the deaths of three men."

He looked at her with a supercilious grin, awaiting her response. With a smile of her own, Aphia placed the book down on the table and pointed to the chapter entitled "Definition and Justification for Self-Defense." The description below read:

> What is **SELF-DEFENSE?** In criminal **law**: The **protection** of one's person or property against some injury attempted by another. The right of such **protection**. An excuse for the use of force in resisting an attack on the person, and especially for killing an assailant.

"Warden Lewis, I am not foolish enough to believe that I will ever be free of this jail or some other place even worse. It is only one of my three sentences which I have come to question: the conviction for murdering my husband. The case relied on circumstantial evidence and hearsay without any consideration that I was defending myself from assault by Henry Greene."

"I am acquainted with that definition, though I can't for the life of me see how it will help your situation. You confessed the murder to your lover. He then told of your confession in a manner which the jury accepted as gospel truth."

His words goaded her to indignation. He was an idiot. A fool. How had someone with such low mental capacity been given such a high-paying job? Yet she held her tongue and continued to smile.

"Sir, it is my hope to prove that I was in danger of my life. The man had thrown me down on the ground and was about to rape me. I had to protect my person."

"Miss Stevens, you are here with us until you leave this earth. As long as you abide by our rules and regulations, it is up to you how you want to spend what free time I give to you. Please be kind to Mrs. Jameson. She is a volunteer and is here to assist all prisoners who wish access to books. Do not take all her time for yourself."

Beneath her smiling façade, Aphia fumed. So, that's what this little visit is about, she thought. Protecting that bitch. She cried on his shoulder about me. Perhaps she does more favors for him than anyone would expect from an old hag.

46

"I'm not sure what to make of your sister," said Nathan to Hattie. "She and Mary have recently become close companions."

"What do you mean?"

"Well, I dropped in to visit Lizzie yesterday on the way back from Portland. Thought she might be a little lonely with Franny away. But she wasn't missing her at all. It appears that Mary has temporarily moved into the second bedroom. The two of them were sitting in the parlor enjoying a bottle of French champagne. They asked me to join them in their celebration. Liz said they were toasting to their long-term friendship."

"I still don't know what you mean. That sounds like a happy occasion."

"Oh, yes. Please don't get me wrong. There was a new intimacy between them. Something that I had never noticed before."

"They have always been close. I remember how Liz would talk so kindly about both Mary and Maeve when she would come home from Saco. When Mary left to be with family in Ireland, it took Liz a long time to get over missing her. They were business partners, you know."

"I knew all that. I'm not speaking about their business relationship. The champagne cork was popped yesterday to toast a personal relationship. At one point they were holding hands."

"Come on, Nathan. Women hold hands all the time. Why Liz and I have walked arm-in-arm our whole lives. The Flaherty sisters slept in the same bed for years."

"That is how sisters are. I know that."

Hattie turned to the window and silently stared out at the large elms on South High Street. She wasn't sure what he was getting at. She had noticed a new familiarity between the two women when the three had lunched recently in Portland. She assumed that their friendship had become deeper as they spent more time working together. Mary's move into Franny's bedroom, however, meant that they were together even more.

"Perhaps you're right, dear," said Hattie. "Their friendship has lasted so many years. I hadn't thought that they might be growing even closer as they age. Older women who have not married often live together as companions. No harm in that."

"I didn't say there was anything wrong, did I? Just wondering about how close they've become. You know—both emotionally and physically."

"Holding hands? Toasting themselves with champagne? They didn't kiss or anything, did they? I didn't know you could be so nosy."

47

When Ethan left to go to Beech Hill Farm at four o'clock, he knew he was going to be very early for dinner. He had already traveled the route that morning, to scout any difficulties along the way. Nothing was going to stand in the way of spending a full evening with Francena. Pulling his pocket watch out as he approached the house, he saw that he was thirty minutes ahead of schedule. That wouldn't do. It would make him appear overeager. He turned the horse around and found a narrow path into a dark glade where he could wait and make sure he arrived exactly on the minute of six p.m.

Franny was sitting on the front porch and saw him approaching the first time. When he turned back, she knew he must be nervous about making a good impression. She herself had been unable to relax all day. Twice she had changed her outfit and re-pinned her hair. Lottie had lent her a lovely long scarf to wrap over her shoulders. The second time Ethan approached she walked to the gate to greet him.

"Welcome, Ethan. I hope you had an easy ride."

"Oh, yes, Miss Francena. No problems tonight."

Nate came out onto the porch.

"Right on time, Ethan. You couldn't have been any more punctual. Right on the dot of six. Please take your horse to the hitching post at the barn door. We've had a couple of visits from a mountain lion recently."

"Thank you kindly. Wouldn't do to have my horse meet a cat."

She watched him lead his ride toward the barn. He was so tall that his head showed above that of the animal. His clean-shaven face was much more handsome than she remembered. So many young men these days wore beards or long pointed mustaches that it was a relief to see he was more modest. As he came up the steps, he doffed his cap and bowed slightly.

"Miss Hallett, you look quite lovely this evening." He blushed as he bowed again. "Please don't take my words in the wrong way. I am sure you always look lovely, not just tonight."

Lottie, who heard their conversation, rushed from the kitchen to the doorway, with her apron corner held over her mouth to cover a laugh.

"Will the two of you please relax. You are not on a date or anything. This is only dinner with the neighbors. Ethan, can I get you a beer?"

"No thank you, Mrs. Hallett. I don't drink alcohol."

Nate stopped in his tracks. "No beer? How about port or sherry?"

Ethan shook his head back and forth. "No, sir. I don't seem to have a taste for those drinks."

"Ethan, please stop being so formal. You know my real name is Nate. My wife is Lottie. Your new friend is Franny."

Both Franny and Ethan blushed to be referred to as new friends.

"Nate, let's not push them into anything too fast," said Lottie with a big grin. "Who knows, they might not get along."

"I guess we will just have to wait and see," he said, leading everyone to their seats at the dining table in the kitchen.

48

After dinner, Lottie excused herself from the table, asking Nate to join her doing the dishes. The two "new friends" went into the parlor to continue what had become an animated conversation.

"I understand that you are a skilled dressmaker. Your brother told me you're very talented and work full-time for your aunt. How did you learn to do that? I ask because my mother used to make our family's clothes. She still sews some for the neighbors."

"My aunt Lizzie has been such a success in her dressmaking business. She came a long way from a very rough beginning here in Waterford. Her mother taught her how to spin thread and make her own cloth. Then she learned about machinery while working in a Biddeford mill. She taught me to follow in her footsteps."

"Mom never made a business out of seamstressing, but she has great skills. When my dad passed, she helped support the house with her income from making dresses."

"How old were you when your father died?"

"Just turned twelve. I had to drop out of school for a couple of years to make some money. That's when I started at the store. Mr. Nason hired me right off. He also made me promise to return to school and graduate."

"You've been working for him since then?"

"Yes, nine years now. He wants me to become his partner at some point. Not sure I want to make that kind of long-time commitment. After all, I am only twenty-two. There is time for me to explore the world before I have to get married and settle down."

"Yes, it's good to experience what the world has to offer. You don't want to end up feeling trapped in a life not to your liking."

They stared at each other for a moment, realizing that perhaps they were revealing more about their lives than they wished. Ethan stood up and walked to the kitchen where Nate and Lottie sat at the cleared table. Franny followed and pulled up a chair for herself.

"I think I'd best be going," said Ethan. "I must be at work early tomorrow."

"Come on, Ethan," said Lottie. "Have a seat. We four can play at canasta for a while. It's still early. The shank of the evening, as they say."

"Thanks for the invite, but I'm not much for card games."

"What do you do for fun?" asked Franny.

"I like to go for long rides in the hills north of the village. Up in Albany, Lynchville, and Stow. The land up there is so undeveloped. So wild. I don't have to ride very far from home to feel like I'm in the Wild West.

Franny looked at him in surprise.

"Can you take me with you sometime? I could borrow Nate's pony and we might explore."

"Sure. That would be a great idea. If you're still around on Thursday, when I'm off, we might ride out to a wilderness area called Albany Basins. It's up Bethel way, not that far."

"I can be here for that. The schedule for my return to Westbrook is up in the air. Perhaps these two might like to join us," she said, pointing to her hosts, who made up reasons not to go.

"It will be like a scene from your favorite novel," Lottie commented to her friend.

49

"I do not understand how you can do such a thing." Maeve could not believe what Mary was telling her. "It isn't natural."

"We're not doing anything immoral or evil. Many older unmarried women live together for companionship. You remember our Aunt Jennine and her friend Liddie. They shared that cottage in Tubber for years. No one in the family ever said a word about it."

"Mary, they were in their nineties. Who would say anything about two old biddies? Their helping each other made it easier for the rest of us. This is different. You and she are only in your forties and both healthy and attractive. If you had a mind to, you could easily find a man."

Mary had not expected such a negative reaction to her announcement that she would soon be giving up her room and moving in with Lizzie. After all the years the three of them had shared, her thought was that Maeve would be happy for them. Not angry.

"You know I've never been happy enough with the men I've met to want to marry. Your life has been so different. You were always attracted to boys. You could have had your pick of anyone you wanted. You were so fortunate to have a man like Will sweep you off your feet and give you the family you always wanted. That's not me."

"Oh, I know when we were girls and a boy would seek to win your favor, you would turn away. You stayed so long in Clare that I thought you might have met someone you liked. Sadly, you returned alone."

"Sadly? Weren't you happy that I returned to live with you, help with the kids? It has been a joy to be here under your roof. For the decade with Da' in Clare it was as if I were all alone. We hardly ever spoke, except when he needed me to do something for him. Here, I am loved by you, your children, and my dearest friend, Lizzie."

"What shall I tell the children? They will think you've moved because you no longer like being here with us. I can't let on that you love another woman, even if it is our Liz."

"If you want me to explain to the kids that it has nothing to do with how I feel about them, then I will."

"No. I will handle it. Faith, Janey, and Owen are old enough to understand. The little ones will be very sad to lose you."

"Lose me? Maeve, I'm not going anywhere. My home will be almost next door where I'm working all the time anyway. I fear that it is you, not the children, who feel deserted. How can that be? I would think you would be happy that I have found a friend who loves me and wants me to live with her."

"In a way, I am happy for you, except for the fact that you are both women. It's not the natural way. It confuses me."

"I'm sorry you feel that way. May you come to accept my decision."

Mary stood from the table and walked toward the back door. Maeve sat with her head lying on her clenched hands. Then she called out to her sister.

"Mary, please forgive me. I will do my best to understand."

50

Leaving North Waterford Village, Franny and Ethan turned to the north and rode four miles on Bethel Causeway. The early morning was warm even for August, with a hazy sun striking through tall pines at a low angle, casting elongated shadows across the road. By the time they entered Albany Basins Road, little more than a woodland pathway, the forest had become so thick it seemed dusk had arrived early. Ethan rode his horse in the lead. Franny followed at a length where branches brushed ahead would not strike her when they snapped back. Several times, she lost sight of Ethan completely.

"We'll have to lead the horses from this point on," he said as he dismounted. "There really is no path from here to a cascade.

Footings vary from sand to hard bedrock, and the way is barely wide enough for one person to pass. When we're almost there, we'll have to tie the horses to a tree."

Franny was glad she had borrowed a denim riding outfit from Lottie, even though it was a little large. Briars and brambles surrounded them, and biting flies zoomed around her head. Her hair hanging long from beneath a wide-brimmed hat kept most of the insects off her face and neck. Ethan offered her some sort of gooey concoction he said would repel the bugs. It smelled so bad she refused to spread it on her exposed skin.

"Hey, are you sure you know the way?" she asked. "The trail has disappeared."

More insects began to swarm around them. They were surrounded by giant boulders piled one atop the other in a rugged sort of stone wall.

"We're almost there. Let's tie the horses here and make the final leg on foot. You won't believe how incredible the sights are in this place."

Foliage was so thick, the boulders so broad and tall, that they lost sight of their animals within a few yards. The grade climbed precipitously so that they had to grab onto trees to hold themselves from falling backwards. Suddenly, a loud sound of rushing water pierced the stillness and clouds of mist rose before them, wetting the towering pines and hemlocks.

Ethan shimmied up a boulder twice his height, using a series of cracks in its surface as hand and footholds. At the top, he knelt and reached his hand down for Franny to grab and make her way up to join him. Together they stared at scenery which must not have changed since the end of the last ice age. Boulders, some as big as houses, some rounded, some roughly broken, were stacked as if they had been dropped from the sky. Water ran over the tops of some stones and through gaps between them. Trees and bushes of all sizes grew in places where the water gushed, some rooted in cracks in the stones. The noise of the waterfall was so loud that they had to shout to be heard.

She couldn't understand what she was seeing.

"What happened here? How could a place like this come to be?"

"I will tell you what my father told me about this magical place. This is the basin of Albany Brook, which runs from the top of Albany Mountain, feeding into Crooked River. The jumble of broken ledge and glacial boulders, called erratics, was piled here fifteen thousand years ago. A massive glacier, ten miles thick, carried blocks of stone from mountains north of here, dropping them in a messy dam as it melted and retreated."

"How come you know so much about this place? Did you study its geology in school?"

"No. Like I said, my dad brought me here many times. He told me many stories, ones he'd heard from his own dad and granddad. He told me that a mighty lake, once trapped behind this dam, spread out from here to Bethel along the path of what is now called Bethel Causeway."

"Years ago, I traveled up to Bethel and Rumford on that road. Was Songo Pond part of that lake?"

"Yes. And Albany Brook, Pattie Brook, and a string of small ponds, as well."

As they spoke, a Great Blue Heron swooped in from above the trees and landed in a large pool at the bottom of the rock formation. Both stopped talking and stared with gaping mouths. The gray bird stood as motionless as a stick at the water's edge. Franny gasped when its beak, like a spear, shot forward and reemerged from the water with a pierced fish attached. Throwing both hands up to her mouth to stifle an outburst, she lost her footing and fell backwards against rough ledge. He leaped down next to her and helped her sit upright.

"Are you okay? I don't see any cut or blood." He felt around in her hair and inspected her shoulders.

"Ouch! Right there where you just touched me. If my arm isn't broken, it will surely have a horrible bruise in the morning. I'm sorry to have been so clumsy."

"You'll be okay. No blood, but a big bruise for sure. You've torn your friend's jacket," he said, rubbing the back of her shoulder again. He helped her to her feet and brushed dirt from her back.

"That's okay. I can easily repair it for her. I'm lucky that's the worst thing to happen. Now you will think me a clumsy oaf."

"How could I ever think that about you, Franny?"

Albany Basins, c. 1910. Photo by Fred Johnson of Waterford

51

Liz passed a cup of coffee across her design table to Mary. To rest from the long hours of work, a midmorning break was now a regular part of the day. As they chatted, there was a loud knock. Mary rose and opened the door to greet Eugene Bailey.

"Mr. Bailey, what a surprise to see you out on such a cold, damp day." She extended her hand for a friendly shake.

He stared blankly at her. "Miss Flaherty, if I can't get out and about in September, what will I do when winter comes? Stay inside, I ask you?"

"Please step in out of the weather. Liz and I were just sitting down for coffee. Can I get a cup for you?"

"No thank you, miss. I closed the store for an hour and must return before people go somewhere else to do their shopping. Is Miss Hallett at home?"

Liz pulled a third stool up to the table and gestured for him to sit.

"Please, have a seat. You've walked a good distance. Your legs might welcome a rest."

He was uncomfortable with her comment about his body. It really was no business of hers how he felt after a long walk. Did she think him an old man?

"No thank you, Miss Millett. I stopped in for a quick visit to say hello to Francena, if she was about, and to discuss having some bespoke holiday garments made for Christmas sales."

"She hasn't returned as yet from Waterford. I can help you with those special orders if you wish."

"I know that you are very busy, especially with your niece away. If she is expected to return soon, I would prefer to speak with her directly about my items. She and I have often discussed how to display the clothing I sell. Together we have designed a set of display racks."

Mary excused herself and left the room, leaving Liz and the merchant alone.

"Eugene, Francena will be back by week's end, I'm sure. Her absence has given Mary and me a very full schedule. If you wish to wait and chat with the young lady personally about your requirements, that will work out quite well for me."

"Then I will return soon. Would you be so kind as to call me on the telephone to let me know when she gets back?"

"Of course. I will ask her to call you herself. May I ask you a personal question?"

He was uncomfortable but said nothing.

"It seems to me that you are interested in more than a business relationship with my niece. Am I correct?"

He blushed at this question. A man would normally speak with the father about his romantic interest in a girl.

"Miss, your niece has been very helpful with merchandising at my store and has made a few suggestions that show she is very interested in my success. She also has been very kind to me personally and led me to believe that we might become good friends. Each friend I have is valuable, and I don't want to lose the opportunity to have another, especially such a young and beautiful woman."

"Eugene, Francena has been a blessing to me from the day she was born. I have watched her grow into a capable young woman who deserves only the best that life has to offer. She is quite unaccustomed to male friendships. If you have some thought of marriage, you must promise to be careful and not to trample on her emotions."

He was shocked that the business visit had now veered into embarrassing territory. Discussing a woman whom he liked with another woman made him very uncomfortable. Without a word he walked toward the door. As he reached for the knob, he turned to her.

"Miss Millett, rest assured that my intentions are honorable. Your niece and I have much in common. Whether that leads us to be more than friends would be hard to tell at this point. You have my word that I respect Francena and will do nothing to hurt her. She is a delicate flower to me."

With that, he left the room. Mary then entered and returned to her seat at the sewing machine.

"My dear," she said, "he is so much older than his years. You'd think he was fifty the way he acts."

"The man is quite lonely, Mary. Though he needs someone to enrich his life, I am not sure Francena is the one to fit the bill."

52

On her return trip to Westbrook after a fortnight's absence, Francena was able to enjoy a night with her parents, the first such visit in nearly a year. Her brother dropped her off on his way to Harrison, and Nathan was to deliver her to Lizzie's on his way to a Monday meeting in Falmouth. Riding in carriages for both legs of the trip was a relief. With her shoulder still bruised and swollen, riding horseback could have been quite painful. As it was, she had to ask the men to tote her luggage and help her in and out of the bench seats. Nate knew how her accident had happened, but her parents wanted to know all the details.

"Francena, dear, how did you happen to fall so badly? Didn't your friend warn you about the dangers of such a wild place?" asked Hattie.

"I can't blame Ethan for my clumsiness. It was my fault. There was so much to see in that beautiful site that I lost my concentration. It could have been much worse if he hadn't been there."

"Does this boy often go out into the forests alone for adventure? If so, he should have known better than to take you where you might get hurt."

"Mom, he's not quite a boy. He's twenty-two and has been exploring the wilds since he was a little kid."

Nathan wanted to know more about Ethan.

"So, his father is dead? How did that happen?"

"I don't know him well enough to ask such a personal question. He will likely tell me about it sometime if he wants to."

"You plan on spending more time with him? Does he have a job? Did he complete his education?"

"Daddy, what's with all these questions? He is a nice young man who is a friend of Nathan and Lottie. He works at the general store in North Waterford. Has done so for a few years. His boss, Mr. Nason, trusts him enough to offer him a share in the business. I don't know how far he went in school, and I really don't care. He is an interesting person who knows a lot about nature."

Hattie interrupted. "You must be more careful with the men you meet. They may not be as kind as they seem at first. Was it wise to wander off into the woods with a man about whom you know so little? We ask these questions because you are our daughter. We want you to find a man who can show you a wonderful life."

"Hey, I'm not in love with the man. He's just a friend. I'm not planning on marriage to anyone real soon. My plan is to return to Westbrook and work with Mary and Auntie to make dresses for the spring. If anyone worth marrying shows up, I'll be sure to let you both know."

Her parents looked at each other and shrugged.

"Perhaps we are overly concerned, but the thought that you may have seriously injured yourself, and, in the process, exposed yourself to a perfect stranger bothers us. We worry," said Hattie.

"Please promise us that you will be more careful about your safety in the future," said Nathan. "And promise that you will let Lizzie know that you may need time to recover. Be honest with her."

The three continued to chat until Franny asked to be excused to have a long night's rest. She knew they loved her and wanted what was best for her. However, they had been married since they were fifteen and never had the freedom she had to take her time carefully evaluating with whom and when she might settle down. She looked forward to being once again in the dress shop and sleeping in her own bed.

53

It was a cold day for the journey to Westbrook, so both Franny and Nathan were bundled up and shared a blanket spread across their laps. She wanted to sit up next to him, not in the passenger seat, as he suggested. So much time had passed since they had been together for a long period that she wanted to chat with him. She snuggled up close to him to stay warm. As they entered North Windham, Nathan turned the carriage off Forest Avenue onto a side road leading to a small teahouse. They both felt the chill of a breeze from the north. He asked the proprietor to place them near the small coal stove that warmed the empty dining room.

"Daddy, I'm so pleased you offered to drive me to Westbrook. It would have been impossible for me to ride without a lot of pain from this shoulder."

"Perhaps you should have stayed with us for a few more days and given the injury more time to heal."

"I so want to get back to my own bedroom. Nate and Lottie were so good to me. And being with you and Mom was wonderful, but my home is in Westbrook."

He smiled and sipped his tea before speaking. "You'll be finding things a little different in Lizzie's house. She doesn't live alone anymore."

"Nate told me Mary has been staying temporarily in the house. That will change when I return."

"You might be right, but I think you best be ready for a permanent change in the household."

She had raised a sandwich to her mouth, about to take a bite. His remark made her return it to the plate.

"Francena, the world is different from when I was a boy. Back then, women were girlfriends with other women, but two women were never a couple. At least, not that I was aware of."

"What are you talking about?"

"Your aunt and Mary are living together all the time, not temporarily. I believe you will find that Mary has moved into your old room."

"What do mean? They are a couple?"

"Your mother does not agree completely with what I am about to say: They are in love with each other."

54

Francena didn't know what to expect when she arrived home. Nathan's comments about her aunt's relationship with Mary confused her, made her wonder whether she would still have her room. Like her mother, she felt that his concerns were overblown. Many older women lived together for support and companionship, and with Mary and Liz working together so much of the time, it made sense. She was sure that with her return, Mary would move back to a comfortable residence with her sister Maeve and the children.

"Welcome home, my lovely Franny," Liz said as she opened the front door. "I have missed you so." She changed her welcome when Mary came up behind her. "*We* have missed you so,"

"And I have missed you, too. So wonderful to be home at last." Franny dropped her valise and squeezed her aunt's hand.

Mary picked up the bag and touched Franny's shoulder. "Francena, you look wonderful. I thought you would gain weight being waited on by your friends for so many days, but you still have your wonderful figure."

Pulling back from the touch on her bruise, Franny cried out, "Ouch! Thanks, but please don't touch that shoulder. I have an awful welt there."

Nathan came through the door carrying the rest of his daughter's luggage. He set the bags on the floor, kissed his sister-in-law on the cheek, and shook Mary's hand.

"Please, ladies. Would one of you help take these bags to Franny's room? She can't do it herself, and I must run. I have an appointment in town and don't want to be late."

When Mary picked up two bags and headed up the stairs, Franny breathed a sigh of relief. If she didn't have her old room, why would the woman carry her luggage up to it? Dad must have been wrong, she thought. He can be such a worrywart.

Liz led her niece into the parlor. "Dear, please come and rest yourself on the sofa. You've had a long ride. That injury must have made the trip more tiring."

"They wanted me to stay in Bridgton for a few days to rest up. I couldn't wait any longer, regardless of the discomfort." She avoided using the word pain, afraid it would make people think the bruise was worse than it really was.

"We can take care of you here. Let you rest and recover for a few days. Tell me, how did you hurt yourself?"

She began to tell her story and, when Mary came down the stairs and sat on the arm of the sofa, both women listened intently. At the end of her story, Lizzie reached out to touch Mary's hand.

"My dear, we shall have to care for this darling girl for a few days. It wouldn't do to have her return to work bothered by such pain."

"It isn't really painful, Auntie," said Franny. "Only uncomfortable."

"Whatever you want to call it," said Mary, "you will want to rest the bruise for a while. We want you to return to work, but not if you risk reinjuring your shoulder. We two have been doing very well for a couple of old ladies. No reason why you would have to push yourself."

"Old ladies! Who are you calling an old lady?" Lizzie asked. "I haven't felt this good for several years!"

"Please, ladies. Don't worry yourselves about my health. I may not work a full day, but I want to get back in the swing of things. I have missed my home and my work. My craft. Now, if you don't mind, I would like to go upstairs and rest on my comfortable bed."

As she climbed the stairs, there remained a bit of doubt in her head that her room would be the same as she had left it. Not until she opened the door and took a deep breath did she know this was her home once again. She removed her shoes, sat on the bed, piled one pillow on top of the other, and gently laid her head back. There was her writing desk by the window. The books on her bookshelf were just the same. Two dolls made by her grand-mother sat together on the rocker Auntie had given her. All was back to normal. She fell asleep.

55

Aphia's dream states were becoming so frequent that they did not take place only while she was asleep. Several times, her mumbling and ranting had made the prison staff concerned that she was insane. Recently, she had been left alone in the library studying an old English law journal. Suddenly, she jumped up, threw the book across the room, and turned over her chair. Her eyes were closed tightly, yet the vision of a rustic cabin in total disarray was clear. She had no idea where she was, but the anger within her heart was vivid. Who lived here?

The elderly librarian returned to the room to find Aphia walking around in a daze, mumbling to herself. "Prishoner Shtevens, what ish wrong wit you?" she shouted, backing out of the room.

She returned with a male guard who pounded on the main desk with his night stick. "Prisoner, sit down immediately, before I clap handcuffs on you."

Aphia became aware that she was no longer alone. "I'm okay. Just fell. I was getting the dropped book. Tripped on my chair." Both staff members stared at her as she wobbled across the room to pick up the volume and right the chair. "I'm fine. Really. Please don't send me back to my cell. This is my study time."

The ugly man left the room, and the old lady took her seat once again. Aphia reopened the journal to the passages on circumstantial evidence. As she turned a page, she noticed that her hands were stained purple, as if she had been handling ripe elder berries.

I think that place was Bert's home, she thought to herself. I must have left him a message.

56

It was two weeks before Christmas and no snow had fallen, not even a light flurry. Most people were complaining, but not Bert Learned. He still had winter squash lying on the ground and firewood to be split and stacked where it would be easy to reach once the snows arrived. The supply of hardtack, dried beef, and bacon in his cupboard would not get him through the winter. One more trip to West Bethel village was needed before travel became difficult.

Bess was amenable to carrying him down to the store, so the journey was easy. He left as the rosy dawn broke and returned six hours later, just in time to light a fire for the evening. Opening the door into the dark hovel, he gasped and stood back in shock. His chair and table lay smashed on the dirt floor, dishes and pans strewn about, clothes scattered. When he pulled a curtain away from the one window, the extent of devastation became clear. His little potbelly stove had been tipped onto its side, and lengths of stovepipe lay atop his bed. Someone had destroyed what little he owned.

"Oh, my God," he moaned and knelt on one knee with his head in his hands. "Who would do such a thing? Someone has done this to scare me away.

"What will I do now?" he wondered aloud. "Am I supposed to start all over again? At my age? Who would do this to an old man?"

He had no neighbors he could complain to or go to for help. It had been his choice to live alone on the seventy-acre lot. As far as he knew, no one even knew he was there. If a stranger had come across the shack by accident, he would not have done such damage. This was more than simple vandalism. Who would have done this to him to deliver a message?

Clearing the bed so that he might at least have a place to sit, he spied a wooden firkin, its handle hung on a nail driven into a rafter over what had been his sink. A bunch of green leaves was gathered in it, arranged like a neat bouquet centered with a single cluster of withered purple berries. As he went to reach for it, a memory of poison herbs entered his mind.

A whisper formed on his parched lips. "Aphia. Was it you, Aphia? Did you do this to me in revenge?"

How had she found him deep in the woods where he had escaped from her so many years ago? This must be her revenge for testifying against her in the murder trial. How could she hurt him while still in jail?

He did his best to repair the damage, culled through his belongings and found a few things to keep. With winter here, he had to find a temporary place to live. He saddled up his Bess, packing food and bedroll. As he traveled southward, he realized that this might be the end of his hermit's life. He decided to head to Waterford and take a room until spring, perhaps a room in a farmer's home. He certainly could not afford a hotel.

Crossing the Lynchville Bridge into North Waterford, he spotted a familiar-looking man walking toward the sawmill. It was Nathan Hallett, in town to meet the mill owners.

"Ahoy there, Mr. Hallett!" he shouted out. "So relieved to see a familiar face."

"Bert, what brings you back to civilization? The last time I saw you, you were cursing that animal of yours for bringing you into the civilized world."

"Civilization has much to offer in the winter. My cabin has been ransacked by a hooligan. I'm looking for a cheap place to rent for a short time. There's nothing like that up in Chatham, I'll tell you."

"You're not likely to find a room here in North Waterford. I'd suggest you ride on a bit further on Greene Road to South Waterford. There's a lady there, a good friend of mine, Mrs. Mary Monroe. She puts up people each winter at her Bear Mountain House. Not very warm. It is a summer hotel, but it would be better than sleeping in a farmer's barn. That's unless you can afford the Alpine House."

Bert reached deep into his pocket and pulled out a small purse of coins. "This here is my worldly fortune. If I open it, you might see moths fly out. A hotel is not in my future."

"You tell Mrs. Monroe that I told you to see her. She has a good heart. What happened to your home, Bert?"

"While I was shopping for winter food, that cursed bitch Aphia destroyed my cabin in revenge for how I ruined her life."

Nathan raised one hand and placed it on Bert's bony chest.

"Stop giving that woman evil powers. She's in jail, sir. Behind bars for life. There is no way she could get to the New Hampshire woods to find you. You, Maeve, Lottie, and even Lizzie are creating this illusion that everything bad that happens is caused by her."

"Friend, what you say makes logical sense. However, I think there are just too many coincidences about these accidents, deaths, and vandalism that make me believe she has strange powers. She appears to me and the others you mention in dreams, too. I think she works her evils in her sleep."

"Bert, I admit I can't disprove your foolish conclusions." Nathan smiled. "Please make your way to Bear Mountain House before it gets dark. You don't want to be out and about when the witch is sleeping."

57

Len Monroe watched a tall, thin man enter the long driveway, leading a horse that could barely put one hoof in front of the other. It would have been a comical sight if the pair had not been approaching his doorway. At this time of year, old men from Waterford and Harrison, geezers whom his mother had housed before, often dropped in to see if there was room for them to stay for the winter.

"Hullo, young man," Bert said in as loud a voice as he was able to muster after walking most of the way from North Waterford. "Can ya tell me if this is the Monroe house?"

"Yes, sir. It is. What can I do for you?"

"Lookin' for Mrs. Monroe. A friend, Nathan Hallett, sent me to see her."

Len knew that his mother had already retired for the evening. "Sir, she ain't around right now. Can I help you? I'm her son, Leonard."

"I'd be lookin' for a place to stay."

"For the night? I'm afraid the inn is closed for the season."

"Nathan tells me you take in roomers for the winter. That's what I'm lookin' for."

Len looked carefully at the stranger and nearly burst out laughing. Bert looked like a scarecrow. His pants were so patched that the original fabric had nearly disappeared. They didn't even reach the tops of his worn-out boots. He wore a heavy coat with no buttons, and his snarled hair hung down below his shoulders from beneath a straw hat which appeared to be held together with safety pins.

"Mister, I'm afraid we are full up for the winter. Since it's getting dark, I'll let you stay in the barn for the night. No charge for that, but you'll have to leave in the morning. If you have twenty-five cents, I'll feed you a good breakfast before you leave."

Bert was very disappointed, but accepted the young man's offer for a refuge from the chilly night. Len led him to a small cot at the rear of the barn. Bert tied Bess in an empty stall, ate a dry piece of bread he had packed in his coat pocket, and lay down on the cot. His feet extended over the end of the bed.

After a night of disturbed sleep, he rose early enough to eat a morning meal of cornbread with strawberry jam and a cup of strong coffee. He really had no idea where to go, but as he walked to the end of the driveway, he recalled an invitation once extended to him by old friend Lizzie Millett. If he ever needed a place to stay, she had said, come to her big house in Westbrook. It was a long way off, and he was not sure he could get there in one day. He could think of nothing else to do. The horse was rested enough to carry him at least part of the way.

He made it easily through Bridgton, and just before reaching Naples Causeway across the south end of Long Lake, the nag began to weave back and forth. Bert nearly slipped off several times, so he dismounted at the bridge to give both of them a short rest. He tied the horse to a maple tree and sat down on a park bench to stare out at the dark-blue waters.

Suddenly a man shouted out to him. "Bert! Bert Learned, is that you there on the bench?"

Turning to face the busy roadway, he saw Nathan sitting in his carriage, waving to him.

"For the love of Pete," said Bert. "Who would imagine I might see someone I knew out here on the open road."

"I thought you would be ensconced with Mrs. Monroe by this time. What are you doing in Naples?"

"On the road to Westbrook I am. Was no room at the Monroe place. All full for the season, said the son. I'm trying to make it to Lizzie Millett's place by end of day. She invited me to stay there a while back."

What a coincidence, thought Nathan. This man must have a guardian angel following him around. "I'm on my way to the same place right now. Can I give you a lift?"

"What a godsend you are, my friend. I'd surely take your lift if it weren't for my Bessy here. You'd be hard-pressed to lift her into the carriage seat."

"Hitch her to the back of the rumble seat. She'll likely trot right along without you on her back."

Bert attached the nag to the rear railing of the chaise and pulled himself up next to Nathan in the front.

"Bert, I don't know where Lizzie is going to put you. Her house is pretty full right now with both Mary Flaherty and my daughter living there, but, if she invited you, she must have something in mind."

Having the old lame horse tied to the rear of his carriage slowed the journey much more than Nathan had thought it would. Usual travel time from Naples Causeway to Westbrook was four hours. After five hours, they were only in North Windham. He had counted on Bert to keep the animal moving—until the man fell asleep in the rear seat as soon as they lost sight of Brandy Pond. Although not having to make conversation with the old man was a blessing, he himself was required to stop every hour to give Bess a drink of water. At one water stop, the horse lay down on the road and refused to be roused. Nathan shook Bert awake and told him that once the mare was back on her feet, he would need to either ride her the remaining few miles or lead her by hand.

"Git up, worthless bag-o-bones! You've had an easy time of it on this journey. Don't make believe you're tired."

Bert yanked on the reins until Bess finally stood again. He straightened her saddle and tightened the girth so that he might mount her. After he climbed up and coaxed her to move, she wouldn't stir.

"Damned beast. I oughta just give you to the next person who comes along."

It was clear that he would need to walk the rest of the way.

"Bert, I'll ride along to Lizzie's and let her know you're coming. It's nearly dark. She might think I've decided not to arrive this evening. Does she know you're coming?"

"No, sir. Not at all. I'm sure she will remember her invitation from a couple of years back. You tell her Old Bert can sleep anywhere. Even in the barn if need be."

"I'll tell her that and ask her to hold dinner for you as well," said Nathan as he drove away. Looking back at the man pulling with all his might on the horse's reins, he wondered if those two really would reach Westbrook that night.

58

Eugene couldn't have been any happier. Unusually mild weather through November and now December had allowed masons to complete the foundation of his new house. Carpenters were then able to complete the framing of a spacious raised cape behind the store. It was the house he had been thinking about for years, but he'd never been motivated to spend resources to make his dream come true. A single man might be satisfied to live in a little apartment behind the store. Now that he was thinking of marrying, a wife would want a place with more room and modern amenities. Will Cain's old crew was doing the work. Maeve had made sure they would do the job at a reasonable price for such a prominent citizen.

Eugene was so excited when the project finally began that he often neglected work in the store. Several times, customers had to holler for him to come to their service. As the framing began to rise, he wanted to show the structure to others, especially Francena, who was still away. Worry that she might have moved to North Waterford bothered him, but he was sure, if he asked for her hand, she would accept and move back to Westbrook.

As he sat at supper one evening, the phone in the store rang and he went to answer it.

"Hello, Mr. Bailey speaking. How may I help you?"

"Oh, Eugene. This is Francena Hallett. My aunt told me you requested that I call you once I returned. I've been home for two days but am resting up."

"Miss Francena, how wonderful to hear your voice. How was your time away? You were gone for quite a while."

She thought it odd that he would question how long she had been in Waterford. After all, he had no claim on her time or how she lived her life.

"It was wonderful to be with my best friend. We had so much to catch up on. Her farm on Beech Hill is so rustic. A great getaway."

He thought North Waterford was backward and old-fashioned. *Rustic* was too complimentary a word. He had to question how such a delicate young woman would be drawn to staying there more than a short time.

"Miss Francena, now that you are back in the civilized world, perhaps we might get together. I have quite a building project going on here. You might find it interesting."

Hmm, she thought. Civilized world? His attempt at humor failed on her.

"Auntie had told me you are putting up quite a house behind the store. So fortunate for you that the weather has cooperated. When will the place be completed?"

"Yes, quite a house indeed. Unless it snows soon, the place will be closed in within the week and the men will be able to continue inside work through the winter. I was thinking that you might join me for a light lunch in my apartment one day soon. While there is still a good deal of daylight, we could walk around inside the house."

"I'm working again. Perhaps on the weekend. Is this Saturday okay with you?"

"Oh, yes. That would work very well for me. You might be able to make a few suggestions about the interiors, design ideas that might help me set the style for finishes."

"Aunt Liz and Maeve are the designers in the family. Have you questioned either of them?"

"You are the one I wish to have as a consultant. No one else. I trust that you will help me make my new home quite grand."

59

E than stood at the Beech Hill Farm back door speaking with Lottie. He had taken the opportunity of another sunny early winter day to ride out to visit Franny.

"She's left again?"

"Ethan, she's been gone for nearly a month. You knew she wouldn't be staying with us much longer, didn't you?"

"I guess so. Must have lost track of the days. I thought she would still be here."

She stared at him with a grin on her face. What a silly assumption. He must have a lot on his mind.

"After her fall, she stayed around for a couple of days. I tried to convince her to stay until the swelling went down on her shoulder. She wouldn't hear of it. Had to get back to work."

"Hopefully, her family will make her rest for a while. She had a bad fall there."

"You must have taken her to a wild and wonderful spot. Her description of it made Nate and me want to go there sometime."

"I don't think she was ready for a wild place like the Basins. I explained it all to her beforehand. What to wear. How careful to be walking the trail. Still, some of the responsibility for her injury falls on my shoulders."

"No one is at fault. Accidents like that can happen even to people who are fully prepared. She will get over it. Her aunt will make sure she takes it easy."

He looked around with his hands behind his back, then turned to peer at the top of the hill.

"It is surprising that she would want to go back to the city, when all around this house are radiant natural beauties. Look at that rocky face, the trees pointing into the dark-blue sky. I would not leave here for all the gold the world might offer."

Again, she looked at him and smiled.

"You are more of a country boy than I imagined. Franny needs the stimulation of being surrounded by people and working at her dressmaking. During the days after the hike with you, she began to act bored and talked about life in Westbrook all the time. She'll come back again, don't you worry. When she does, it will only be for a visit. She'll never live in a place like North Waterford."

"Don't say never. That's a long time. You can't tell what might happen if she had a good reason to stay."

"What reason would that be?"

"Oh..." He hesitated for a moment. "Perhaps a good friendship?"

60

Snow swirled around the corner of the porch, then up against the front door. Nate stared through the parlor window wondering how long it would be before this first snowstorm of the season would let up and he could shovel a path to the barn and finish his chores. Lottie sat behind him on the sofa, reading *The Virginian*, which Franny had left behind. She had reached a chapter where the heroine falls into a flooded stream and is rescued by a handsome stranger. The cowboy rides into the river, pulls the damsel out, then rides away before the woman can thank him.

After marking her place with a strand of yarn, she looked up at her husband.

"Nate, please come and sit with me for a moment. You stare into the storm, pacing back and forth like an impatient young boy who wants to go outside and play. Let's chat for a while. Get your mind off the snow."

"You know the cow must be milked. We need more firewood. I just want to get my chores done before it gets dark."

He crossed the room and sat beside her. She leaned against him, reaching to brush a stray curl that had fallen across his forehead. What a handsome man I have, she thought.

"What do you want to talk about?" said Nate.

"You know how much I love you, don't you?"

"Don't you tell me that all the time?"

"Not often enough. I am so fortunate to have you in my life. As a matter of fact, I think you saved my life."

He laughed and took her hand. "What do you mean? How did I do that?"

"You know what I mean. After Clarence died and I lost the baby, my life was miserable. You cared for me and brought hope back to me. You saved my life. Thank you."

"You are very welcome."

"I've always hoped there would be a way I could express my love to you."

121

He placed a kiss on the palm of her hand and put his arm around her shoulders.

"Well, I have a surprise for you, and I hope you will be pleased. I am pregnant."

"What? How? I thought you couldn't have another child. Dr. Rowan said it would be impossible."

"I'm as surprised as you. I wasn't sure until I missed my period for the second month."

He stood up and walked back toward the window, acting like the news didn't please him.

"Nate, are you not pleased?"

When he turned to face her, she saw tears running down his cheeks.

"Not pleased? How could I not be overjoyed? A child! My God! But I am concerned about you, my love. How will a pregnancy affect your health? Won't there be danger?"

"Perhaps. I'm not sure. When the winter breaks, I will see the doctor. There will be precautions to take. We can deal with that in due time. For now, it makes my heart sing to be carrying your child. It is a gift that you so deserve."

"I have so many gifts already, Lottie. I have you. I have Con and Francis to love me. I do not want to lose any of you."

"Don't worry. You will not be losing anyone. We will have a strong family of five soon, and the fifth will be yours and mine, not Clarence's."

"Clarence is gone, my love," said Nate. "When we first were wed, the fact that he was the boys' father sometimes bothered me. Now it never enters my mind. I am content with what we have together."

"Do you not want me to have a baby?"

He rushed to her, sat down, and drew her close in his arms.

"You didn't listen. I am both pleased with what we already have together and also overjoyed by the gift of sharing a child with you. I love you so."

She began to cry on his shoulder. Through the sobs she whispered, "We have saved each other's lives."

He was so happy that there was nothing else to say. His heart swelled with love, yet a small seed of fear over what might happen to Lottie lay planted in his mind.

61

Franny was accustomed to Eugene arriving at her door on foot. His store and apartment on Brook Street were only a mile distant. So it was a surprise when a one-horse, brightly painted gig pulled up. When he stepped down, she saw that he was dressed to the nines for a lunch date: tan tweed business suit, colorful checkered waistcoat, spats, and a felt derby hat. He wore one of the Irish linen shirts topped off with a sky-blue bow tie. She hoped he would not be disappointed that she was wearing her work clothes. It was still the workday, and after lunch she planned on returning to the shop. When she opened the door, he bowed with an arm across his knees, hat brushing the spats.

"Why Mr. Bailey, how handsomely dressed you are today. I might think we were going to a fancy Portland restaurant instead of your own dining room."

"I'm not too early, am I? Did you have enough time to get ready?" He wondered why she was still wearing her work dress. There were even a couple of common pins stuck in the sleeve just above her wrist.

She could tell that he was judging her outfit. "I'm sorry for not dressing more neatly for our date. I've been working all day on a new dress Aunt Lizzie designed. Right after lunch, I plan on returning to the job until it's finished. Did you want to see the dress?"

He followed her to the sewing machine. The assembly table next to it was littered with odd-shaped pieces of fabric and tissue paper. He had no idea what was going on and thought the place looked a mess. It was clear she was in the middle of a creative process he did not understand.

"Francena, you will have to show me the dress when it's complete. I really don't know what I'm looking at. Please, let's head back to Prides Corner so that I can show you my new house before lunch."

Franny grabbed her coat and gloves, hollered up the stairs to Liz that she would return soon, and followed him to the carriage. He kindly helped her up to the passenger seat, then walked around to the other side. As he climbed up to the seat, Liz lowered the second-floor apartment window and shouted to her niece.

"Franny, your father just rang me to say that he would be coming for a visit tomorrow morning. He has something important to discuss with us."

"What is it?"

"Something to do with your brother and Lottie. He didn't say much."

"I'll be back in an hour or so. I'll ring him up then."

On the short ride to Brook Street, Eugene talked on and on about his new house and what a wonderful home it would be for a family. She paid little attention to him, wondering what it might be that her dad wanted to discuss. Something must be wrong.

"Francena, what do you think about a garden? Should I have vegetables or only cut flowers? I've never had one before. Have you?"

Surprised that he had bothered to ask for her opinion on something, she asked him to repeat the questions.

"My dear, are you paying attention to what I'm saying? I was asking you whether I should have a garden or not. You've had a vegetable garden for several years, haven't you?"

"Lottie and I had a wonderful garden behind the dress shop. When she married Clarence and moved to Waterford, I kept at it for a while. There hasn't been time recently."

The conversation continued as he drove the carriage onto the construction site. No one was working today, so they had the place to themselves. After he helped her down, she inspected the house for a moment before leaving him to walk toward the rear of the building.

"You could have a great large garden here. It's so sunny, and the trees are far from the house. Was this a pasture before?"

He remained behind her, standing at the front steps, sorry to have brought up the idea of horticulture. It was the house with which he wanted to impress her, to win her over. He hadn't built the place for himself only. With three bedrooms, a large kitchen, two bathrooms and a wraparound porch, this house was made for a large family.

"Please come with me to see what's inside. The rooms are very large," he said as he climbed the front steps.

She joined him at the front door, which was untrimmed, the shims used to level it still sticking out. When he opened it, the frame wiggled so much that they both thought it might fall over. He closed it very carefully, not wanting to cause any damage.

Rough framing was exposed everywhere. Extension ladders stood against the walls of the first floor where plaster was being spread. Scaffolding was mounted where a staircase was rising to the second floor. Window openings in the walls were boarded up. Sawdust was everywhere.

"I guess my choice of outfit was appropriate," said Franny with a giggle. "Be careful you don't rip your suit."

Although he found her tone offensive, he didn't want to ruin their first date with a row.

"My apologies for bringing you into such a mess. I asked the men to clean the place up before they left yesterday. As you can see, they didn't pay much attention to my request."

Feeling that her joking might not have been the best thing to do, Franny became more serious. He hadn't reacted as if he understood her humor and seemed to be offended. She wanted to be at peace with him.

"Oh my, Eugene, I didn't realize how large a project you had made for yourself. Please show me the rooms on this floor. Is there a full basement?"

"Oh, yes. Please come this way to see the kitchen. There are no appliances installed as yet. The rough plumbing is already in place."

When she entered the kitchen shell, its size made her stop in her tracks.

"A real working kitchen here. I didn't know you like to cook that much."

"I don't really cook too much for myself. Just planning ahead. Speaking of cooking, why don't we go next door and have lunch. You do want to get back to your work."

As they walked to the store and entered the rear door to his apartment, she looked back at the house. From this perspective, it looked so huge that she guessed it must be the biggest house in the neighborhood.

His small dining table was set for a formal luncheon, with a clean white tablecloth and neatly folded napkins, fine china plates with delft blue bands around the edges, even fine silverware. She was surprised that a bachelor would go to such lengths for a simple bite to eat.

"Eugene, you have outdone yourself. What a lovely spread. I doubt if I could do any better."

"Thank you so much, but I take no credit for the place settings or lunch itself. I've a woman from the neighborhood who does my housekeeping. I had her prepare everything for us. If you would be so kind, would you please bring the sandwiches in from the kitchen? I'll pour us each a tumbler of ale."

She was surprised at the offer of a drink of alcohol. To her knowledge, he had always been a teetotaler.

"Please, no beer for me. I must get back to work soon and need to have a clear head."

He turned toward her with a look of disappointment.

"One small tumbler isn't enough to make one drunk. I thought, if we shared a drink, it might make the occasion more relaxed. However, you must know your own limits."

He poured a glass for himself from the dark glass growler and lifted it to his nose.

"My neighbor woman's husband brews this himself. Sure you won't try a tumbler?"

She refused his offer again as she went into the kitchen. There she found two wooden serving trays set out on a soapstone counter. One held two small plates with ham and cheese sandwiches, the second held slices of apple pie topped with wedges of cheese. She picked up both and returned to the lovely table. He was already seated, sipping on his glass. Setting down the trays, she placed two dishes in front of him and carried her meal to the other chair where a glass of water had been placed.

"Francena, it was a pleasure to have you visit my grand house." He raised the glass and made a toast. "To us, my dear. To us."

Not sure that she wanted to encourage him any further, she left her glass on the table.

Noticing that she was not participating in his toast, he took a deep swallow of the tan brew and refilled his glass.

"My dear, please forgive my familiarity. It is not my wish to offend you in any way. I only want us to be friends."

She picked up her water glass and clicked it against his.

"Yes, then, to our friendship."

62

Daughter Janey reminded Maeve so much of Will. The girl was so handy with tools that even at an early age, she had accompanied her late father to job sites. As she grew, her talents made it possible for her to create gifts for the family at holidays and birthdays, things like birdhouses, dollhouse furniture, and signs. By the time she was in her teens, she was making full-size furniture: chairs, small tables, and lovely boxes. She had also inherited from Will his tendency to be a perfectionist. At times she would be quick to criticize her family members if, in her own opinion, they misbehaved. It was not only her siblings to whom she directed criticism, but also her mother. Maeve relied on her to assist in raising the other children, but when Janey's complaints were aimed in her mother's direction, Maeve often took issue. When the girl went off to Bridgton Academy to complete her high school grades, Maeve missed her help. She also felt some relief from unfair criticism, except on weekends.

"Mom, I've been thinking about this Stevens woman," Janey began while the two were bringing firewood into the kitchen. "She must be a very tormented soul. Don't you agree?"

Four years had passed since Aphia Stevens had accidentally shot Will to death, and Maeve was still grieving his loss. She wasn't sure where her daughter's question was leading.

"I'm sure she is. Lizzie says that Aphia is ravaged by guilt going back to when she was younger than you and deserted her own family. Your Aunt Mary is of the opinion that the woman will never be able to escape her demons."

"She must feel guilty about stealing Auntie's fiancé, don't you think? And then she killed him!"

"Remember, that may have been an accident. Even though she was convicted of her husband's murder, the jury relied on the testimony of one man who wasn't even a witness to the crime."

"Still, she must carry some guilt for the act. How could she not? And there was that other man who was found buried in her pasture. My God, how many men has she killed?"

"If you listen to Lottie Hallett, you could add a fourth death to her list. She believes Aphia somehow killed Clarence up in Ontario."

"So, that would be four men dead at her hands. If so, no wonder she is tormented. She must be close to insanity!"

The strange discussion seemed to have ended as the two continued in silence to fill the two wood boxes with armfuls of dried splits. When they were finished, Maeve drew a kettle of water and placed it on the range for tea. Janey cut two pieces of fresh-baked bread from a loaf in the pantry. As the two sat down across the table from one another, Janey picked up the discussion again.

"Mom, sometimes I'm still so sad about Dad's death that I start to cry. Sadness sweeps over me at the strangest times. In the middle of a lecture, his face might come to mind, and the tears come. There's no controlling the grief."

"I know, dear. It is often the same for me."

"How long will it take to get over this sadness?"

"Grief is different for each person. Yours may last longer than mine, but I doubt it. You have your father's resilience. I know my sense of loss may last as long as my love for him."

"But that would mean you would never recover."

"Could be."

The two sat in silence, each stirring the sugar in their teacups. Janey then noticed tears on her mother's cheeks.

"I'm sorry to have made you cry. Please forgive me, but I need to ask you one more thing. Then I will leave you alone. On the day of Dad's burial, you and Lizzie stood above the open grave holding hands. You said something about a custom back in Ireland where people often forgave others who had done them wrong as a way of relieving their own hurt feelings. Do you remember that?"

Maeve was surprised that the girl would have recalled that conversation.

"Yes, I do recall that moment. The people back home often said that a person who is wronged might never recover from effects of a crime against them until they forgive the one who hurt them. I believe that to be true."

"Perhaps we might feel better if we forgave Aphia Stevens for her awful deed. It might be worth the effort if we were able to find peace."

Oh my God, thought Maeve as she stared with wide-open eyes at her daughter. How much she is like her father!

63

Franny carried the completed prototype dress to Lizzie for inspection at her desk. As the women mounted the dress on a mannequin, both noticed that the seams were uneven at one shoulder where the arm joined the bodice.

"Auntie, I am so sorry to have made that mistake. Please forgive me. I have not been myself since noontime." She began to roughly tug at the garment.

"Don't be so hard on yourself. It is easy to fix. We all make mistakes once in a while."

Franny sat down hard in her chair. She began to sigh deeply and put her hands up to her face. "Auntie, I don't know what to think. Perhaps if I tell you what's on my mind, it will help me understand my dilemma."

"Of course. I may not be able to advise you, but at least I can listen. Your Uncle Moses used to say I am the world's best listener."

"Well, here is my problem. You know that I would like to meet a man and start a family. I haven't kept that a secret—though I probably should have."

"My dear, your parents have told me about your wishes, but only in passing. You can trust that I haven't told a soul. Not even Mary."

"Thank you for keeping things private. I sometimes think that everyone wants me to find a good husband. Feels like there is pressure on me to wed."

"That is likely your own pressure, but please go on."

"I suppose that's true. I see Lottie in a happy marriage at last. She and Nate are made for each other. It makes me want to find the same fulfillment. But when I meet a man who might be right for me, I am always finding fault with him. He is too young. Too old. Too self-centered. There's always something."

"That must be frustrating for you."

"Take Eugene Bailey for example. He is reliable, and at thirty-two, very mature. He certainly has the wherewithal to take care of my material needs. But he isn't much fun to be with. And he's so set in his ways."

"You know I married a man who was nearly twice my age. Moses certainly was set in his ways, yet he was so endearing. He cared for me and gave me the space I needed to be myself. Wouldn't Mr. Bailey do that for you?"

"See? You called him Mr. Bailey, not Eugene. Even you can see he is much older than his age. I do not believe he has it in him to do what Moses did for you. Yesterday, we toured his grand new house. His castle. It's a mansion built for a king and queen, and it's very clear to me that he wants me to be his queen. She would stay at home and cook in her big kitchen, play in her garden, raise the children."

Her voice had become quite agitated.

"Franny, please calm yourself. There's no need to get so upset with a man who is obviously trying to be friendly. You don't have to marry him. There are others."

"There is another boy who might care for me. He is younger than me, but oh-so-handsome. I met him in North Waterford with Lottie. He's a friend of Nate's. I was with him when I fell and hurt my shoulder. Ethan Blaine is his name. He clerks at a store in their village."

"How do you know he cares for you? You've spent very little time with him."

"That's true, but I've enjoyed his company the few times we have been together. He knows so much about nature and has taught me a lot. We've gone riding in the wilds around his town of Albany, north of Waterford. He's a great horseman."

"Sounds as if you might have a good friend in this Ethan. How old is he?"

"I'm not sure, but my guess would be four or five years younger than me. When I say he is young, it isn't so much in years as it is in terms of maturity. He's like a colt who wants to run free until life teaches its lessons to him. He would be so much more exciting to be with than Eugene, but a life with him would not be without risk."

"Franny, dear, whose life *is* without risk? You can only stay safe if you make no decisions."

The young woman looked at her aunt, whose words made so much sense.

"I know you're right, Lizzie. It is up to me to either choose between one of the men life is offering or remain a single spinster until the right man comes along."

Then she laughed, removed the dress from its form, and returned to her sewing. As she worked, a thought came to her mind. What if the right man never does come along?

64

Lizzie and Franny sat on the porch swing waiting for Nathan to arrive. It was so late in the day that the sun had already set, and the early evening was turning cold. Both were wearing heavy woolen cardigans and knit hats pulled down to their ears. Snow had yet to fall in Westbrook, but they knew it would be coming soon. When at last his carriage entered the long driveway off Forest Avenue, Franny jumped from the seat and ran out to greet her father.

"Daddy, you're so late. We thought you might not get here tonight. Aunt Liz rang your home and talked with Mom. She said you left right after breakfast. We were getting worried."

Nathan climbed down from his carriage.

"Sorry to worry you all. I stopped to help a friend and it slowed my pace. Lizzie, you'll never believe who is on his way to visit you—your old friend Bert Learned. I would expect him to show up after dark," he said, pointing back at the road. "He is riding that horse that's about as old as he is."

"What? He still rides that old Bess?"

He laughed out loud.

"He doesn't really ride her much, I'd say. They sort of walk along side by side most of the time. I met him resting on a bench along the road in Naples. When he told me he was on his way here, I knew that if I didn't help him, he'd have to sleep on the ground by the side of the road tonight. As it is, he still might have to do that."

"Why is he coming here? I thought he was up in New Hampshire somewhere."

"He told me that you invited him to stay here if he got into trouble. Sounds like he's without a home for some reason."

"I remember making that offer, but it was years ago. Things are different now, but I'm sure we can work something out."

As the three of them climbed the steps and went into the house, Franny asked her father, "What's the mysterious news you have for us? Mother would give neither of us a hint."

In the kitchen, he pulled a pressed-back chair away from the table and sat down hard. He appeared to be exhausted from the trip.

"Well, it's Lottie. She is pregnant."

"No! How can that be?" said Franny. "The doctors said she could never have another baby."

"Yes, I know. That's what we all thought. Nate told us they are both surprised and very happy about it. Hattie and I are worried about her health. She is supposed to stay in bed most of the time for the next few months, especially during the final trimester."

"Mom would know a lot about a rough pregnancy. I remember how she had to stay in bed for weeks before Nate was born."

"This is different, Franny. Your mom suffered from toxemia, which is not uncommon. Your friend damaged her uterus. An infection grew inside her and left scars that would usually make it impossible to get pregnant."

Recalling the tough time Hattie had when she was pregnant with Nate, Liz remembered that a local midwife had skillfully attended her sister throughout the ordeal.

"Nathan, do you know if Agnes Hodgson is still practicing? Remember how she tended Hattie during that very rough pregnancy? I think she saved her life and Nate's, too."

"Yes, that's one of the reasons I'm here. The woman is in her seventies, but still working miracles. Hattie thought we might consult with Mrs. Hodgson to make sure we have a good plan in place before Lottie reaches the second trimester. The other reason is to talk with you, Liz, about the possibility that Lottie may have to stay here to be near the midwife during the last couple of months of her term."

Before Lizzie had a chance to answer, someone began to yell loudly in the driveway a few yards from the house. Franny ran to the window and saw Bert Learned swatting his horse with his ragged hat. The animal lay on the lawn.

"Darn you, Bess. Get up right now!" he hollered. "You can't be that tired. I haven't rode you but a bit since we left Windham. Get up on your four feet."

The three of them went out to stand on the porch. Nathan called out, "Ho, there! Bert, give the nag a chance to rest. She'll get up soon without all your shouting."

"No, I think she's breathed her last. Her eyes are shut tight. Chest ain't rising at all."

Nathan walked to the horse and held his hand to its snout. Indeed, it was not breathing. He pressed his hand hard into the neck. He felt no pulse.

"Bert, I'm afraid you're right. Your Bess is dead. Come inside and sit yourself down to rest. We will take care of her tomorrow."

The old man held what was left of his hat to his heart and began to say the Lord's Prayer. Then he fell to one knee and placed his hand on Bess's forelock.

"You been a great friend, Bessy. Sad to see you go. You got me this far. Now I got to make it on my own."

65

For six months, Aphia had been reading every law book and journal that was available to find a way of overturning her conviction for the murder of Henry Greene. She theorized that there had to be a way to prove that her trial had been unfair. Her lawyer may have failed to defend her properly. Jurors may

have been misled in some way. At first, she found it very difficult to make sense of the intricate reasoning used in trial sum-
maries and legal essays. Terms used by the experts were sometimes given in Latin or Greek or, more often, archaic English.
In time, she began to understand the logic behind criminal law
and how many shades of meaning one could make out of the
simplest law.

Warden Lewis knew that she would be incarcerated for the
rest of her life and that the search was a waste of time. Yet he
came to take a personal interest in this woman who was so attractive and intelligent. He began to borrow books from judges and
lawyers who were his friends, lending them to her in return for
good behavior. This new source of more modern jurisprudence
gave her a new understanding of the law. One day she made a
further request that only Lewis could grant.

"Warden, would you be willing to provide me with court
documents pertaining to all of my convictions?"

"I'm not sure that would be permissible under Maine law."

"How could it not be allowed? I have read that a defendant
has the right to question whether her lawyers may not have used
exculpatory evidence which might have affected jury decisions.
How can I evaluate my lawyer's judgment if I can't see what
evidence was used?"

Surprised that a prisoner would know what types of evidence
might be used in a trial, he stared at her in silence, pulling on his
right earlobe.

"Once you were convicted of the crimes, you stopped being
a defendant and became a prisoner. You have lost many of your
rights under the Constitution."

"Lost my rights, you say. And what rights are those? The right
to a fair trial? I believe I still have the right to question the actions
of my lawyers in bringing only one witness against me and not
cross-examining him properly."

Her voice got louder, and her fingers drummed on the table-
top. She did not want to lose control and verbally abuse him, thus
risking the loss of his assistance.

"Prisoner Stevens, if you don't mind, I would like to address you by your first name, Aphia. The name has a certain flair to it. So different. I looked it up. In Greek it means 'all-important' or 'clear-minded.' Did you know that?"

He smiled and winked at her, thinking he was being clever.

She knew that he was looking for something from her. That was why he was becoming personal. This had happened to her before. Men, even perfect strangers, might seem to become friendly when they were really seeking intimacy.

"No, Warden. I didn't know that," she lied.

"If I help you get the information you request, could you do me a simple favor?"

Smiling and tilting her face to one side, she asked, "What favor would that be?"

He folded his hands across his ample stomach and smiled.

"Join me for a private dinner at my home here on campus. Since you came to Thomaston, you've not had as good a meal as I can arrange for you."

"Sir, if you can do me the favor I ask, I can certainly return one for you."

66

Mary was confused and angry. Her shadow, cast by the light of a bedside lamp, loomed large against the door of Lizzie's bedroom. She strode back and forth at the foot of the bed, still wearing her nightgown and slippers. Liz was beneath the covers, propped up in a sitting position by two pillows. The book she had been reading lay open on her chest.

"I don't see why you must let old Bert move in with us. I realize that it is your house, but things change over time. It was years ago that you gave him the invitation."

"I see no reason why we can't give him a comfortable place to live, at least during the winter. You don't want him sleeping outside, do you?"

In exasperation Mary threw up her hands. When Bert had been given Francena's room, the girl had to move up to the second bedroom on the third floor next to Mary's. Until now, Mary had bitten her tongue to keep from saying anything that might lead to a row. She had to say something because the peaceful life the three women enjoyed had been disrupted by Bert's constant chatter and noisy manners. The straw that broke the camel's back had happened during supper, when he fell asleep at the table and snored through the entire meal. Franny had poked him several times with no effect. They continued to eat through his wheezing, trying to enjoy the meal even though they were unable to hear each other speak.

"I thought he was going to die at the table. Now I've got dyspepsia and can't sleep. You know I love living here with you, Liz, but Bert's presence is driving me to have second thoughts."

Liz closed the novel and placed it on her nightstand. Then she reached out for her friend's hand. Mary pulled her hand back and continued to pace back and forth.

"Liz, you can see how his presence is upsetting Francena. She hardly said a word at the table and ran off to bed while we did the dishes. We both love you. Do not force us to leave because of that man."

Her voice became so loud that Liz was afraid Franny would hear her from the third floor. She held her index finger to her lips.

"Hush, dear. Please. Let's not keep everyone else awake."

"Everyone? You mean Franny. Bert is probably still asleep at the table. I couldn't wake him if I was shouting in his good ear."

She began to giggle at her own joke.

Liz swung her legs to the side of the bed and stood. She, too, was giggling. By the time she put her arms around Mary, neither could stop laughing.

"I'm sorry," said Lizzie. "I might have at least discussed letting him stay here with you before I agreed to his request. This is your home, too. Please forgive me."

"I do forgive you. I'm sorry to threaten to leave you. It's just that he is so annoying. You are right to protect the old man from the hardships of winter. I would have probably made the same decision if you had asked me. Knowing that he will only be here for a short time makes it easier to accept."

Liz smiled and said softly, "I guess that was our first real quarrel."

"Yes, love. Let's go back to bed," said Mary as she left the room.

67

In the spring, Maeve started working full-time in the shop, using the third old Singer. It had not been in operation for a long time and needed a thorough cleaning and lubrication. Several parts had to be replaced by a specially trained technician who owned the Lewiston Singer dealership. Liz introduced him to the other women.

"Ladies, this is Charles Van Dam. He is here to get that old machine up and running again. I may also ask him to give the others a once-over to see how they're holding up. Please make note of any mechanical problems you've been having with your own machines and give it to me."

Charles was a handsome man with a full beard and slicked-back hair. Maeve thought he looked to be around fifty years old.

"Mr. Van Dam, I have had this clunker working some," she said. "It misses a stitch now and then, and it came to a complete stop yesterday when the bobbin threw all its thread into the presser and jammed everything up."

"Well, Mrs. Cain, let me have a look at that. What did you do to get the bobbin out and rewound?"

"Well, sir, I lifted the foot and cut the bobbin thread. Then I pulled out the bobbin and rewound the whole thing. It won't do to have that happen all the time. It took almost thirty minutes."

"Don't worry about that problem. Just a couple of adjustments should keep that from bothering you in the future. I'll have to remove the housing from the base. Might as well inspect the gears. They always need some lubrication."

As he worked on her machine, Maeve sat next to Liz. They chatted until Maeve became intrigued by the efficient way the repairman worked. He wiped down the entire machine with a clean white rag which he then laid across the top of his toolbox. All the tools he would need were neatly lined up on top of the cloth in the order they would be used. He studied the machine for a moment before testing a screw with a small screwdriver. When the screw wouldn't turn, he took a copper oil can from the tools display and applied a squirt to the offending screw. He wiped his hands and smiled over at her.

"This old thing hasn't been cleaned for some time, perhaps never. But don't you worry, ma'am. We see this all the time. Good thing Singer makes a great machine."

She liked his manner, his smile, his confidence. He reminded her of Will—not his personality or appearance, just the way he had everything organized ahead of time. The two men would have gotten along well.

"Ma'am, have you been working here for long? I was here some months ago to service the other machines. The two ladies were the only ones here."

"I used to work here, before my husband and I decided to have five children. Doing something like that doesn't leave much time for work."

"No. I bet it doesn't. Pardon me for saying this, but you look too young to be a mother of five. Your husband is a lucky man." He returned to his project, lifting the housing, brushing dust and bits of thread from the base.

"You need no pardon for such a compliment, though I think it is more like flattery. Thank you very much. I'm afraid my husband is no longer with us; he died four years ago."

Charles stopped working and turned directly to her. His face showed genuine shock and concern. "Mrs. Cain, I am so sorry to hear that. My condolences for your loss."

Looking into his eyes, she saw that his concern was sincere.

His words were trite, what everyone said to one who had lost a loved one. Yet there was something about the way he peered at her that showed he really was feeling sympathy for her.

"Mr. Van Dam, please call me by my name, Maeve. May I address you as Charles?"

"Yes, of course, Maeve." He smiled for a second. "What a lovely name, Maeve. Maeve. Maeve. You must be Irish."

68

A tall, heavy-set matron tapped on the bars of Aphia's cell door, interrupting the prisoner in her review of a large envelope of pages containing notes from her murder trial.

"The Warden wishes to see you in his office following breakfast. I suggest you clean yourself up before that."

With a smiled pasted on her face, Aphia stared at the woman. Her true opinion of the matron remained the same as it had been ever since the bitch had poked her with a nightstick the day she entered the prison three years before.

"Of course, Miss Johnson. Should I wear my best outfit, the taffeta dress and pumps?" she asked sarcastically.

"Stevens, you may be able to pull the wool over the warden's eyes, but I know how angry and vengeful you really are. Just comb your hair and wash your face. And don't mouth off to me."

"Why, I was only joking with you. If I sounded offensive, I apologize."

"Harrumph!" bellowed the woman as she whacked the bars with force.

"Be ready right after breakfast. He'll rue the day he took an interest in your case."

69

Warden Lewis opened his office door for Aphia. He smiled and gestured her in with a wave of his arm. She felt his greedy eyes staring at her body as she walked past. The office stunk from what she recognized was a combination of cigar smoke, whiskey, and sweat.

She went to the small wooden chair directly in front of his desk. Before she was able to sit, he pointed to a much more comfortable chair with a padded leather seat next to his own chair. Once she was seated, he walked behind her and took his seat, brushing against her shoulders as he passed.

"Aphia, dear, have you had an opportunity to look at the trial notes which I procured for you? It took quite a lot of string-pulling to get those from the state archives."

"Yes, Warden. I'm sure it did. There hasn't been time to read everything. It looks to be very comprehensive. Thank you so much."

"Justice Johnson of the Supreme Court was reluctant to release records which are usually sealed. He was very curious why you wanted them. When I told him your reasoning, he laughed at what he called your 'fantasy' that you would get the third conviction overturned. He and I both agree that you are on a fool's errand. You were convicted of three murders. Getting rid of one will not get you released."

"I realize that, Warden Lewis. My only goal is to be cleared of Henry Greene's homicide, to clear my name of such a faulty conviction."

Fantasy, indeed, she said to herself. Are all these men so pompous?

"Aphia, please call me Bernie. It is short for Bernard. If we are going to be friendly to one another, at least we can use our given names."

"Friendly to each other? Sir, I am not quite sure what you mean by that."

"Well, I did what you requested. Now it is time for you to do a favor for me, Aphia. What a beautiful old name that is."

She frowned and peered at the man. He was at least twenty years her senior and very obese. His nose was red and bulbous, with black hairs coming out of both nostrils. Though the room was a comfortable temperature, the starched collar of his shirt was damp from sweat beneath a tightly knotted four-in-hand. It was clear that the only favor he wanted was for her to become his mistress. She needed to decide whether there might be any advantages in doing so.

"My paternal grandmother's name. It goes way back in the family. I've been told it came from ancestors over in Scotland, though I can't be sure."

The warden was pleased that their conversation was becoming more casual. Surely she knew where this all was leading. She has kept herself in better shape than the librarian, he thought. And after all, a younger woman would be better in bed.

"Aphia, can I offer you a bourbon, or perhaps a tumbler of sherry?"

He pulled open a desk drawer which she could see was set up as a bar. There were two crystal carafes, an assortment of glassware, even a large jar of what looked like pickled pigs' feet. She almost burst out laughing.

"Sir, if I said yes to either beverage, wouldn't I be breaking the rules for prisoner behavior?"

"Aphia, my dear. I am the one who sets the rules. I may break them if I want. Besides, we might break a few more rules in the future."

70

"Nathan, there's someone at the door," said Hattie. "Could you get it?"

When he opened the door, a well-dressed gentleman removed his bowler hat and introduced himself.

"Good day, Mr. Hallett. I hope I have not disturbed you."

The man looked familiar, though Nathan could not place

him. His outfit was overly formal for travel: worsted trousers, spats, a gray waistcoat, and a bright-white linen shirt held tightly together at the throat with what looked to be a silk tie. Draped over his arm he carried a tweed storm coat.

"Not at all, sir. What can I do for you this fine day?"

"You may not remember me, but we have met several times at my store at Prides Corner. I am Eugene Bailey. Your wife has often been a customer when she is in Westbrook visiting her sister and your daughter, Francena."

"Oh, yes. I do remember you. Please come in, Mr. Bailey. I will tell my wife you're here."

"Thank you; I appreciate your hospitality. No need to disturb her if she is busy at something. I came to speak with you."

Nathan thought it strange that a man he hardly knew had driven all the way from Westbrook on a Saturday afternoon. This was likely the busiest day of the week for him.

"Well, then. Please come in and rest yourself in the parlor. Can I get you a glass of water? You must be parched from the road."

"Yes, thank you. That would be good," he said as he sat on the sofa.

Hattie accompanied Nathan when he returned. She wore a dirt-stained apron and carried a pair of garden gloves.

"Mr. Bailey, what a pleasant surprise. Please excuse my appearance. I've been working in the conservatory."

He rose from his seat to greet her.

"You are a gardener, like your daughter. Wonderful hobby. I must consider a conservatory for my new home. I wouldn't think of it myself. As an unmarried merchant, I don't have much time for hobbies."

Nathan sat in the easy chair, while Hattie sat on the chair's arm. There was an awkward silence for several moments until she said, "Franny has told us that you're in the midst of building a grand new home."

"Oh, yes. Nearly completed. I may be able to move in soon. Definitely before summer."

"You must be so pleased. What a lot of work it must be to build your own home. And such a large one. She said it has three bedrooms."

He was pleased that the girl had shared so much information about his new house with her parents. It showed that she was keeping an eye on the project. The fact that the conversation was leading directly to the reason for his visit helped him relax. He sipped the water.

"Mr. and Mrs. Hallett," he began.

Nathan interrupted him. "Please call us by our names, Hattie and Nathan. Let's not be so formal. May I address you as Eugene?"

"Oh, yes. Of course."

It was good to be less formal. After all, if he was successful today, the three of them might soon be family.

"Thank you, Nathan. I have come to visit today to ask a favor of you. It concerns your wonderful daughter. She and I have been spending time together over the past several months making selections of interior finishes for the house. She has given me guidance on where to locate a garden and offered to help me set it up. She is such a helpful and intelligent woman."

"Indeed she is," said Hattie, who was surprised to hear her daughter so appreciated by a stranger. "We have raised her to be very capable of expressing herself and assisting others. She is also very talented, as you can see from how well she does at her trade."

Nathan said nothing. He knew where this was going and didn't want to get in the way.

"Nathan, Hattie, I am somewhat older than Francena and some would say set in my ways. I am also quite sound financially, with a successful business, investments in land, and shares of other businesses. I would be able to offer your daughter a secure and happy life. Do I have your permission to ask for her hand?"

The two stared at each other for a moment before Nathan spoke.

"Eugene, this is quite a surprise. Neither of us had any idea that she was interested in marrying anyone in particular. Did you suspect anything, Hattie?"

"No, not really. Have you discussed this with her?"

"Not directly. We have spoken of the future. I believe we both enjoy each other's company."

"I appreciate your asking us for permission to have our Franny as your wife," said Nathan. "It is highly honorable of you. However, I think you should ask her directly. Asking the father is a time-honored custom. I myself asked Hattie's grandfather for her hand many years ago because she had no father other than him. Things have changed since then. Fathers do not give their daughters away except at the marriage altar."

Eugene placed his water glass on the coffee table, looking as if he was preparing to leave. Hattie saw that he was embarrassed by her husband's comments. She stepped over to the sofa and placed her hand on his shoulder to keep him from rising.

"Sir, do not think that we disapprove of you as a prospective son-in-law. You are a very successful man, and I'm sure you would make some young lady a wonderful husband. Hopefully, when you express your wishes to Franny, you will be accepted. Nathan is correct. The old way of arranged marriages is a thing of the past. Or at least it is in our family."

Bailey smiled but stood, despite her effort to make him stay a while.

"Hattie, I thank you for your kind words. And Nathan, I am sure what you say is correct for most young people today. My parents, God bless their memories, raised me according to the old ways, and the old ways die hard for some people. I will follow your suggestion and speak with your daughter directly about my desire to have her as my wife."

As Eugene grasped the doorknob, Nathan came to his side, offering his hand. The merchant took it in his and said, "Sir, do you approve of me as being worthy of your Francena?"

"Yes. If she accepts your proposal, we will be pleased to have a wedding here in our house. Thank you for your visit."

71

Spring's earliest warm days on Beech Hill were a blessing after a long Maine winter. Lottie sat on the back-porch bench staring at the pasture, which appeared to be a small pond of melted snow. The kitchen garden had been muddy for a week or more with brown remains of last season's weeds sticking up through standing puddles. Already her stomach was bulging with the new baby. For the past two weeks, she had been unable to sleep comfortably for more than two hours at a time between spasms of pain which shot through her shoulders and upper back. Nate was taking care of the boys most of the time so she might nap as needed during the day. The plan had always been for her to stay in Westbrook for the final weeks. Now it was likely she would have to leave much sooner.

As she shifted her weight to one side to relieve the discomfort in her legs, a voice shouted out from the front of the house. It couldn't be Nate. He had taken Con and Francis with him to the village. She tried to stand to find out who it was but couldn't lift herself off the seat.

"Hello!" she shouted. "I'm behind the house." There was no answer, so she shouted out again as loudly as she could. "Hello! Hello! Whoever it is, please come to the back of the house."

Ethan Blaine poked his head around the corner of the house and waved his hand. "Mrs. Hallett. Um, Lottie. Are you okay?" He saw that she was sweating and her face beet-red.

"Oh, it's you, Ethan. Please come over here. Perhaps you can help me stand and get back into the house. I came out to enjoy the sun. Now I've got a chill."

Even with his assistance, she had a rough time standing. He let her grab hold of his shoulder for support while they walked into the house. As she dropped down into a hard wooden chair, he saw how large her abdomen had become.

"Are you okay? Is there something I can do?"

"No. I'm more comfortable now. Please don't worry yourself. You didn't know that I am pregnant, did you?"

"I knew. Nate told me a while back. I didn't realize you were so far along. When is the due date?"

She didn't feel comfortable sharing the facts of her condition with someone she barely knew. Still, he could see for himself how she was faring.

"Not for another four months or more. I wish it were sooner."

"I'm sure it is none of my business, but you look like you're in pain."

"No more than usual, really. It comes and goes. Can you draw me a cup of cold water from the pump?"

By the time he returned with the drink, she was standing with the table as a prop.

"Thank you, Ethan. Now what are you here for? I know you didn't come to watch me go through a difficult pregnancy."

"Sorry to bother you. I came to ask if your friend Franny was planning to visit you soon. I want to speak with her about something personal."

"No, she hasn't been here since before winter. I doubt she will be visiting soon. I'm going to visit her myself for the remainder of my term. If you would like me to deliver a message, I will do that."

"As I said, it is something kind of personal. Maybe I will write a letter and you can carry it for me. When are you leaving?"

"As soon as I feel well enough for the journey. If you want me to get a letter to her, please be quick about it."

"I'll get it to you by end of day tomorrow."

72

With all three Singers in top shape, the shop was whirring along at a pace not seen since Liz and the Flaherty sisters first opened the business more than twenty years before. On most days, Mary, Maeve, and Francena each sat at her own machine working to complete designs put together by Lizzie with her niece's help. Liz manned the phone and met with customers who ordered bespoke dresses and with clients who ordered shirts, dresses, and waistcoats in commercial lots. Bolts of Irish linen were stacked against the rear wall. Millett's American Designs was once again thriving.

Nathan continued to travel throughout New England and New York and often visited, either delivering supplies or picking up goods to be delivered. One day, he popped in unannounced to bring alarming news. He bounded through the door without a knock.

"Dad, what a surprise. You weren't expected until later in the week," said Franny. She saw the distressed look on his face, rose from her work to hug him. "What is wrong? You look a fright."

"Franny, it's Lottie. She has taken a turn for the worse. She is bedridden. Can barely walk, her legs are so swollen. Her Waterford physician says she may lose the baby. Worse than that, her own life is threatened."

He sat down in Franny's empty chair. The four women gathered around him.

"Should she come here now, instead of waiting?" asked Liz. "Mrs. Hodgson might be able to help her."

"That's exactly what I suggested to Nate, but their doctor thinks travel would be very risky. He says that even a shorter trip to our house would not be without danger."

"We can't let her stay up there in the hills," said Franny. "Perhaps if I go back with you, I could help."

"My dear daughter, we must figure a way to get Lottie here safely. That is the best thing for her. That is my opinion, and I think both Nate and Lottie agree. Hattie would travel with them to Bridgton, where we would keep watch over her until she recovers from that trip. Then we could hire Dr. Edward Abbott's ambulance to bring her here. It's designed to travel much more safely than any wagon or buggy."

The women all were impressed by his thorough plan.

"Nathan, you have done your homework," said Mary. "I didn't know there was a horse-drawn ambulance anywhere around here."

"Neither did I," he said. "I know there are several that work out of Massachusetts General Hospital in Boston. Apparently, Abbott purchased one from the same manufacturer. It has been well-used in Bridgton."

"When will Lottie be moved to your house?" asked Franny. "If Auntie doesn't mind, I would like to travel to Waterford to help."

"The first leg of the trip will happen as soon as I get home. When she arrives, I will ring you, Liz, to let you know. Franny, how will you get there?"

"Oh, I think my friend Mr. Bailey has a carriage he will lend me."

"I'm sure he will be cooperative. Have you spent any time with him recently?"

"How do you know him?"

Nathan was unsure if he should let the cat out of the bag by mentioning the merchant's visit. He was surprised the man had not immediately asked Franny for her hand after returning from Bridgton a week ago.

"I have occasionally run into him in town. Don't know much about him, though. Surely he would help out a friend in need."

Franny thought her father was acting coy with her, that he knew more about Eugene than he let on.

"I'm sure he will say yes to me."

73

Warden Lewis sat at his desk, waiting for Aphia to arrive. The time given for her appointment, 2:30 p.m., had come and gone, and he was perturbed.

"What could be keeping her?" he muttered. "Does she think I will let her visit me only when she wants something? This is not a one-way street. She owes me a favor."

At 3:30 he left the office and strode as fast as his fat legs would carry him to the cell block where she was housed. Finding her cell empty, he shouted to the matron on duty, "Guard, come here immediately!" but no one came. He waddled to the guard station, where someone was supposed to be on duty every minute of every day. It was empty. He pulled a set of keys from his bulging jacket pocket and opened the door that led to the parade ground. Many prisoners, both men and women, were gathered in clusters talking and smoking cigarettes. There was no guard present. As soon as he entered the yard, all conversations ceased. The males and females separated, going to stand at opposite sides of the open space.

The door behind him opened. Out stepped a male guard and a female matron, both smoking, something which he specifically did not allow while they were on duty. He turned to the couple and cursed.

"Damn it! What the hell are you two doing? You have allowed prisoners of both sexes to fraternize in the yard. This is expressly forbidden. I could have your jobs for this! Now, make the prisoners return to their cells immediately."

Everyone in the yard stared at Lewis. As he berated the staff members, the prisoners snickered and elbowed each other. Then they lined up according to cell number and prepared to exit the space. Suddenly the warden's shouting stopped. His face grew red as an apple, sweat running down and wetting his collar. He grabbed his left arm above the elbow and fell on his knees, then on his face. The male guard knelt, rolled the man over on his back and felt his wrist for a pulse.

"My God, Grace," he said to the matron. "His pulse is racing as fast as the hooves of a running horse. What should we do?"

Grace knelt and put her hand to Lewis's nose. "He's also panting like your horse. He's been struck down by apoplexy."

The prisoners gathered around the man and began to give the guard all sorts of instructions on how to deal with the situation.

"Sit him up."

"Raise his arms."

"Let the devil die."

One woman stepped forward and knelt above the man's head. She began to lift his arms.

"Stop!" shouted the matron. "Leave the poor man alone. Back in line there with the rest."

"Ma'am," said the woman, "I learned this Silvester technique when I was an army nurse. If we do nothing, he'll die."

She continued to lift the arms above his head, then crossed them back across his chest. Nobody else had any idea what to do, so she was allowed to repeat the maneuver several times. At last, the prisoner turned to the matron and said, "I'm afraid the warden is dead. There is no pulse."

At this very moment, Aphia Stevens entered the yard and stood over the corpulent body. She had been hiding behind a stack in the library, hoping that something would happen to keep Lewis from collecting his "favor." She smiled, thinking about how often her wishes came true.

74

Franny had not seen Eugene for at least two weeks and assumed it was because the interior finish work on the house was taking so much of his time. As she approached the corner of Brook Street and Portland Road, she glimpsed a CLOSED sign hanging on the store's door. It was strange for him to close the place on a Friday, when everyone needed food for the weekend. Stepping up onto the porch, she saw "Back at two o'clock" handwritten on the sign in smaller letters. When she went to the rear of the building, she saw that the clapboard siding of the new place had been stained a pastel green, just as she had suggested. His head appeared in an open first-floor window.

"Francena, so nice of you to visit," he called out. "Please come see how the kitchen turned out. It is just as you designed it."

They met at the front door, which was ajar allowing the smell of paint to escape. Walking through the entryway, she was able to catch glimpses of the parlor with its huge stone fireplace, rose-patterned wallpaper, and light maple floors. At the kitchen door, she turned toward him clapping her hands together.

"How were you able to get so much completed since the last time I was here? This place is almost ready for you to move in. You must be overjoyed."

"The men are not quite done with the second floor, so I'll wait to show that to you in a week or so. Yes, this house is nearly in condition for a family."

She looked at him in some confusion. He had no family. Was he thinking of renting the place to a local family? Before she could ask him what he meant, he took her hand in his.

"Please come with me, Francena. I have something else to show you."

He led her out the rear door into a sunny conservatory whose glass walls looked out at an area that had been plowed and harrowed.

"This is the garden you wanted. Is it large enough?"

She smiled and joked, "I think you'll be looking for a good gardener to care of this for you. One who isn't afraid to get his clothes dirty."

"I am hoping you will be my gardener, Franny."

"I may be able to help out once in a while, but you know how busy I am."

He surprised her by kneeling on the floor. She thought he was looking for something he had dropped, until he took her hand again and kissed it. How could he be doing this to her?

"Franny, I know you may think me a stuffed shirt, a man who is not terribly exciting to be with. However, you have become so dear to me over the past year that I want you to be with me, to help me live a better life. Will you marry me?"

"Eugene, I am honored to be asked. And surprised! Am I to be the family who moves in?"

"My dear, building this house has always been about you, trying to please you. Look around. Everything is done exactly as you wanted, down to the finest detail. This place is already as much your home as it is mine. It suits you to a tee. I know I am much older than you and set in my ways, but with you as my helpmate, I will become a better person. You know I'm financially comfortable and will be able to provide you a life free from money worries."

"I know that, yes. But I earn a comfortable wage at the shop."

"Though you would not need to work any longer, it would be acceptable to me that you continue at your craft for the time being."

"Dear me. I don't know how to answer you. I came here today to ask to borrow your carriage and for a trip to Waterford to bring my dear friend Lottie back to Lizzie's. She is with child and having a very difficult time. She'll need my help for the next four months, at least."

He rose from the floor, still holding her hand.

"Of course you can borrow the carriage. Perhaps I can drive you to your parents' lovely home. My proposal has been too impetuous, hasn't it? Please forgive me. I might have waited for a better moment."

"I like men who are impetuous, who do things on the spur of the moment. You have surprised me. Shown me another side of you. Don't apologize. Please give me some time to consider your proposal. You have made me feel very important. A good man has asked for my hand—how marvelous!"

He might have been offended that his marriage proposal had not been accepted, except for the fact that Franny made him feel that he was appreciated. He was sure her acceptance would come after Lottie's emergency had passed. It would only mean a small delay in his plans.

75

After giving his wife a small meal and a dose of laudanum to help her sleep, Nate returned to the kitchen to wash the dishes. He heard a loud knock, and when he opened the door, Ethan was standing there holding a small envelope.

"Come in," he said quietly. "Please keep your voice down. I'm hoping that Lottie will get a bit of sleep tonight."

"I'll be as quiet as a mouse, and I'll be gone before you know it. Your wife told me a few days ago that if I wrote a letter to your sister, she would hand deliver it for me. This is it. Hopefully, I am not too late."

"No, you're not too late. We're leaving for Westbrook tomorrow, weather and her health permitting. I will take the letter for you. Have you and Franny been corresponding?"

"No, but I wouldn't mind it if we did. I thought she would be visiting you much more often. Mrs. Hallett told me that your sister is so busy with her work that she hasn't much time to travel."

"Why don't you visit her in Westbrook? It isn't that far away."

"Don't like the city too much. I've been to Bridgton a couple of times. And once to Norway. Too crowded. Dirty streets. In Norway, they don't clean the horse shit off the street but only once a day. Portland must be even worse."

"She doesn't live in Portland, Ethan. Her aunt's house and shop are in Westbrook. They're a few miles from the city."

"I'll think about it sometime. I guess I'm a bumpkin, or what they call a hillbilly. Tell Francena that if she is amenable to having me visit, she can mention it to me in a return letter. Till then, I will be staying put in the country with all its wide-open spaces."

"Franny will be here tomorrow if you'd like to stop by. She's staying tonight with her family in Bridgton."

"Won't I be in the way? You must have arrangements to make. Lots of things to pack for a long journey."

"Most everything is packed and prepared. We're going to Bridgton on the first day. It will be a test of how well Lottie will do on the road. We won't be leaving until after lunch. If you drop by in the morning, you might be able to speak with your friend directly."

Ethan smiled, remembering that he had referred to Franny as his "new friend" many months ago.

"Okay, I will come by late in the morning. Give her time to arrive. See you then."

Nate watched the young man trot out to the hitching post and leap onto his horse. As he rode away, mud from the gravel road splashed up from the animal's hooves. When his hat blew off, he grabbed it from the air and shook it before placing it back on his head.

76

"**M**om, come quick! There's a funny-looking man out back. It must be that funny old man who is staying with Lizzie," said Janey who was on vacation for a few days.

From the window of her second-floor bedroom, the girl watched Bert hobbling on a cane out of the woodland path which led from Lizzie's place. He was so flushed by the exertion that he stopped at the foot of the steps, removed his hat, and dabbed sweat from his brow with a gray handkerchief.

"Dear, you might at least greet the man at the door," Maeve said. "He's usually exhausted by the time he gets here for a visit. Likes to sit and chat for a spell. He's a good man. You'll like his stories. He and your father were good friends long ago, you know."

The girl was not sure she wanted to sit and entertain the man, but she did go to the door.

"Mr. Learned, please come in. My mom is in the parlor. Right this way."

Bert smiled at the beautiful young lady who met him at the door. He didn't recall ever having seen her before. Her dark hair was cut short above the ears so that her beautiful facial features were clear. She was quite tall for a woman. She reminded him of someone whom he couldn't quite recall. He followed her into the next room, keeping an eye on the movement of her hips and shoulders. Who was it that was tall and moved so smoothly like her? Then it came to him. She was very much like Will Cain, her father, his old friend.

"Bert, please take a seat. It's a warm one today. You must need a drink of water," said Maeve. "Janey will get you a cold glass, won't you, dear."

He took his usual seat in a wooden high-backed chair next to a window that looked out on the path into the woods and down to the granite quarry. He had often walked along the edge of the thirty-foot precipice that dropped into the deep, water-filled pit. Recently, though, he had avoided getting too close for fear he might lose his balance, fall, and drown.

"Your daughter is so pretty. She's the spittin' image of your Will, isn't she? She walks just like him. Rest his soul. She has his deep-blue eyes, too."

Janey returned with his water and took a seat on the sofa next to her mother. She sat with her legs folded back beneath her.

"Whoa, missy! How can you sit like that?" asked Bert. "My legs have forgotten how to bend at the knee. They would break right off if I tried to do that. Good to be young."

"Mr. Learned," the girl began, "you know Aphia Stevens, don't you?"

"Yup. I probably know her better than most people. Lived with her for a while back in Waterford."

"Was that at Nate and Lottie's farm?"

"Yes, Beech Hill Farm it was called then. Don't know what they call it now."

"I believe they still call it that. Don't they, Mom?"

"Yes, you're correct. Tell me, dear daughter, where are you leading with these questions? That was so long ago. Bert has probably forgotten most of what happened back then."

He straightened his head up with a snap and took a long draught of cold water before speaking again. "Not so! I remember much of those days. My relationship with that woman began so well. We got on like two halves of an apple. She was the most beautiful woman I had ever been with. Thought I was in heaven for a while, I did."

"Have you seen her recently, since she went to prison for killing Dad and those other men?"

"Just the once. Right after she was convicted and locked up for life. I went there to bid good riddance to the evil woman she had become."

Maeve figured out what Janey was doing by bringing up a discussion of Aphia.

"Bert, this young lady seems to have an odd idea burrowing in her brain. She thinks we might all visit the witch and forgive her for all she has done to ruin our lives: me, Lizzie, Lottie, and you."

"It's not an odd idea!" Janey protested. "After all, you are the one who brought it up at Dad's funeral."

Bert looked askance at her for a moment.

"Why would you want to do a fool thing like that? She's best left alone, if you ask me."

"Bert, Mom said that back in Ireland, where she and Aunt Mary were born, there's a saying that if you don't forgive the ones who hurt you, you keep the hurt deep in your heart forever. Forgiveness frees both the sinner and those sinned against from torment."

"Young lady, that might be true back in the old country. Here in the New World things is different."

Maeve thought for a moment, then said, "I've spoken with Lizzie about this, and we both think what Janey says does have some merit."

"Perhaps," he said. "But it seems foolish to me. I'll have to ruminate on it."

77

At break of dawn, Franny approached Beech Hill Farm. With all that was happening in her life, she hadn't slept very well recently and left Bridgton before her parents awoke. By the time she pulled up to the gate in her borrowed carriage, she was hungry for some breakfast. Nate, who had also been up half the night, met her at the door with a cup of coffee.

"How's the patient today, Nate?"

"Not sure. I haven't looked in at her for a few hours. Last time I checked, she was still asleep, though I could see that she was sweating profusely. Her pillow was soaking wet."

"Has Dr. Stimpson been here recently? What does he say about our plan?"

"He checked in day before yesterday and gave me more pain killer. He doesn't think she should be moved, but he understands why we're doing it. He's heard of Agnes Hodgson and believes her treatment might be a good thing for Lottie, if she survives the journey. I'm worried about her."

"If she's awake, may I see her?"

"Yes, please follow me and keep as quiet as possible. We don't want her to wake until all is ready for the trip. I still have to dress the kids."

When they walked into her room, Lottie was already awake and propped up on a pillow. Her face was so swollen that Franny could hardly recognize her beautiful features. She reached out a hand whose fingers were so puffy that the knuckles could not be seen.

"Oh, dear girl, you look a fright. Please don't exert yourself." Francena had tears in her eyes as she spoke.

"I must move. Can't stay here. Must get ready to leave." Her voice was muffled and hoarse, as if she were out of breath. She pulled at the blanket and revealed her legs, swollen and covered with red sores.

Franny turned to her brother and gestured with her head to the door. When they were in the kitchen, her words exploded.

"Nate, look at her! She's in no condition to go anywhere. If we take her out of bed and on a journey, she will surely die."

"We must, or she will die right here under this roof! There's nothing else to do. I am at my wit's end. At least in Westbrook she will have better care."

"No! No!" she stamped her feet and squeezed both hands into tight fists. "I forbid it! Moving Lottie will kill her. We'll do nothing of the sort."

He sat hard in a chair, making the joints creak as if to break. He began to cry, something that Franny had not seen him do since he was still in short pants.

"What will we do? I don't want to lose my darling Lottie. What will you do?"

Franny was also crying now, her anger having melted in sadness.

"I will stay here with you and nurse her until she either has the baby, God willing, or has another stillbirth."

"But you are not a physician or a midwife. What can you do?"

"I will do what needs to be done to save her. Now let me visit with my friend."

78

Next morning, Franny and Nate sat down at the kitchen table and ate a hearty breakfast of eggs, bacon, and biscuits that Nate had prepared. Neither had slept very well after staying up half the night discussing care for Lottie. It wasn't as if there was no medical care available in Waterford. Dr. Stimpson was nearby, and there were several experienced midwives in Waterford Flat. Reluctantly, he agreed at last to delay the journey long enough to see if the two of them might work together to provide enough care at home.

As they sat at the table over a third coffee, Ethan knocked quietly on the door, opening it enough to be able to peek inside.

Nate gestured for him to join them. "Come in and join us for a coffee."

Franny stared in his direction, trying to focus her tired eyes.

"Hey, Ethan, what are you doing here so early?"

"I wanted to catch you before you left again. Every time I come to see you, it seems like you have just left."

She smiled at him. "I didn't know you got out of bed so early in the day. What time is it, anyway?"

"Don't know. I've never liked wearing a watch. Mr. Nason gave me a gold Waltham for Christmas, and it's still in the cloth bag. All I can say is that it is exceedingly early."

Nate excused himself to check on the boys. As soon as he left the room, Ethan walked to Franny's side and put his hand on her injured shoulder.

"Have you had any problems with that? I often think about your fall. I'm so sorry for what happened."

Pushing his hand away, she grimaced, then grabbed the hand again.

"It gets tired occasionally and is sensitive to the touch. My doctor found nothing broken—just a deep bone bruise, and it will eventually heal completely. No need for you to be sorry, Ethan. It was my own fault for losing my balance."

"I might have had second thoughts about bringing you to the Basins. Such a wild place for such a cultured girl."

He put his arm around her shoulders, carefully avoiding the spot of the injury. This time she did not pull back, letting him pull her close. They turned to look into each other's eyes.

"Franny, I've missed you. Our times together give me happy memories. Isn't there a way we might see each other more often?"

"Looks like you will easily be able to spend time with me. We are not traveling to Westbrook as planned. I'll be staying here for a while to nurse Lottie. Maybe you can help out."

As she said that, she thought of Eugene's marriage proposal and how complicated spending time with another man might make her life. Still, what harm could there be in having a friend?

Even if she were to wed one man, she would still be free to have male friends, wouldn't she?

In his pocket, Ethan carried the letter he had written the day before in which he suggested that he might enjoy traveling to Westbrook to visit her. Now, hearing this new plan, he was relieved that he wouldn't have to leave the safety of his home and venture into the crowded life of the city.

Nate entered the room carrying Francis in his arms. The boy was still dressed in the travel outfit of short pants, woolen socks, and a sweater from the day before. He had slept in them.

"Ethan," said Nate, "did you write that letter to my sister here that we discussed? Though our plans are changed, I'm sure she would enjoy reading what you had to say."

Franny laughed and held out her hand. "I love letters. Did you really write one to me? Men don't usually write good letters. Please, can I read it?"

Embarrassed that he would now have to show her the letter, he slowly pulled the envelope from his pocket and handed it to her.

"Yes, here it is. But please don't read it out loud. It's a private message, you know."

"Okay. I'll save it until later when I am alone."

79

Later that morning, Franny returned to Lottie's room to find her friend sound asleep. The swelling in her hands, which lay atop the covers, had lessened. Not wanting to disturb her patient, she sat on a small caned chair in front of the closed window, pulled the envelope from her pocket, and began to read Ethan's letter. It took up barely half of a single page, but she was surprised at the tiny size of his neat writing. Several ink blotches, finger marks perhaps, marred bottom corners of the paper.

Dear Miss Francena,

Too much time has passed since the last time we were together. Maybe you are angry with me for the neglect I showed you by allowing your injury in the Basins. I am sorry if that is the case. Nate says you are going to be taking care of his sick wife for a time in your Westbrook home. If it is permissible and you forgive me, could I visit you there in the city? Then I could apologize in person. I don't get out that way very often. If you might show me around, it would surely be very much fun.

I hope you are healed from your fall.

Yours,
Ethan Blaine.

She had never received such a sweet letter from a boy. It made her heart flutter. Folding it and placing it back in her pocket, she stared out the window at the small unmown pasture and the grove of tall hemlocks near the old mica mine site. A melancholy feeling came over her. Was it the emptiness of this rural setting which caused it? This had suddenly become her home once again for several months, far away from the life she loved. No, that wasn't the cause. The feeling came from another dilemma in which she found herself. Two men were pulling her heart strings so taut that she was held up in the air, hanging between them.

I have been looking for the right man for so long, she thought, and now I must decide before it's too late and one or both of them give up on me.

Lottie let out a loud snore, bringing Franny's attention back to the reality of responsibilities suddenly brought to her. The rest of her life would have to wait.

80

Mary and Lizzie prepared the storeroom behind the kitchen hearth for use as Lottie's convalescent room. Bolts of fabric, boxes of large one-pound thread spools of many colors, rolls of ribbon, and small cans of pins had to be removed and set around the workshop. One wooden box of sewing machine parts left behind by Mr. Van Dam was so heavy that they had to ask Maeve to help them. When the room was empty, the three women cleaned every surface and placed a double bed opposite the room's single window. They thought it would be good for Lottie to see the outdoors but not be exposed to drafts from the open window.

Mary and Maeve spread new sheets on the bed while Liz unrolled an old hooked rug made by her own grandmother. A chair and bedside table would be needed, but neither household had spares.

"Maeve," said Mary, "this mattress and box spring held up well in your musty old basement. Haven't they been down there since Will passed?"

"Not that long. I couldn't think of giving up the big bed for a long time after his death. Young Willy and I took it apart and stored it wrapped tight in a canvas sack. That was less than a year ago."

"Are you sure you'll not be using it again?"

Maeve looked at her sister with a questioning expression. "Whatever do you mean, miss? Why would I be needing a large bed?"

"I'm only thinking on the future. You've been spending quite a bit of time with that repair man, haven't you? Who knows what might come up?" She held out her fist with her index finger straight up.

"Come up? What do you mean by that?" said Maeve.

Lizzie stood in the doorway with arms akimbo. She snickered, then put her hands over her mouth to stifle a laugh.

"Mary, what a horrible thing to say! Come up, indeed."

"I'm only thinking about how a man often has no control over his emotions. You know what I mean."

Maeve began to smile. She grabbed a pillow and threw it at her sister.

"And you think a good Christian woman like meself would not hold the man off?"

"Knowing how flirty you are, you might hold him *on* you instead of off."

The two women fell on the bed and wrestled with each other as they must have done when they were children. Lizzie jumped on top of them and the three jostled each other until they were all out of breath.

When they had separated and rested, Maeve was the first to speak.

"You see what a fine strong bed this is." She stuck out her tongue. "Will and I made a lot of children on it."

81

Eugene assumed Francena would eventually accept his proposal, so while she was on her mission to rescue her friend Lottie, he decided to make the move into his new house. Why would he stay in the cramped little apartment when he had such spacious accommodations available just a few steps away? It didn't take more than two nights' work to pack all his clothes and personal goods in wooden crates. Then a local farmer with a large flatbed wagon and two strapping sons was hired to move all his belongings, including furniture.

When they were finished, he realized that all his stuff barely filled two of the first-floor rooms.

"We'll need a lot more furniture to fill this place," he murmured to himself. "I wouldn't be surprised if she would want to throw out half of what I have and replace everything with cleaner, more refined pieces to match her tastes."

He set up his single bed in what was supposed to be the parlor, knowing that a double bed with matching accessories would be needed. Neither did he bother to hang curtains or pictures. Francena would want to decorate. He wasn't sure he even liked the art and drapes that he'd brought with him.

I can put up with temporary living for the few days until she returns, he thought.

82

"Mary, could you please pick up the phone?" Liz shouted to her partner, who was working in the shop.

"I have it already, dear. It's your sister. Wants to speak with you about something important."

Knowing that the call might well concern Lottie's condition, Liz rushed to the kitchen and picked up the handset from the wall-mounted phone.

"Hello. This is Liz."

"Good day, big sister. Hope you're feeling well today." Hattie's voice came in loud and clear.

"Fine and dandy, Hattie. And you?"

"I want to share some news with you about a change in plans. Franny refused to allow Lottie to be moved. The whole plan is off."

"What do you mean, she refused to allow it?"

"I wasn't there, but Nate called from the village. He tells me that when she saw how ill Lottie was, she put her foot down and wouldn't go along with his plans. I guess she is much worse than we thought."

"What does Nathan say about this?"

"He left for Waterford just minutes ago to see for himself. Can I have him call you when he returns?"

"No need of that. If the move is off, then it is off."

"I'm sorry you went through all that trouble to set up a room for her. That must've been a bit of work."

"Not too bad. Maeve and Mary helped me."

"I'm sure you'll figure out something to do with the extra bedroom."

"Maybe you might visit for a change and stay in the room. I haven't seen you in ages."

"How are you and Mary getting along?"

"Doing fine. Why do you ask?"

"Just wanted to make sure you're happy. That's all."

"No need to worry, little sister. Thanks for letting me know about the changes."

"I'll keep you posted. Say hi to Mary for me."

At the end of the call, Liz walked into the new bedroom and sat on the side of the bed. She wondered why Hattie would be worried about her and Mary's relationship. As she thought about it, she realized that Hattie had not been to visit since Mary had moved in.

83

With the three women in the house making sure he had more than enough to eat, Bert had developed a small pot-belly. He gained so much weight that his worn overalls pulled tightly across his arms, legs, and waist. Lizzie made a new pair for him, much fancier that the old, with linen trim on the cuffs and pockets.

"Miss Lizzie, you can't expect me to wear this dandy's outfit," he said, inspecting the pants and a new long-sleeved cotton shirt. "Folks around here will think me dressed like a rich man."

"You seem to forget that, since you never venture out, we three and the Cain family are the only people who ever see you. You deserve to dress better than that old costume you've been wearing for years."

"What I deserve, you say? I can't say I ever did anything to deserve the royal treatment you all give me. Being here has surely put a few months back on this old man's life. I'll miss your kindness when I'm gone."

"Where are you going?"

"Well, I think our deal was that I would stay here only until spring came, wasn't it? Don't want to upset anyone by overstayin' the welcome."

"Don't worry about our 'deal,' as you call it. Now go upstairs and try on these new clothes. I want to see if they fit well enough."

When he returned, she was pleased to see that the overalls were a good fit. He had the sleeves of the shirt rolled up to his elbows.

"Why do you have a belt on over the pants?" she asked. "They'll be secure with just the shoulder straps."

"Oh, I'm afraid I'm a 'belt-and-suspenders' man. You can't be too careful in keeping your pants up, you know. Somethin' could always fail."

Mary entered the room and complimented his new outfit.

"Bert, don't you look like a prosperous farmer in those clothes! You always reminded me of a scarecrow in your old outfit."

"It wasn't crows I would scare off. It was good people like yourself that I frightened. They wouldn't know what to make of me. Up in the woods, that was all right. Might keep people away from me."

Mary smiled and stepped toward him, straightening a twist in one of the shoulder straps.

"I'm afraid you're right. When you first arrived here, I didn't know what to make of you. Thought you were crazy. After the past few months of your company, I agree with Lizzie. You have also become an old friend to me."

He tried to bow gracefully, but instead bent at the knees as if making a curtsy to her. She laughed out loud and bent at the waist, sweeping her arm across her chest, hair nearly brushing the floor.

"This is how a gentleman makes a bow."

"Is it, now? Guess I'd have to be a gentleman to be able to do it right."

She approached him again, took one hand in hers and raised up on her toes to place a kiss on his cheek.

"Bert, it is good to have you around. I hope you can stay with us for a while."

Liz stood apart from them, watching, and smiled as she remembered how much Mary had disliked him when he first arrived. Perhaps, since Lottie would not be using the first-floor guest room, he might stay there. It would be better for him than having to climb stairs.

84

Nathan was shocked at Lottie's condition. He arrived thinking he might be able to convince his daughter that moving her friend would be the best plan. When he saw how weak Lottie had become, it was clear she needed to stay put. The first thing to be done was to get a respected doctor to suggest a course of treatment. After the local physician recommended by both Ethan and farmer Kimball prescribed a course of treatments that sounded like they might work on a horse, Nathan said that he would ride back to Bridgton and see if his friend Dr. Abbott would agree to take on a new patient.

When Nathan returned with Abbott, the doctor asked to see Lottie alone, entered the room, and closed the door behind him. After nearly an hour, he emerged without his jacket, shirtsleeves rolled up, wearing a pair of yellow gloves. He asked Nate to bring him hot water and went back behind the shut door once again. Another thirty minutes passed before he stepped out of the room. He gave Franny the gloves wrapped in a towel.

"Please wash these immediately in very hot water. Your father has explained to me that you are to be the main caregiver for Mrs. Hallett. You are not a trained nurse, so it's important that you learn how sanitary we must keep her surroundings. I've worn these rubber gloves while touching her. She has a serious condition. Any exposure to germs and bacteria might make her condition worse. If *you* are exposed to the infection, *your* health may be endangered. You are to wear surgical gloves while you are with her."

Nate asked, "Doctor, what is her serious condition?"

"Your wife has an infection in her blood, or sepsis. This is complicated by the fact that she suffers from preeclampsia, which likely arises from the difficult pregnancy last time. This time, her condition may be even more difficult."

Nathan recalled the traumatic days Lottie had spent in Westbrook. "Edward, she nearly died last time. I want her to get the best treatment possible."

"You may want to call on Agnes Hodgson in Westbrook. She has handled every type of complication that comes with pregnancy. There are many mothers and children who owe their lives to the woman."

"Yes, yes, I know the woman. It was she who cared for Hattie and delivered Nate. She saved their lives," said Nathan.

"Would she be willing to visit Lottie once in a while to see what she could do to help?" asked Nate.

"Son, that was back more than two decades," said Abbott. "She's now in her seventies. I've not heard of her traveling much at all; stays pretty close to home. She went to cases in Portland several times, but that was years ago. Your dad might convince her to consider a bit of an adventure." Abbott smiled at Nathan, then looked at Franny.

"Young lady, perhaps you might visit with Hodgson yourself, get some suggestions to make your care for your friend more professional. What do you think, Nathan?"

"Francena is very intelligent. She might learn a lot from Agnes in a short time. I'll call the woman when I get back to Bridgton."

85

Mary hung the CLOSED FOR LUNCH sign on the front door and then sat at her worktable to eat a salad. There came a loud knock at the door. "Can't they read the sign?" she said aloud as she went to the door. Opening it, she was surprised to see Eugene standing there holding his hat.

"Sorry to disturb your meal," he said, noticing the napkin in her hand. "Like yourself, I take a little private time for lunch. Unfortunately, that means I often must run errands, rather than eat, and return before there is a line of customers at the door."

"Well, what can I do for you?" she said in an impatient voice.

"Miss Flaherty, is Miss Francena at home? I know she was to be away, but only for several days."

Realizing that he had not heard of the change in plans and that it might upset him, she asked him to step inside.

"I assume you haven't heard about the big change in plans."

"No. What has happened?"

She related all that she knew about the new arrangement and then said, "So Franny may not be returning anytime soon. She is going to nurse her friend until either she has the baby and returns to health, loses the baby, or dies herself. A very difficult situation for everyone."

He said nothing for a long moment, then turned to leave. As he opened the door, she saw him turn toward her and stare down at the floor.

"Are you all right, Mr. Bailey? You look like you have lost a family member."

"No. No. Nothing like that. What you say is very disappointing. I was looking forward to having Francena help me set up my new home."

"Oh, she'll be back. Can you wait for a couple of months? Is there anything that Liz or Maeve or I could help you with?"

"No, thank you. I will make do for the time being. She has my carriage and horse, you know. I will need it sooner or later. I walked here today and will more than likely be late returning. I must hurry."

He walked quickly down the steps and out to the street. Mary called out before he disappeared, "I will take the matter up with Nathan. Perhaps he can get the carriage back to you soon."

86

Such a sudden change of plans left Franny at a loss over what to do about clothes, books, and things she would need in Waterford. She also worried about who would do her work in the shop. Nathan offered to drive her back to Westbrook for a short visit to return the horse and carriage and pack up her things. She could only stay for a day or two because Nate was anxious to get back to his work for local farmers. He had not been able to work at all so far in planting season, and the family resources were shrinking.

Franny also knew that Eugene awaited an answer to his proposal, and it was unlikely she would be able to avoid him. What could she say about being his wife? There had been little time to think about the prospect while arrangements were being made to move Lottie. Now that her own future was set for the short term, the decision needed to be put off further. It wasn't fair to make him wait to know her answer, and it was unfair to herself to make a commitment while under such duress.

Her dilemma was so distracting that she talked very little to Nathan as they traveled to Westbrook. By the time they reached the house, it was dark, and Nathan had given up trying to coax her out of her mood. Lizzie was sitting on the front porch when they arrived. She rushed down the steps to hug her obviously bothered niece.

"Auntie, I'm so sorry to desert you again."

"Girl, you stop apologizing right now. I don't want to hear a word about how sorry you are. You've had a long journey and are tired. We will discuss matters later."

When Franny reached for her duffel, Nathan snatched the bag and placed it over his shoulder.

"Liz is right. No need for you to feel apologetic about what you've decided to do. You're a regular Clara Barton, in my opinion."

Mary came to the door, an apron covering her housedress.

"Yes, drop your coats in the office, take off your boots, and come upstairs. I've made a meal for you."

From the second-floor landing, Bert gestured to everyone to come upstairs.

"Miss Francena," he said, "you are my hero. What you're doing for your friend is a true labor of love. Not many would do the same."

Franny looked up at him and began to cry as the burden of her worries flooded forth. To her relief, these people—even Bert—were not blaming her for abandoning them. They understood her motives. Hopefully, Eugene would feel the same.

87

Warden Lewis's death was both a win and a loss for Aphia. His death meant that she wouldn't have to worry about his lascivious intentions toward her. But it also robbed her of the connection needed to continue her research into overturning the conviction for murdering her husband. With his help, she had gathered defense, prosecution, and judge's notes from the trial; not everything, but enough to be able to question whether justice had been done.

She culled over the documents in the library day after day, struggling to make out the handwriting. There was no longer any time for her to exercise in the yard. All her free time was taken up by the tedious task of trying to figure out the rationales of the case on each side. Neither lawyer had put much work into the case, most likely because she had already been convicted of two other murders. The judge had made very few notations, and those that were legible didn't make any sense. It was clear that the man was bored, scribbling notes about other cases in the margins. One of his notes was a shopping list.

Going back to *Black's Law Dictionary*, she found a section pertaining to a Writ of Habeas Corpus—the way in which a prisoner might be able to appeal a conviction once they are serving a sentence. If she could prove that her own lawyer had provided "ineffective assistance" during the trial, or that the prosecutor had failed to disclose evidence which would have proved her innocence, a new trial might be set. It was surely a long shot, but with all the information in her large file, Aphia was sure that such proof had to be there.

It may take me a long while to find the evidence I need, she thought with a smile. After all, I have nothing but time to do it. And I'll make sure those relatives of Lizzie Millet don't get to stay in my house.

There had to be something she was missing. Maybe, if she could objectively and completely recall what happened that day of the incident and list them in sequence on a page of her notebook, it would help to make evidentiary omissions clearer.

This will not be easy, she thought. I've tried to block out memories of what happened. How he attacked me in my herb garden... The bastard tried to rape me. It was the only way he would ever get to have sex with me. He pushed my face down to the ground then tried to roll me over. As he ripped my shirt, I tossed him aside face first into the aconite bed. He didn't know I was so strong. When he sat up, he had a mouthful of the poison leaves and started spitting them out, but I knew it was too late. His face was stained green. I knew he had been poisoned.

Often, when she had been living alone back at Beech Hill Farm, Henry had come to her in nightmares where he would rise from the ground and dance on top of the shallow grave in which she had buried his body.

If only I hadn't buried him, the sheriff could have seen the stains on him. It would have been easier to explain how things happened. But there still must be a way to show that I'm innocent. There has to be reasonable doubt.

One more time, she reviewed her defense lawyer's notes and found a list of questions he had used to cross-examine Bert Learned, the prosecution's only witness. There was one entry that made her stop and reflect.

Mr. Learned, you are the only witness, and your story of what happened is completely based on what the defendant told you. Isn't that correct?

What was his answer? Where would she be able to find it? Perhaps some mention was made in the judge's notes...

Reviewing those notes, she found mention of one direction made to the jury before their deliberations began. The judge had said, "Please keep in mind that the evidence presented here today by the Prosecution is solely third-hand, based on Mr. Learned's recollections of what the Defendant told him about, many years after the death of Mr. Greene. The Defense has called this 'circumstantial evidence.'" In the margin beside this statement was a scribbled comment: "Pattern of Stevens's past behavior much more important."

"This is it!" she said out loud. The librarian looked at her and held a finger to her mouth.

88

Nathan drove the carriage up to the front of Bailey's Store. From what Mary told him, the man who might be his future son-in-law was annoyed by the length of time his primary mode of transportation had been gone. He was surprised to see that the OUT TO LUNCH sign was still hanging in the door at two p.m.

Hearing someone shouting behind the big new house, he walked down the long driveway toward the building. In the rear of the house, he spied Eugene turning soil in what looked to be a large garden. The man was complaining out loud each time he dug a spade of dirt from the ground and spread it behind himself. His tweed pants and polished shoes were covered with dirt, as dust and weeds flew all about him. Nathan stood unnoticed for a time until he called out to the gardener.

"Eugene! Do you want any help?"

Bailey turned, held one hand up in a gesture to make his guest stay back.

"Mr. Hallett, no need for both of us to get filthy. Gardening is a lot more difficult than I imagined." He threw the spade on the ground and walked away from the plot. "I've sold these shovels for years. Never tried to use one. I guess it must be an acquired skill."

"Do you know what time it is?"

Eugene pulled his watch from his pants pocket and shook it.

"Damn, is it really two thirty already? I've been at this for nearly two hours. I hope your daughter is better at this type of work than I am."

He walked very quickly toward the store with Nathan following behind. Seeing his carriage returned, he turned to Nathan.

"Wonderful! Thank you so much for bringing it back. Your daughter is a good friend to be willing to spend several months taking care of your daughter-in-law. It's too bad she must stay in Waterford to do it."

A woman customer stood at the door and frowned as the merchant approached.

"So sorry to have kept you waiting, Mrs. Josephs. I hope you haven't been here very long."

He removed the sign and opened the door as she waved a shopping list in his face.

"I know, I know. The store is supposed to be open all day. Let me see your list. We can fill it together."

After standing patiently for a moment, Nathan began to walk around the place looking at the merchandise. He noticed a rack of shirts and vests set in the rear next to a shelf of men's boots and hats. There was a hand-lettered sign above the garments: MADE IN WESTBROOK AT MILLETT'S AMERICAN DESIGNS.

"Do you sell many of these clothing items? They seem a bit out of place with all your other merchandise."

"Sells very well, especially the shirts. I have one on right now. Did you want to buy one? They're made by your daughter, you know."

Seeing that his customer was getting impatient, Eugene returned to cutting a wedge of cheddar for her order.

"No, I have several already. She does a great job on them."

"And on everything else she does, as well. She practically designed my new house. I'm looking forward to her return to help me complete the inside."

"You might use a little help on the garden, too," said Nathan with a chuckle as he left the store.

89

The day after Franny left for Westbrook, Lottie awoke feeling much better than she had for a week or more. Pulling back the covers, she swung her still swollen legs to the side of the bed, where they dangled for a few minutes. She wanted to get out of bed but didn't want to move further until she was sure her legs would hold her. As she sat there, Con poked his head through the door.

"Mommy, are you trying to get up?" He ran into the room and grabbed hold of her arm. "Would you like to sit over on that chair?"

"You might want to get your father to help me. I'm tired of being in bed."

"I can help you. Put your feet down on the floor and I'll help you stand."

First one foot, then the other, touched the cold wood. When she leaned forward to lift herself, Con took both of her hands and pulled as hard as he could to move her forward. She nearly fell, grabbing onto the headboard to catch herself.

"Con, you really are a strong little boy. Can I lean on you to get over to the window? It looks to be a sunny day."

Together, the two of them slowly trudged across the room. With each step, she became more confident that they would make it safely. Lottie was able to prop herself up with both hands on a small table by the window while Con positioned the chair so that the garden and pasture might be easily seen. When she dropped down onto the upholstered seat, the floorboards creaked, and Nate ran into the room to see what had happened.

"Lottie, what are you doing? You're not supposed to out of bed."

Con stepped away from her side and began to cry.

"I'm sorry, Daddy. Mommy wanted to look out the window," he said through his tears.

Nate knelt next to the boy and put his arm around him.

"Don't cry, Con. You did nothing wrong. Looks to me like you were able to keep your mother from falling."

"Yes, he did," said Lottie. "He is so strong. What a good boy. Come here for a kiss."

Both Nate and Con came to her side as she hugged her son and placed a kiss on his cheek. Nate made a point to shake the boy's hand before turning to Lottie and taking her wrist to check her pulse. It was racing.

"Why did you get up? Your heart is beating so fast. The doctor said you were to stay in bed on your back until he could see some improvement."

"Nate, I feel so much better today. Isn't that an improvement? Where is Franny? I want to thank her for helping me get better. She's been sitting here next to the bed for days."

"She's gone back to Westbrook to get some things she needs. She'll be staying with us until you have the baby. My dad is taking her to see a midwife to learn a few things about how to care for you."

"How can she afford to do that? She works for a living. Has her own life. It's unfair of us to have her put her future on hold."

"You know I must work. We need to have money coming in. Having my sister here will make it possible. Lottie, she loves you and wants to help us both."

She put her arm around Con and hugged him as tightly as her strength allowed. Francis then came to the door, and seeing his brother getting so much attention, he ran to his mom and tried to jump up onto her. Nate swept him up in his arms and carefully placed the little boy on her lap.

"Okay, boy," he said, "you can sit there for a *few* minutes. We don't want to make your mom tired, do we?"

As Nate stepped back, he wiped tears away from the corners of his eyes. He prayed that such a loving family would be able to stay whole forever.

90

Franny had given herself two days to visit with the midwife, get what belongings she would need for a long visit, and check in with Eugene. With such a packed schedule, there was little time to sleep or enjoy the company of her aunt. The first day was spent collecting clothes, books, and toiletries, enough to fill a large trunk which Lizzie had stashed away in the basement.

"Auntie, I'll only need to borrow this chest for the duration of my stay. Do you have a place to temporarily store the things you have inside it until I get back?"

Lizzie knelt in front of the chest, pulling out an odd collection of items and stacking them on an extended gateleg table. There were old books whose pages were tattered and torn, two handmade dolls with faded clothes, and a box of old letters. From the very bottom, she carefully picked up some folded fabric with a rose pattern. Pieces of thin pattern paper crinkled as she placed it on top of the pile.

"Oh, look at that fabric. Is that linen? It's so beautiful," Franny said as she touched the cloth.

"Yes, that's the finest linen I could find in Maine back when I was making my wedding dress. I never got to finish it." She patted the folded material, brushing away specs of paper. "Life would have been so different if I had been able to use it."

Franny had been told by her mother the sad story of how nineteen-year-old Lizzie had been abandoned by her fiancé. How angry she must have been when the man married Aphia Stevens instead!

"That must have been a bad time for you. Mom says that you could have become a very bitter woman. Instead, you rose above the experience and threw yourself into a new life."

"You know, dear, finding the right man is only one part of a happy life. I have found such fulfillment in my work and family. Then there were my happy years with your uncle Moses. No use crying over a dropped stitch."

Each grabbed a handle of the trunk and carried it up the steps. As they climbed Franny thought of the wisdom in her aunt's words.

"I must see Eugene now. I owe it to him to be honest about my feelings," she said to herself. "He is a good man, but I'm not sure he's the right one."

91

Janey Cain was back from school for the summer and beating the drum once more to forgive Aphia Stevens. She felt that having Bert as a neighbor gave momentum to her campaign to convince Lizzie and Maeve to journey up to Thomaston Prison for a visit. Since Bert had lived with Stevens and knew her better than the others, his presence might make access to the prison easier.

"Mom, it was your idea. Why do you keep denying it?" she said to Maeve one evening.

"Yes, it came up at a moment of grief. I was under a great deal of stress, you know. The woman had just killed your father. As time has passed, I've had second thoughts. There were many customs and beliefs in the old country that don't really fit the way we live in America."

"I've discussed the idea with Lizzie, and she has not closed her mind to the idea. She wants to see what everyone else thinks. Have you discussed it with her or Bert?"

"Bert? Why him? She didn't rob *him* of a person he loved."

"Mom, she robbed him of happiness when she drove him out of her life. Look what happened to his life after she shamed him. I've already spoken with him about the plan, and he is completely in support. He told me it would give him a chance to put his relationship with her behind him."

"Oh. I don't know. Let me think about it for a while. You know we would have to wait for a few months, to get Lottie along with us. So we have some time to plan."

"Mom, I spoke to Franny about representing Lottie. She was reluctant to do that without getting her friend's permission. She suggested that Nate, as husband, might be a better representative."

"My God, dear. You've been touching all the bases. I will speak with Lizzie about your plan. I'm not agreeing, only willing to discuss it."

92

Franny rose before dawn on the second day of her visit. As she dressed, a rosy-red sun cast its hot light through her bedroom window. She knew it was going to be a warm and humid summer day, so she put on a light dress and grabbed a yellow sun hat from the closet. Whisking down the stairs and through the kitchen, she grabbed an apple from a basket on the sideboard and filled a thermos with cold water. Her plan was to walk to the store right at the time it opened. The discussion she had planned would be best done in the store, not the house.

She passed the deep pit of James Pride's quarry just as the workers arrived. Two high cranes and the men who were operating them were reflected in the reddish groundwater at the large hole's base, creating a panorama that brought her to a stop. When the loud pumps were turned on to remove the water, she covered her ears and hurried down the road toward Brook Street.

The store was not open when she arrived, so she took a seat on one of the porch benches, ate her apple, and took a drink of water from the thermos. She thought about stepping out back and looking at the big house…but then it might tempt her to meet him there. She stayed put.

At eight thirty she heard the house door slam and waited for him to appear around the corner of the store. He was smartly dressed in light-gray cotton trousers, one of her white linen shirts, and a tweed vest. She liked the clothes he wore: a respectable outfit, yet practical for a merchant who might get flour, seeds, or oil on his garments. He appeared to have lost a little weight since she last saw him, and he walked a bit more briskly than she remembered. When he saw her, his face lit up in a broad smile and he waved.

"Francena, my dear, you have returned. What a pleasant surprise!" He bounded up the steps and grabbed both her hands in his. "Miss Flaherty said you would be gone for months. I'm so glad to see your beautiful face."

"Oh, you are such a dear to say that. I fear my features must show how tired I am. I'm in town for only a short while before returning to North Waterford."

Turning his key in the door, he hung the OPEN FOR BUSINESS sign and invited her to step inside. The old electric stove that had formerly been in his apartment kitchen had been installed against the wall behind the counter. He placed a kettle of water on it to heat.

"I'm making tea for myself. Can I make a cup for you? This is where I have my breakfast each morning. Tea and one of Mrs. Canby's scones from the cooler. Please join me."

He set two high stools at the counter, poured the tea, and brought her a buttery scone on a small plate. She watched him as

he took a seat. Being with him was less uncomfortable than she
had feared. Perhaps having the new house had changed him. He
said nothing for a moment while dipping his scone into the tea
and taking a bite.

"I respect what you are doing for your friend," he started.
"There are few people who would do the same—make a drastic
change in their life to help another in distress. It has made me
think the world of you."

She sipped the tea. "Eugene, how could I not help Lottie? She
is one of the dearest people I know. I love her. I venture she would
do the same for me. I have been thinking much about you during
the past few days. We have an unanswered question dangling
between us. Can we talk about your proposal?"

Her bluntness shocked him. He had planned to bring up the
subject of their marriage but had not figured a way of doing so
that wasn't uncomfortable. She certainly was an unusual woman
to speak of the matter so openly.

"Franny, I have thought of little else in the time you've been
away. Although the move into the new house has improved my
life, I have done very little to make myself comfortable. This
house is yours as much as mine."

"I appreciate your gratitude for the help I gave in designing
the house. It makes me feel happy. However, you should not wait
for me to return before making the most of your new home. I may
be gone for four months."

"I can wait," he said with a sigh. "What is four months apart
compared to a life together?"

Franny frowned. This was not going very well. She wanted
to have this conversation result in a comfortable agreement
between them.

"My dear Eugene. As much thought as I have given to your
proposal, I have not yet reached a decision on how to answer. My
life is a jumble of unfinished patterns, like the design of a new
dress. Each day brings new problems to overcome, new tasks to
learn. Sometimes I just don't know what to think."

Moving back in his seat, he folded his arms across his chest and sighed deeply.

"So, you are still thinking about what to answer. I am sorely disappointed in that. Yes, you are to be away for a while. I can accept that and wait for you to return. I assumed you would have already decided to marry me when you returned. Now you tell me that is not the case."

"I have not decided. It's that simple. Once things in my life quiet down, there will be time to choose. Please accept that I cannot choose at this time."

He stood and collected the teacups and plates, tossing the partially eaten scones into a wastebasket behind the counter.

"My dear Francena, take all the time you need to make your decision. Only know that I may not be able to wait for the answer."

"What do you mean?"

"I am not sure what I mean, but I must ask you to leave now. There is work to be done to get ready for my customers."

As she walked back to the street, her attention was drawn to the edge of what appeared to be a cultivated area. Curious as to whether he had actually attempted to make a garden in her absence, she turned toward the rear of the new house and was amazed to see that he had not only cultivated a very large garden, but several rows of small plants were already peeking up through the soil.

Her attention was then drawn to the building itself, whose windows were unadorned by curtains. Through the rear windows, she could make out crates of his belongings stacked against the kitchen walls. Obviously he had not unpacked, even though it had been a month since the move. She thought how odd he was to put so much effort into making a garden, when he had not even gotten settled indoors.

I know he tilled and planted this garden for me, she thought. How sweet. He really is a good man.

93

Roy Lord, a friend of Ethan's father, owned rocky Harndon Hill in Stoneham, where locals were allowed to search for minerals and crystals. Ethan had been there many times. It was only an hour's ride away from North Waterford and an easy climb to reach the naked slope where specimens of various crystals were often found. Several neighbors had collected mahogany-gray smoky quartz, blue topaz, and pale blue-green aquamarine specimens to display on their mantels. Thinking that he would soon be able to spend a lot of time with Francena, Ethan decided to hike to the top to see if he might collect a beautiful crystal to give her as a gift. She already had a small collection of rough gemstones found up near Rumford.

He set out from home early on a sunny summer morning with a pack on his back and two small buckets tied to his saddle. The buckets were light metal and banged into each other as he rode along. Equipped with a chipping hammer, several short, iron star-tipped chisels, and a small, folded camp shovel, he was sure that he would find a specimen that would show Francena how much he appreciated her friendship. If the crystal was pure enough, he could have a friend cut it into a jewel she might mount in a ring or pendant.

The Lynchville Road had recently been rolled and was quite smooth. By the time he reached Stoneham's Keewaydin Lake, many washouts slowed the pace. Several times he dismounted and led his horse across intermittent streams, evidence of some recent heavy rains. When he reached his destination, it was already noon, and the sun was beating down so brightly that he had to cool himself by dipping one of the buckets into a spring at the foot of the hill and dumping it over his head. Halfway up the slope, the angle of incline became so steep that he had to dismount and lead the horse slowly toward the exposed rock face. Shady pine woods along the narrow trail became thinner as he neared the mine, until he reached an open area where very few trees grew. The largest had been cut down and pushed to one side, a sign that Mr. Lord was attempting to create a bona fide mining operation.

In the center of the clearing, he discovered an open pit, the result of dynamite blasting. The surface was littered with rough broken stone.

What luck! he thought. This should make it easier to find some good specimens.

As he stepped onto the wall of the pit, it collapsed under his weight, sending him sprawling into the rubble ten feet below. His shirt and jeans were torn and there was a cut on one hand.

As he lifted himself into a seated position, one of the buckets rolled down the drop-off, landing to his left. He reached to pick it up and noticed that several small pieces of stone had fallen into it. Looking into the bucket, he gasped and let out a cheer so loud it spooked his horse. Sitting loosely in the bucket where two brilliant crystals of gemmy topaz the size of his thumbnail. Held up to the sunlight, they both were transparent, perfect specimens.

94

Nate arrived much earlier than expected to get Franny for the trip to Waterford. The summer sun had just broken the horizon with a shout of red and yellow. His sister was still packing, while Liz and Mary were both sitting at the kitchen table in their housecoats finishing breakfast. Knowing that he might disturb someone, he tapped softly at the door before entering.

"Nate, is that you already?" asked his aunt as he entered the kitchen.

The sight of the two women in their bedclothes embarrassed him, and he turned his face away from them.

"Sorry to disturb you. I'll wait out on the porch for my sister to get ready. I came a little early to beat the heat at least on half the journey."

"She will be a while getting ready, Nate. Yesterday was a very tiring day for her. After the training visit to Mrs. Hodgson's, she didn't return until after nine o'clock."

Mary stood and went to the stove to get the coffee pot.

"Nate, please come have a bite to eat and a good cup of coffee. You must have missed breakfast to get here so early."

"No, no. I don't want to disturb you." He was hungry but didn't want to sit with two women who weren't fully dressed.

Lizzie noticed his awkwardness.

"My boy, we are family, aren't we? I don't think you should feel like you are being a peeping tom by sitting with us. After all, neither of us is baring much skin."

He smiled and entered the room to enjoy the cup Mary filled for him, still keeping his eyes on their faces and not their bodies. As Mary refilled Nate's cup, Bert entered from the first-floor bedroom. He was fully dressed to face the day.

"Young Nate, so wonderful to see you once again. How does that wife of yours do today?"

Nate thought the man looked much healthier than the last time he had seen him. He no longer wore that ridiculous tattered outfit. He had also gained some weight. Life here with the ladies certainly seemed to agree with him.

"Thanks for asking. She's been feeling a bit better the last couple of days. Actually got out of bed and is walking around in her room once in a while. She still has a long way to go."

"She's not deserving of this. That girl has gone through so much in such a short time: lost her husband, lost a baby, and now this. She's sure lucky to have you as a husband and Miss Francena as a friend. You two will get her through."

Lizzie put a plate of poached eggs and toast down in front of her nephew. "Is anyone with her today, while you're away?"

"She's alone with the boys. Con can get her water, food, and medications while I'm away. He's such a good boy. I couldn't arrange for anyone to stay with her. All the neighbors are so busy with planting, and the first haying has started. The reason I came so early is that I want to get home before the boys' bedtimes."

As Franny came downstairs, Bert excused himself to take his morning "constitutional." He smiled and wished her a safe journey. She was dressed to travel in denim pants, a short-sleeved blouse of green cotton, and a wide-brimmed gaucho sun hat hanging down behind her shoulders on its chin cord.

"Hi, brother. I'm ready to roll when you are. Getting an early start on such a warm day makes sense. Let me have a bite to eat and then we can get along. Oh, could you get my duffel and chest onto your wagon?"

"You haven't changed a bit, have you? I've been carrying your luggage as long as I can remember. Where is everything?"

"Upstairs on the landing. Don't forget that little leather satchel. It has all the supplies the midwife gave me yesterday. Such a dear boy."

95

During the first month Franny was away, the work of running a thriving business fell more heavily on Lizzie's shoulders. Some weeks, she worked seven days, and it was beginning to affect her health. Her eyes were getting worse, and she was tired most of the time. There were times when she fell asleep at her desk while doing the bookkeeping.

"Lizzie, dear, why don't you take a couple of days off. Or at least work half days for a while," said Mary after a day when her partner had dozed off several times. "You are not looking yourself these days. It does you no good to sleep sitting at your desk."

"I've thought about doing that, but there is so much to do."

"No matter," said Maeve. "Wasn't having me here all week meant to make life a little easier on both of you? Mary's right."

"You know I'm correct," said Mary. "Please do us all a favor and go upstairs to take a nap. We two sisters can handle the place. Trust us."

Liz stood from the table and shuffled her feet to keep her balance before grabbing the back of her chair. Mary jumped up and rushed to her side, putting an arm around her to keep her from falling. Maeve wrapped an arm around Liz's waist and together they led her to the steps and then up to her bedroom. Maeve went to get a glass of cold water from the kitchen, while Mary helped Liz lie on the bed, loosening her dress and removing her shoes as she did so.

"Stay here quietly and rest," whispered Mary in Lizzie's ear. "I will call Dr. Rowan and see if he can come by to check you out."

"No. No need of that. I will recover with a little rest. Wait and see."

Mary could hardly make out her words and leaned closer to hear. She did not have a fever, but her face was flushed.

"Okay, my dear. I'll not call him right now. But if you don't rest yourself, I'll have no choice."

After Maeve returned with water, the sisters covered their friend with a light throw and went back down to the shop.

"I'm worried about her, Maeve. She never stops. Always go, go, go. That's her. When Franny is here, you'd think Liz would let youth be served, give more of her own work to her niece. But no. She gives Franny more rest time than she takes herself."

"Do you speak with her about it? You're with her much more than anyone else."

"I do. She won't listen. She thinks she is still in her twenties and able to run, run, run all the time. She appears to most people to be a calm and peaceful woman, but deep down, she is driven to be a success."

"And she has been that. No question."

"Yes, 'tis the truth. And her success has made life better for all of us who love her. Think about where we might be if we'd never met her. I'd be stuck back in Clare. You'd have never met your Will."

They returned to their machines, and no further words passed between them until just before five. As Maeve began to clean up her work area, she reminded Mary of a conversation they had shared the day before.

"What do you think of that weird idea my Janey is driving about visiting Aphia Stevens? When I brought it up yesterday, you ignored me."

"'Weird idea' is a good description. Have you ever heard of such a cockamamie plan? Let the woman rot in jail, I say. Let her go to hell."

"I've been thinking about it. Perhaps her plan is not so silly. I told her I would bring it up with Lizzie. It was her loss of Henry Greene that brought Stevens into our lives."

Mary slammed a pair of scissors on her worktable. "You see how tired she is. I do not want you to bring up such a horrible, misguided adventure to her. Not now, not ever."

96

The first two weeks of living on Beech Hill were exhausting for Franny. Caring for her dear friend took most of her daytime hours. Lottie was able to get out of bed each day to sit in her chair at the bedroom window for an hour or so, allowing time for freshening the bed linens and bathing. All meals were served to her in bed. Herbal tinctures and teas prescribed by the midwife had to be prepared and given to her daily, along with doses of laudanum and blood thinners provided by Dr. Abbott. Franny had to care for the rest of the family, as well. She had been wrong to expect that Nate would do most of the work taking care of the boys. He was getting so much field work from John Kimball and other local farmers, as well as hours each week for Roy Lord at his mica mine, that he was gone most of the time. Con was very helpful for a six-year-old, but Francis was still in diapers and needed nearly constant attention.

Her brother, tired from hard work, did take over for her each evening, caring for the boys and putting them to bed, making his own dinner, and sitting with his wife for a while before stumbling into his bed. This provided Franny with time to go for an occasional walk. And she was able to read sometimes, either in her bedroom or, when it was too warm to stay inside, sitting on the back porch with light from a kerosene lantern.

One of the books she had brought with her was a recent gift from Aunt Lizzie, *The Luck of Roaring Camp and Other Tales* by journalist Bret Harte. It was a collection of entertaining short stories that took place in the American west during early years of settlement in California. Her aunt knew the tales would appeal to her because they were "cowboy" stories, which always excited her interest. If sleep took her before completion of a short tale, it was easy to start at the beginning again next day.

One late afternoon, sitting on the back porch, she was reading a story called "Mliss," which takes place in the Sierra Nevada Mountains. She looked up from the page to rest her tired eyes, staring across the pasture, where the hay was turning brown. When she returned to reading, it was to the following passage:

> The long dry summer came. As each day burned itself out in little whiffs of pearl-gray smoke on the mountain summits and the upspringing breeze scattered its red embers over the landscape, the green wave which in early spring upheaved above Smith's grave grew sere and dry and hard.

She looked back toward the top of Beech Hill and thought, how different that mountain scene is from what we have here in Waterford. Even now, when the soil is dry and parched, the green on the pines makes me feel cool. The mountains there in California are so much taller. They must be something to see. I shall go out west sometime…

♥

Ethan arrived in front of the house, and Con, who saw him coming up the steps, opened the door.

"Young man," said Ethan, "is your Aunt Franny here?"

"Mr. Ethan, yes. She might be asleep on the porch out back. She is so busy." He held his forefinger to his lips in a sign to be quiet.

"Oh, I won't disturb her, if she's napping. No, sirree."

As he rounded the corner of the house, Franny looked up again from the book and waved.

"Oh, Ethan, please come sit with me and look at this wonderful view. As the sun sets, its rays light the tops of the pines. What a lovely place."

Sitting down next to her, he took her hand in his.

"I have missed you, Franny. Did you read my letter?"

She smiled and touched the back of his hand.

"What a sweet letter! Yes, I read it and was wondering when you might come for a visit."

"Well, now I don't have to travel miles and miles to be with you. You've made my life so much easier."

They both stared across the field to the graying mountaintop.

"And happier, too," he added.

"Have you ever been to California, Ethan?"

"You're kidding, right? I've only been to Portland once in my life. Travel is not something I like to do. Visiting you in Westbrook would have been okay because I would be with someone I like, not because I want to go somewhere to see the sights. Staying home and scouting around Oxford County is really all I want to do."

"You old stick-in-the-mud! I read about so many places out west that would be great to visit—majestic mountain ranges, rivers running through deep canyons, skies that go on forever."

"You are a dreamer," he said, still staring at the hilltop, beyond which stars were coming out. "Me? I'm happy with what I have here in my little piece of the big world. The natural places around me sometimes take my breath away."

"Well, I agree that the world around us is wondrous and beautiful. It's just that you might appreciate them even more after being away for a while."

"Listen to you, Franny. You must be reading another cowboys-and-Indians book."

He picked up the Harte volume and turned to an illustration of men sitting around a campfire.

"I could take you to fantastic campsites with views that make your heart stand still. Come with me sometime."

"Afraid I'm not going camping anytime soon, but I'll keep that invitation in mind."

97

E ugene sat at his new dining room table, an antique mahogany piece recently purchased in Portland. It was part of a Chippendale set that included eight chairs with cushioned seats. Though the six-hundred-dollar cost was much more than he wanted to spend, he had decided to make the most of his life by completing the move into his new mansion and filling it with furniture more attractive than the pieces he had used in the apartment. There was so much space to fill.

He even hired an architect from Gorham to make sure the place was designed tastefully. Donald Pratt came highly recommended by several customers who said the man had the unusual ability to make the interior of a building lovely. At their first meeting, the two men walked through the chaotic mess of unpacked crates. Pratt warned that he saw no use for most of the old furnishings.

"Mr. Bailey, I am not one to reuse ugly elements just because they are here," said the architect, as he turned a pressed-back chair upright and took a seat. "Please sit down. We need to reach an agreement before I might begin working for you."

Eugene sat on a large chest which he pulled away from the kitchen door.

"An agreement, sir? What type of agreement are you suggesting?"

"Well, making your wonderful house into a comfortable home will definitely be an expensive project."

"How expensive do you estimate the job to be?"

"If you ask me that question, you may not want to hire me."

"You must have some idea of what you usually charge for a project of this sort."

"Mr. Bailey, it has been a pleasure to meet you, and I hope your new house will be comfortable. I don't think my services will be a good fit here."

As Pratt rose and walked toward the front door, Eugene carefully thought about what the man had just said. After a moment, he said quite loudly, "Sir, please sit down so that we might continue our discussion. You must understand that I have never approached such a project of this scale. My concern with a budget comes from years of running a business. Those who have followed your advice are very satisfied. I will not bother you for an estimate any longer."

The man hesitated at the door, giving his potential client another moment to think. It was as if he had been through this situation before. Turning back, he began to walk around the parlor with a hurried stride. He turned several lamps on and off, picked up several paintings and peered at them to see if they were signed.

"I will be pleased to draw up concept sketches for you and partial lists of essential furnishings. My charges for this preliminary work will be approximately two hundred dollars, half of which would be paid today. We may meet again in two weeks to review my plans, if that is acceptable to you."

Afraid that a hesitation might drive the man away, Eugene nodded in agreement and reached for his wallet.

"Mr. Pratt, I look forward to reviewing your plans. If you have the time when you return, perhaps we might go through more of my things and see what might be used."

"I don't think that will be necessary. From what I have seen, nearly everything must be replaced."

Now, a month after that first meeting, Eugene found himself in the middle of a predicament. Pratt had completed a set of incredible plans, and he had approved them. The two of them were running to Portland once a week to purchase furniture, art, and accessories which would make the house as beautiful inside as it was large on the outside. Nearly every day, moving vans, some pulled by three horses, arrived and delivered bespoke goods as well as items that he was sure had not been ordered even though everything had a signed work order attached. Work men and women painted and papered, then rolled out oriental rugs as large as the entire old apartment behind the store.

The place was becoming fit for a king. However, moneys being spent were in the vicinity of a king's ransom. Eugene's life savings were nearly gone, and he had taken out a second mortgage to keep things moving toward completion. Pratt was a complex genius with the design skills of an artist and a complete lack of financial control. He had never established a budget, just spent as much as he wanted of the other man's funds. The debt was becoming so large that the idea of bankruptcy began to loom large in Eugene's mind.

If only I had waited for Francena to return, things would be much simpler, he told himself. Her taste and style are more in keeping with mine. Four months is not that long a wait. What was I thinking?

Turning off the kitchen ceiling light, he walked into his dark study, lit a lamp on his desk and reached into the bottom drawer. He pulled out a bottle of rye whiskey and poured a tumbler full. A drink or two before bed were always helpful in allowing him to find peace in his sleep.

98

Lizzie lay awake peering out the bedroom window at the starlit sky. For seven nights, she had been unable to get her usual good night's sleep. She tossed and turned, got out of bed, and walked around in the dark until first rays of dawn pierced the window. Each morning, Mary met her in the kitchen to share breakfast. Liz had no appetite, leaving whatever was set in front of her and returning to her bed.

Maeve was also concerned about her friend's condition. She herself had suffered from short periods of insomnia that had only lasted a night or two, especially following Will's murder. It was clear to both sisters that Lizzie needed to see a doctor. However, she wouldn't agree to make an appointment, preferring to let the problem take care of itself.

"I don't feel sick, just tired. That's all. The problem will be solved as soon as I can get a few good nights."

Mary frowned across the table at her and stood up to collect the uneaten toast and jam.

"Have you looked in a mirror recently? You don't look yourself. There are bags under your eyes and crows-feet on either side of your mouth. Maeve and I are both worried about you."

"You two are so dear, but I'll be fine. I remember my mother would sometimes go nights without sleep during the winter. She stayed up all night spinning thread at the fireside, worrying about Hattie and myself keeping warm."

"Liz, what do you think is keeping you awake?"

"I don't know, my love, but it will go away. Wait and see."

"I don't want to wait and see. You must get some medical attention, perhaps a sedative of some sort would help. Let me call to make an appointment."

"No! I'm sorry. I must heal myself. If I can't sleep by the end of the week, you can have your way. Now, I will try to rest on the sofa."

As Liz left the room, Maeve and Janey entered the shop and called up to Mary.

"Sis, can we come up to speak with you two?" asked Maeve. "Janey has an idea about what might be causing Lizzie's problem."

"No, I will come down," Mary answered. "No need to disturb her. She's trying to nap."

At the bottom of the steps, she noticed Bert Learned standing at the shop door, a bouquet of wildflowers in his hand. He held these out to her.

"These are chamomile flowers. I picked them growing wild over near the quarry. If you make a tea with them, it may help her sleep. Years ago, I remember how Aphia used the brew to let me sleep on restless nights."

Skeptical, Mary took the flowers, sniffed at them, and dropped them on a design table.

"I'm sorry to be so rude, Bert. Anything that madwoman did with her concoctions has no interest to me. Liz needs a sedative, not a bouquet."

"Wait, Mary," said Janey. "Natural remedies have been relied upon for ages."

Maeve picked up the bouquet and placed it under her arm.

"Dear sister, please don't be angry. What Janey says makes some sense. I remember how our Granny used to make teas all the time for us to use when we were sick or feeling weak. Didn't they work back then?"

"I don't give a hoot about 'back then.' The magic potions of the sidhe can't work as well as modern medicines. You three are foolish to believe otherwise."

Janey sat on the lowest step.

"Aunt Mary, I don't want to make you any angrier, but Bert and I have been discussing how to bring Lizzie back to health. We think that her anger against Aphia, hidden all these years in her subconscious, has finally come to hurt her, make her sick. He believes the anger Lottie also feels toward the witch is also contributing to *her* problems."

Mary was aghast. She pulled the flowers from under her sister's arm, threw them on the floor and crushed them with her feet. The astringent aroma filled the room.

"Not this again! What is wrong with you people?" She began to walk in circles around the broken blossoms. "This is about that stupid idea of visiting the woman and forgiving her, isn't it? You are all crazy."

Bert put up his hands and left the room, while the others backed away. They had never seen Mary so angry. Yet Maeve wanted to make a point.

"You can't deny that Stevens has hurt this family so much and that we all either hate or fear her. One way or another, we need to rid ourselves of her influence...before something else more sinister than insomnia happens."

99

Valley Road between Waterford Flat and the village of North Waterford ran between Rice Hill and the eastern flank of Beech Hill. To Eugene's left, he viewed a clear pasture full of brown Guernseys. Beyond them, a white farmhouse and a large red barn sat below a grove of tall pines. To his right, he caught sight of the Crooked River running beyond acre upon acre of freshly cut hay. He stopped his carriage, stepped down for a rest, and caught sight of a cluster of small houses that lay ahead. The air was so fresh here in the country. It cleared his head after such a long ride from Westbrook.

He had departed before dawn after a restless night spent tossing from one side of his bed to the other. In the month since Franny left, he had found it more and more difficult to get a good night's sleep. Not knowing what the future held for the two of them, or even if there *was* a future together, made him worry that he had made a fool of himself because of her. He needed to speak with her, to find out how she felt about him. As he returned to the carriage and moved forward into the village, he wondered where he might ask to get directions to Nate's farm.

At the crossroads in the center of the village, he tied his horse to a hitching post in front of Nason's Country Market, where a tall young man stood in the open door smoking a cigarette. He looked to be about twenty years old, wore a long tan apron over blue jeans, and had several days' growth of whiskers. *He* wouldn't have allowed a clerk to appear at work with such a slovenly appearance in his own store. Standards must be much lower here in the back woods. When the man greeted him with a smile and opened the screen door for him, he saw that at least the man had good manners.

"Good day, sir. Quite a warm day, I'd say."

"Oh, yes. Quite warm," said Bailey.

He took a quick glance around the shop. An old potbelly stove stood in the center of the room with a chimney so crooked it looked ready to fall. Green vegetables, wilted from the heat, sat in wooden boxes on the counter in front of a cooler full of what looked to be firkins of butter. Several strips of flypaper covered with dead bugs hung from the ceiling above the cash register. This place was not at all to his liking.

"Son," he began, "can you kindly provide me with directions to Mr. Nate Hallett's Beech Hill Farm?"

Ethan didn't recognize this man who wore a pair of light-gray slacks, a white cotton shirt, and a tweed waistcoat.

"Sir, my name is Ethan Blaine. You must be new to town. I haven't seen you around. Are you from Bridgton?"

"No, I am not from this area. My name is Eugene Bailey. I live at Prides Corner in the town of Westbrook."

"Westbrook? Wonderful. I have a friend who lives in your town. You might even know her. Name is Francena Millett. Ever hear of her?"

"Why, yes. She is a good friend. As a matter of fact, it is she I have come to visit. She is staying with the Halletts."

"Oh, yes. I can tell you how to get there. Follow that road across the way out past the church. After a mile or so, you will come to a large old willow tree where you must turn to the left. From there the road will rise steeply until you reach a flat area where the surface turns rough. Continue on until you begin to see the outcrop of Beech Hill's summit. The house is a brown shingle place with a red barn larger than the house. That is their house. Would you like me to show you the way?"

"How can you do that? Aren't you open for business? A customer might show up while you were gone."

"Don't get many customers here at this time of day. Most

come first thing in the morning or on the way home when the dowel mill closes at the end of day."

"Ethan, I am a storekeeper myself. It wouldn't do for me to take you away from the place during business hours. I am sure you have chores to do here. Cleanup, stocking, that sort of thing."

The young man studied his visitor carefully, wondering how Franny could befriend such an older gent. He didn't seem to be her type, although her life back in the city must put her in contact with a lot of different people.

"Mr. Bailey, do you mind if I ask if you are a friend of the Halletts? Do you know Franny's Aunt Lizzie or Nate's parents in Bridgton?"

Eugene was surprised that this man would know Francena well enough to use her nickname. Perhaps it was common for people out here in the country to be less formal.

"Oh, yes I have met all of Francena's family. Her aunt is a regular customer. It was she who introduced me to her niece several years ago. Francena works at Miss Millett's shop making apparel which I sell at my own store. This shirt I'm wearing is one of her pieces." He unbuttoned his vest to display the material. "Very fine material. The best Irish linen."

Ethan noticed the man's belly and smiled. This must be a friend of the aunt or of Nate's parents come to check on Lottie's condition, he said to himself. Not a close friend of Franny's.

"I'd like to have one of those shirts. Mr. Nason doesn't sell any clothing here. Most women make garments by hand for their families. Maybe I can pick one up from you when I get down to Westbrook to visit Franny."

"Do you come to our town often?" He took a new interest in the boy. Why would Francena have any wish to entertain such a young ruffian?

"Never been there, but I would enjoy visiting the place. Especially now that I have met two people from Westbrook."

Ethan held out his hand to shake with his new acquaintance.

Eugene ignored the gesture and turned to leave. An old grandfather clock near the door showed him that it was three o'clock already. He had spent too much time with this lad. The directions seemed to be clear. Old willow tree. Turn left. Rough road. Brown house in sight of the rocky hilltop.

"How long will it take me to get to Francena?"

"Twenty minutes would be my guess. If you don't get lost. Can your quarter horse handle the rough road?"

"I'm sure she will do very well. Thank you for your help, young man."

As the stranger mounted his wagon and headed toward the church, Ethan couldn't help wondering what such a man would have in common with Franny.

100

What a festive family day it was! At the break of dawn, Lottie got out of bed by herself and sat in her chair watching the sunrise. When Franny entered the room to serve breakfast to her patient, she could see from the color in Lottie's cheeks that health was returning to her friend.

"Franny, it is a wonderful summer morning. Look how high the sun is at such an early hour. I've not felt this well since you arrived. Can I go outside for a while today?"

"Wouldn't that be an occasion! Let me speak with Nate. See if we can arrange a place for you to be comfortable. The boys will be so excited."

"I will be comfortable sitting on the back porch, looking out at my mountain. Even if only for a few minutes."

Nate was overjoyed. "Of course. How wonderful! We can make a party out of it. Wait till I tell Con and Francis."

Franny put her hand on her brother's chest.

"Let's not get carried away. She may only be able to stay outside for a few minutes. We will have to keep an eye on her and make sure she doesn't overdo it."

"Okay. I will make it clear to them, especially Con, that they won't be able to get her to play tag with them."

He then grabbed his sister in his arms, placing a kiss on the top of her head.

"This is all because of you. Her getting better is because of your care. You are an angel."

"Nate, she has a long way to go. Like you, I am very pleased to see her acting like her old self. But we must be very careful; she is just too fragile."

He exited the kitchen through the rear door and placed a small side table and three chairs on the grass facing the porch. Then the two of them went to the second-floor bedroom to get their patient. They were surprised to see her standing at the door fully dressed, with a wool shawl wrapped around her shoulders. Her breathing came unevenly, but she stood straight and tall. There was a big grin on her face.

"I know you two think I won't be able to stay outside very long. You will see how strong I've become. I want to spend the whole day with my family outdoors. Such a sunny summer day! Who wants to stay inside?"

Nate and Franny stood on either side of her, taking hold of her upper arms to steady her for the walk downstairs. She gently pushed Franny's arms away, taking hold of her husband's arm.

"You will see that I can make it down the steps with only a bit of help from Nate. I'm stronger than you think."

Slowly, the three of them made their way down the stairs, into the kitchen, and out to the bench. Con was already seated in one of the chairs, and he clapped his hands together to applaud his mother's appearance. She let go of Nate's grip and bent to take her young son's hands, only to lose her balance and grab the chair arms to keep from falling. Con stood and put his arms around her waist, helping direct her to the bench.

Franny rushed forward to help, but she stepped back upon realizing that Con had saved his mom from falling.

"Con, what a wonderful strong boy you've become. You kept your mom from falling. Thank you for doing that."

The boy blushed, then smiled and stood next to the bench patting Lottie's shoulder. "Can Mommy read to me?"

"Of course I can, my darling. I will read to you all day if you want."

He raced into the kitchen, returning with a stack of books. She looked at each one and selected one they had started before her illness, *The Tale of Peter Rabbit* by Beatrix Potter. Con had liked the book even before they read it because Potter was the last name of the author, same as his father's name. As she began to read, Nate brought Francis out and seated him next to his brother. He gave Lottie a glass of cold water and took a seat. Franny stood aside, studying the family gathering before her. She was so happy that her efforts to heal her dear friend seemed to be effective thus far.

If only I can be so lucky to have such a wonderful family. Lottie must have such joy in her heart, she thought.

Lottie proved to be very resilient. She read book after book to the boys, stopping occasionally to catch her breath, eat lunch, or rest her eyes by staring across the field at Beech Hill. The moment was so special that they all stayed together until the sun dimmed behind a layer of high clouds spread across the summer sky. Franny noticed Lottie begin to shiver.

"Dearie, I think it's time for you to go inside. There's a chill now in the air. Come Nate, let's get her back to her room."

Lottie stood and placed her arm in his for support. As the couple reentered the door, the boys formed a procession behind them. Francis grabbed onto the hem of his mother's dress. When a knock on the door brought the procession to a halt, Franny went to the door. Opening it, she was shocked to see Eugene standing there with a bouquet of wildflowers in his hand.

"My God! What are you doing here?"

He cleared his throat and passed the flowers to her.

"I came to visit you. To see how you are doing up here in Waterford. I have missed you."

Lottie stumbled, and the bouquet fell from Franny's hands to the floor as she rushed to help steady her patient. When Nate was able to support his wife alone, Franny retrieved the flowers.

"Nate, Lottie, this is my friend Eugene Bailey from Prides Corner in Westbrook. He owns the general store there."

"I would shake your hand," said Nate, "but right now I have to get my wife back to her bed."

Con stepped out from behind his dad and eyed the stranger.

"We had a fun day outside with Mommy." He put out his small hand for a shake.

Eugene, who was embarrassed to have shown up at such a bad time, bent down to shake the boy's small hand.

"And what's your name, young man?"

"Conrad, sir."

As Franny and Nate went upstairs with Lottie, Con took hold of the man's hand.

"Please come with me to the kitchen. We can sit at the table for a few minutes. This is my little brother, Francis. Sometimes we call him Franny, but that is Auntie's name." He giggled.

"Conrad, I will wait here for your aunt to return, thank you. It is Francena I came to visit."

"Oh, that's right. That's her real name, but we don't call her that."

At that moment, Franny rushed down the stairs and placed an affectionate kiss on Eugene's scratchy cheek. Today was the first time she could remember ever seeing him unshaven. He wore no tie, and his shirt showed sweat marks from the heat. She sensed his embarrassment at arriving in an awkward moment and led him back out onto the front porch, closing the door behind them. In the window she could make out Con and Francis staring out at them.

"You must be tired from your travel. Did you drive all the way today? Please sit and rest. Have you taken a room at the Alpine for the night?"

"Francena, my dear, I have come only for a short visit and will return to Westbrook tonight. Is there a place we might sit alone to chat?" He, too, had noticed the boys.

"Perhaps, if you're not too tired, we might drive up to the old mine at the top of the hill. It's peaceful and very secluded."

"Yes, of course. I would love to be alone with you."

They mounted the seat and headed out to the road. He reached for her hand and smiled. She pulled back her hand at first. Something about his presence made her uncomfortable. Soon she relaxed, took his hand, and began to think how much he must have missed her.

"My dear, I have thought of you so often these past few weeks, that I had to come and see how you were doing out here in the Maine woods."

"Maine woods? Aren't you exaggerating? It may not be as civilized as what you desire, but I'm happy to be enjoying the peace and quiet. And my loving family. Aren't the boys darlings?"

"They seem to be well-behaved, especially the older one. Are you taking care of the entire household? You know—cleaning, cooking, and care of the children as well as tending to your friend's needs?"

"Yes, pretty much everything. My brother has been working so hard to make ends meet that he is only able to spend a short time with the boys each night."

"I am impressed with your willingness to leave your craft behind and give your life over to being a homemaker. And very surprised. Isn't there a local woman to lend a hand?"

"Why are you so surprised? If you didn't think I could manage a household, why did you propose marriage to me? If we wed, isn't that your plan for me?"

"If we marry? Are you still considering having me?"

Pulling the carriage off to the road verge, he stepped down to the ground and sat on a large boulder marking the old mine entrance. She remained in the seat, looking down at him. He put his elbows on his knees, holding his head in his hands. She thought he was about to weep.

"Dear Eugene, are you so sad? I only asked for time to take care of Lottie before deciding on whether we would marry. Please forgive me if I have caused you such pain."

She climbed down and stood over him, putting her hands on both of his shoulders. When he looked up at her, his cheeks were wet. He stood and reached into his waistcoat pocket to pull out a small jewel box. In it was a gold ring set with a large tourmaline crystal. He held it out for her.

"I love you, Francena. Please accept this token of that love and devotion and say that you will be my wife."

"My dear, dear man, I do not wish to hurt you. I still must wait. Please forgive me."

He said nothing, closed the ring box and returned it to his pocket.

"Come, I will drive you back to your current home."

"Eugene, I will walk back. It is not that far, and I need to clear my head." Tears came into her eyes as she spoke.

He climbed back into the seat and, without a word of farewell, drove away in the fading daylight.

101

"Stop that damn chattering!" shouted a prisoner in the cell next to Aphia's. "Can't you let a woman get some sleep?" Two other women banged on the bars of their cells with metal cups.

Aphia had rolled off her bed and fallen on the floor, where she writhed, entangled in her blanket. She had spent another night embroiled in dreams so vivid that she could not tell if her vision was dream or reality. Hearing the loud shouts and clanging, she cried out as she attempted to unwrap herself from the bedcovers.

"Shut up!" she shouted. "Damn you bitches! Shut up and go back to sleep."

Another prisoner directly across the corridor spit on the floor and spun a tin dinner plate through the bars of her cell, striking Aphia's cell with a harsh clang. The loud noise brought a heavy-set guard running into the cell block with a nightstick raised and her hand on the butt of a pistol still in its holster.

"What's going on? If we can't keep it quiet in here, someone will be moved to isolation. Who is making all the noise?"

The woman who had thrown the dish pushed her nose through the bars and said, "It's Stevens again. She's been babbling all night. Something must be done to make her shut up. Every night it's the same thing. She's driving us all stir-crazy. I haven't been able to get a good night's sleep for weeks."

As the guard approached Aphia's cell, the other six women in the block started chanting in unison, "Move her out! Move her out! Move her out!"

Staring down at the prisoner still trying to extricate herself from a twisted blanket, the matron smirked and ran her stick along the bars with a rat-a-tat.

"Get yourself up, miss. I'm afraid it's time for you to meet the new warden. Come with me. It's too early for her to be in the office, so I'll put you in isolation till daybreak. Give the others a chance to sleep."

Aphia mumbled several unintelligible words to the woman as she tried to stand. It was as if she was still asleep and what was happening was only part of the dream. Once in the isolation cell, Aphia was so cold that she began to shake. The guard handed her three musty-smelling blankets as she slammed and locked the door with a key so heavy that she had to turn it with both hands. She stared at Aphia, who was lying on the concrete floor, continuing to mumble to herself.

There's something seriously wrong with this one, the guard thought.

In her dream state, Aphia is a big, beautiful bald eagle flying above her farmhouse. Down below in the pasture, three little boys hold hands and run around in a circle. Their father claps and sings a song, stopping occasionally to point up at her and telling the boys to look up. She dives straight down at the group as if they are prey, then pulls up at the last second a few yards above them. The man waves his arms as the boys fall on their faces in the tall grass.

"I have put a fright into them. Perhaps they will want to leave my house now. But where is the mother, that one

who stole the place with her late husband, the miner? I hope she is either dead or has deserted the family. It is what these friends of Lizzie Millett deserve, as much pain and suffering as possible."

That same morning on Beech Hill Farm, Nate laughed when Con came bounding into the kitchen flapping his arms and making a screaming noise, like a bird of prey on the hunt. He often imitated the birds seen around the house and in the pasture. The boy ran around the room several times before landing himself at the table for breakfast.

"Conny, what kind of bird are you today?"

The boy tucked his hands under his arms as if he was a roosting eagle and made quiet clicking noises.

"Don't you recognize me? *Click. Click. Click.* I am that big old eagle we saw last night behind the house."

"Son, what are you talking about? We were asleep last night. You must have had a dream about an eagle."

"No, no, Dad. You must remember. You kept it from diving down to pick me up in its claws. I was scared last night, but you saved me. Now I am the eagle."

Nate set a tumbler of milk on the table in front of his son and patted the boy on his shoulder. Con possessed an incredible imagination.

102

For several weeks following Eugene's sad departure, clouds of worry and doubt about her own future dimmed the moments of joy Franny usually enjoyed with her adopted family. Her bothered mind was filled with thoughts about what might happen to Eugene and doubts that she would ever find another good man to ask for her hand.

Nate approached her one warm afternoon as she was bringing laundry in from the clothesline. He stood at a distance for a moment and thought he saw her wiping tears from her eyes with the corner of a white sheet.

"Francena Hallett, you are so sad most times of late. I miss your smiles."

He grabbed the end of a sheet. Together they folded it and placed it in the laundry basket.

"Dear brother, I don't know what to think about my life anymore. What will become of me once Lottie has your new child? Will I return to Westbrook and work for Lizzie for the rest of my life? I don't want to be an old maid spinster."

"What can I say, Franny? You are still such a young woman. And so beautiful. So smart. Things may not have worked out with Mr. Bailey, but you know there will surely be others."

Picking the basket up, she walked toward the house. When Nate gently lifted the heavy basket from her arms, she stopped in her tracks and began to weep.

"You are such a kind brother," she said between her sighs. "You've always been good to me, even if I might not have mentioned it often enough. In Lottie you have found a partner who rewards your kindness. A love that fulfills your life. I'm not sure the same will happen for me. The men I meet do not satisfy me. They are too young or too old. Too headstrong or too reticent. Perhaps I set my standards too high. Am I wrong?"

"I can't judge your standards. If they are too high, there is plenty of time left in your life to work things out. Please don't give up. You are only twenty-seven."

Again, she wept. He set the basket on the bench and returned to her side.

"Franny, I saw Ethan today at the store. He asked after you. Wanted to know how you were doing and if Eugene ever found his way here. He seems to like you. Why don't you take the carriage into town and visit with him?"

Franny stopped crying. A visit with Ethan might be just the thing to dispel the doldrums of doubt.

"Can you do without me tomorrow?"

"Sis, you've been my angel these many weeks. I am to work for John Kimball tomorrow, but I will ride over early to let him know my family needs me at home for the day. Don't concern yourself with that. Stay away the whole day if you like. A break and time with a friend will lift your spirits."

♥

Next morning, Nate put his quarter horse into the shafts of the family wagon at break of dawn for his sister's use. When Franny arose, the sun was barely awake. She found half a loaf of sliced bread and a thermos of water on the table next to a note which read, "A good friend is a blessing. Enjoy the day. Nate." How fortunate was she to have such a dear brother?

Watching a hazy yellow sun rise above the eastern horizon, she knew that this would be a hot and humid day. Across the Kimball pastures, she saw a low cloud of fog blanketing the village below and high thin clouds gathered to the north above Albany Mountain. At the Congregational Church, she pulled to the roadside, drank from the thermos, and thought about how she might approach Ethan.

I don't want to be too forward, she thought, but not overly formal, either. After all, I want him to know that I enjoy his company. He can't think I'm making any sort of commitment other than to spend a day together.

At the four corners, she stepped down from the wagon. The dusty street was filled with people on their way to work at the Haskell Mill. Several men recognized her, doffed their caps, and waved them in her direction. Across the street she saw that the door to Nason's was already opened, and the storekeeper was placing hand-lettered sale signs in the large plate-glass display windows. To her disappointment, when the man stepped into the doorway, she saw that it was Tim Nason, not Ethan.

"Mr. Nason," she called as she walked across Valley Road. "Isn't this a lovely summer day?"

The man didn't seem to recognize her at first. In fact, he turned his back to her as if he hadn't heard her greeting. She called out again. This time he turned and put his hand up to his ear.

"Oh, young lady, sorry. I didn't hear you. These old ears don't work sometimes." He put both hands up to his ears and smiled. "Yes, yes. A wonderful day. Best to be out and about early, I'd say. By noon the heat will be stifling."

"Sir, is Ethan Blaine working today? I wanted to give him a message."

"Ethan? You want to see Ethan, you say? He's right inside. I'll get him for you. Who is it that's calling?"

Ethan then stepped into the doorway.

"Mr. Nason, I'm right here. This is my friend, Miss Francena Hallett. Don't you remember her? She's living at her brother Nate's farm for a while."

"Oh, of course. Miss Hallett. You've been shopping here several times. How is your brother? Is his wife doing any better?"

"She's doing well enough for me to take a day off. Ethan, what are your hours today? I thought we might go for a ride if you're free."

The two men stepped inside the door for a moment. When Ethan returned, he smiled, removed his apron, and donned his cap.

"What a great idea! Nason has given me the entire day off. Where do you want to go?"

"Wherever your free spirit might lead us. You know so much more about the area than I."

"Huzzah!" the young man cheered, waving his cap. "You may have been through Waterford Flat before, but I bet you never really stopped to see what is there. It's an easy ride, so we can take your wagon. Let's go."

Ethan helped her up to the passenger end of the bench. He wanted to handle the horse because he knew she would stop at every viewpoint along Valley Road, making the journey take much longer than he wanted. He turned the wagon to the south and with a snap of the reins drove so quickly out of town that a huge cloud of dust rose behind them to momentarily dim the sunlight.

Waterford's Lake House c. 1890

"Ethan, come on. Slow down! No need to frighten all the chickens in the village. We have the whole day to ourselves. Let's enjoy the time, not rush through it."

"I have a few sights to show you. If we lollygag, I won't be able to fit everything in."

"You are so excitable," she said.

Even at such a rapid trot, there was much to look at as they rode along the eastern slope of tall Beech Hill. He pointed out the herds of cattle grazing on the browning grass of two large farm pastures, explaining that the brown cows were Guernseys, the black-and-white, Holsteins. After they passed one white farmhouse set at the top of a winding driveway, Ethan slowed the horse and reined it into a narrow woodland path.

"We will go slower here until the way becomes too narrow. This trail leads to the face of the hill where a naked granite ledge stands high above Plummer Hill and Waterford Village. There may be a bit of walking to reach the pinnacle. Did you wear sturdy shoes?"

Pulling up the cuffs of her jeans, she showed him her footwear, sturdy riding boots. "You don't think I would wear pumps to spend a day exploring with you, did you? I've spent enough time with you to know how to be prepared."

Within sight of the ledge, they had to disembark and make their way through thickening underbrush into the intense sunlight where no plants grew on the naked stone surface. He took her hand and led her to the very edge of the cliff, which dropped eighty feet to a field of broken stone and pale green junipers. Below them, a narrow road wound its way through cleared pastures of hay waving in the breeze and a settlement of small farmhouses on the slope of Plummer Hill. In the hazy distance, she glimpsed the waters of Tom Pond in the Flat. She sat with legs dangling over the precipice.

"My God, you've brought me to the edge of heaven. I expect to see eagles and angels soaring above us."

"I come here whenever the weather is clear and hot, as it is today. The wind from the south brings the coolness of the lake's waters up to this height. Feel how cool it is."

She took in a great breath with arms stretched wide then lay back on the rock to exhale. He stood above her, staring down for a moment at his beautiful friend spread out on the ground.

"Come," he said, "there is much I want you to see today."

She sprang to her feet and ran like the wind back to the wagon, while he lagged behind, watching her. He loved that she acted like a little girl when she was enjoying herself. One moment she might be somber as a parson, and the next as frisky as a colt. How could she have any interest in that man from Westbrook? They were as different as gabbro and mica.

After guiding the wagon slowly back to Valley Road, Ethan snapped the reins again. Soon they saw houses in Waterford Village set along the banks of a waterway he called Kedar Brook. Two- and three-story buildings lined both sides of a wide road in the shade of stately elms so large their fountains of foliage cast wide swaths of cooling shadows. Unlike the decidedly rural character of North Waterford, this village and its wide green common reminded Franny of the High Street neighborhood in Bridgton where she had been raised.

As they turned the corner onto the main road, one building, a very ornate structure, caught their attention. He told her it was the Lake House, a century-old inn and tavern recently redone in what he called the Queen Anne style. There was a wedding ceremony taking place in front of the two-story building, and three fancy carriages pulled by white horses were tethered to granite posts. Not wanting to disturb the group of ladies and gents gathered around a formal fountain, they pulled their wagon off the road in front of a general store across from the inn.

"I've been through this village several times before, but I never noticed this wonderful building," said Franny. "The long colonnade and balcony across the front with sets of double columns. Such fretwork and the lovely turret rising into the roof. What a romantic vision in this rural setting."

He pointed to the high shingled roof.

"Look up there at the two attic rooms with their balconies. I bet those are the bridal rooms. They have green shutters to keep out the light and noise from the street for the wedding night."

Franny blushed as he winked at her.

"What noise would there be coming from the street in this place?" she asked. "Besides the sound of waves on the lake, that is. Nothing loud enough to disturb a passionate couple."

He looked at her without a smile, then helped her to the ground like a gentleman.

"You never can tell what might be happening here in town on a wedding night. Especially in a fashionable hotel full of guests who have been toasting the happy couple at the reception. Some peace and quiet might be essential."

"You said they have a good restaurant here. Why don't we stop for lunch?"

"Franny, the party has gone inside. Let's look at their fountain."

They walked to the inn's cut granite water fountain roofed with a copper dome green with verdigris. Its cascade threw droplets into the air. Shining like diamonds in the sun, these fell back into the surrounding pool, the bottom of which was covered with copper pennies and silver coins thrown into it by guests.

Two large-leafed water lilies with creamy blooms the size of a person's head floated on the surface.

"This is a good place to sit for a moment," said Ethan. "A friend of mine was married here last June. A perfect place for a wedding. They said their vows right here at the fountain. He and his wife didn't have money to go inside the building for the ceremony, so the owners were very gracious to allow the party to stand around the fountain and then have a picnic in the garden."

"How wonderful. This would be the kind of place where I would have my own wedding. It's so peaceful and beautiful."

"Planning on getting married any time soon?"

"Not right away," Franny said with a smile. "I'll have to find someone who might enjoy this spot as much as I do right now."

"Anyone I know?" He took a penny from his jacket pocket, kissed it, and flipped it into the pool.

She didn't like the way this conversation was going. Her goal for the day was to free her mind of what had happened with Eugene. Perhaps if she ignored his comments, he might drop the subject.

She asked a question to change the subject. "This is such a beautiful village. Do you want to have lunch here?"

"Franny, I asked you a question. Are you thinking of marrying anyone in particular any time soon?"

"I wish you wouldn't ask about that. My plans are my own business."

She turned away, walking along a white picket fence toward two eight-foot white wooden gateposts which marked a stone entrance path to the front entry portico.

"Wait. You are upset. Please forgive me." He rushed to the front door and opened it for her. "I ask because I'm curious about that Westbrook gent who recently visited. He mentioned that he was your dear friend. He didn't strike me as being your type."

Standing in the open doorway, she glared at him before turning on her heels and striding back through the gateposts toward Nate's wagon. He let the door slam and walked quickly after her. As she began to step up into the wagon seat, he reached to help her, only to have his arm pushed away.

"My private life is none of your business! If you are going to continue to pry, I insist that we return to North Waterford immediately."

"I'm so sorry. Forgive me. I don't mean to ruin our time together. Your friendship is so important to me. We can't let it break apart. Forgive me."

She turned her face away from him and didn't notice him reach into his jacket pocket. He pulled out a small cloth sack. When he passed it to her, she refused to accept whatever it was he had to give.

"Please take this gift from me. I wanted to give you something to celebrate a lovely day together. Now I have to offer it as an apology. Please forgive me, Franny."

"My anger is not completely your fault. I have been very sad ever since my friend Eugene visited me. He came to ask me to marry him, and I refused his proposal. I wanted to forget what happened for a while today."

"Can we call a truce on discussion of unhappy things for the rest of the day? There are many other beautiful places I wish to show you."

"Yes, of course. Please forgive me for being so touchy. Thank you for the gift. Shall I open it now?"

As she untied the knot, he told her to be careful. Slowly she pulled out the first of two objects wrapped in tissue. When the paper was removed, she gasped at the sight of a beautiful unfinished crystal, a topaz of radiant blue. Removing the second packet, she found an even larger blue crystal nearly the size of a sliver dollar. At first, she was breathless at the beauty of the stones and the kindness of the giver. Suddenly, she changed her mind and rewrapped the specimens, returning them to the sack.

"You are such a dear. Thank you so much. But I can't accept such a precious gift from you. If I do, it will mean that we might be more than just friends."

"What's wrong with that? You said yourself that your engagement has broken off. You are free to do as you want."

"Yes, and what I want to do is be free of any commitments for a while. Can't you understand that?"

Ethan took back the sack and placed it in his pocket again. Without a word, he turned the wagon around and headed back to Valley Road for the return trip. They both knew that their happy day was over.

103

Business in the dress shop did not slow down because Franny was absent and Lizzie was ill. A surge of new custom orders came in for Christmas holiday designs, while designs for the upcoming spring season were being completed. Although the Flaherty sisters were willing to work very long days, their two machines were unable to cut into the growing backlog of work. Janey did her part, working most days, but she was not a skilled seamstress or designer. Faced with the fact that the girl would be returning to school in late August, and that Lizzie might well continue to be unable to work, a skilled helper had to be found. Over lunch one day in late July the two discussed options.

"Doesn't your oldest girl, Faith, know how to sew?" said Mary.

"Heavens! She knows how to darn a sock and hem a skirt. That's about it. She'd probably be frightened the machine would stitch her fingers together. What about Hattie? She worked here for a while back before you returned."

"Really? I didn't know that," said Mary. "I wonder would she be willing to come this far a couple of days each week. I'll check with Liz to see what she thinks."

Without delay, Mary went to Lizzie's bedroom and knocked on the door. Although it was early afternoon, her friend, wearing her nightdress and pink bathrobe, sat at the window trying to read.

"Come in, dear. No need to knock. You know I'm up by this hour."

"Yes, yes, of course you are. But I thought you might be resting."

"I certainly don't need any more time in bed. Seems like all I do is lie there and try to sleep."

"Liz, you know Maeve and I are not catching up on the orders. People keep bringing in pictures of dresses to be made. We aren't done with the ones we already have, even with Janey's help."

"I can work more than I have been, especially with designs, if that would help."

"No, the doctor says you must rest your body and your eyes if you are going to get better. Maeve tells me that your sister is a decent seamstress. She says Hattie used to work here in the shop. Do you think she might lend a hand, at least part-time? It would only be temporary, until Franny returns."

"I'm not sure Hattie has kept up her sewing in a long time, but I could ask. She used to be quite good. I'll give her a call."

Liz left her chair, put on slippers, and walked to the kitchen, where the phone hung on the wall next to the range. Passing the stairway, she looked down at the shop and sighed. When would she be able to get back to her old self? Be able to work along with the Flahertys? She wasn't that old. There was no reason for her to be so tired all the time.

As the operator connected her call to Hattie's home in Bridgton, Liz sat down next to the stove. Mary had a teapot of water heating and had given her a cup of soothing mint, which she had sniffed and sipped. The pungent aroma cleansed her throat and made her cough. When the phone rang, she knew that the call had gone through.

"Dearie, this is your big sister. How have you been doing? Haven't spoken to you or Nathan in ages."

"Lizzie, sweetie, what a joy to hear your voice. You sound well."

"Somewhat. At least I am up and about. Can't keep a good girl down."

"Nathan is here with me. We are both doing very well. I just got a card from Franny. Looks like Lottie is doing better, but there are still a couple of months to go before your niece can return."

"What an angel she is to be her friend's nurse for so long."

"She worries about you and is sorry to leave the shop so short-handed. Nate tells me you have a batch of new orders. That's wonderful."

"He knows because he's the one who keeps bringing in the new orders. Your husband is a super salesman."

"I won't tell him you said that. It will go to his head."

"Actually, I'm calling you to see if you might be able to help us fill all those orders. As you know, I am unable to work like I used to. Maeve and Mary, with a bit of help from Janey, are doing their best to keep up. We were wondering if you might be willing to work here in the shop several days each week. Just temporary, until Franny returns."

"Girl, are you sure I would be a help? You have those big new machines. I have that old Singer, the one you started with and then gave to me. It would take a while to train me."

"Little sister, you were always good at designs. We used to work together with patterns. Do you remember? If you concentrated on preparing the patterns, that would be a great help. You've always been a fast learner, so I'm sure you would learn to run the third machine right away."

There was a long silence on the other end of the line. Liz could hear a conversation in the background. When Hattie returned to the phone, she sounded very excited.

"I think we can work out a way to do this. Give me a day or two to move a few things around. Nathan likes the idea, and I would love to spend a few days with you. I'll get back to you quickly."

"You're sure about this? Don't feel pressured into doing it. I know it may be inconvenient."

"Don't you worry now. A little excitement in my life would surely be welcome. Give my regards to Mary. Goodbye, dear."

♥

The next day, Hattie returned the call and surprised her sister by agreeing to work full-time at the shop temporarily. She also asked if she might live with Liz and Mary for as long as she was working. Nathan would bring her to Westbrook the following weekend on his way to an extended business trip down to Virginia and Maryland. He would be gone for more than two weeks, and when he returned, he might be able to go to Waterford and bring Franny back home. Hopefully, the arrangement would work out well for everyone. The three women working together could make it possible for the shop to catch up. Hattie, instead of being left alone for many days, would enjoy the company of friends and family. Nathan would not have to concern himself about his wife being alone, and Lizzie would enjoy the companionship of her beloved sister.

The most optimistic aspect of the plan was hope that Franny might be able to return home. Everyone knew that Lottie was still in need of her friend's care, even though she had begun to feel better as the end of her pregnancy approached. Her doctor was cautiously positive that she had gained enough strength to handle the delivery. Yet Agnes, the midwife, still questioned the wisdom of letting the birth go full term. If Lottie agreed to a cesarean birth, as the woman advised, the birth would come in less than a month. If not, there might still be four to six weeks until the crisis would be over.

104

Hattie arrived on Sunday, normally a day of rest. Yet, upon entering the house, she was greeted by the rumbling of sewing machines at work. The two women were so busy that they didn't notice her until Nathan stepped into the shop door.

"Ladies, working on Sunday?" he spoke above the din. "Don't you make time for Mass?"

Maeve, who had not seen the man for a while, didn't know what to think about the comment. Was he joking about them being lapsed Catholics? Mary was used to his humor and turned to him with a broad smile.

"We don't have to go to Mass. Our priest gave us indulgences back at Easter. Said we didn't have to go to Mass until Nathan Hallett himself went to church on a Sunday."

He bowed to her. "Touché."

When Hattie entered, both women left their stations to hug her. Maeve placed a kiss on her cheek. "You are so dear to join us. You will surely be a godsend."

"It isn't right that you two should be slaving away with no time off. It may take a few days for me to refresh my skills. I'll try my best to help out. Where is my sister?"

Hearing Hattie's voice, Liz entered the room, carrying her coffee cup. She planned on working in the shop for part of the day and was fully dressed. She wanted her sister and Nathan to think that she was feeling better. As she made her way across the room to give Hattie a hug, the cup fell from her hand, spilling coffee all over the floor.

"Oh, no!" she cried, looking at the spill and then at her sister. "What is wrong with me?"

Hattie rushed to Lizzie's side and put her arm around her shoulders.

"Dear, it's okay. Come! Sit down. Look, the cup isn't even broken."

Mary grabbed a rag and knelt to sop up the coffee. When she stood, Nathan gestured to her to follow him out onto the porch where they might speak in private.

"Mary, she looks so weak, almost feeble. And so thin."

"She has seen two doctors and neither of them has been able to diagnose her condition. One thinks it might be premature senility. The other one said he saw nothing physically wrong with her, no obvious reason why her condition does not improve. I'm beside myself with worry."

"Perhaps having Hattie here for a while will help. They've always been able to coax each other out of their difficulties."

"Let's pray that happens. I have just about given up. What with all the work to be done, it's tiring me out. Maeve, too. Having some help may be a remedy for us all."

By the time they returned to the shop, Hattie had taken Liz back to her room, where the sisters sat on the edge of the bed. Liz wiped her red eyes with the corner of her sheet and held tight to Hattie's arm.

"What is wrong with me? No one seems to know. I feel that I've aged years in the past couple of months. Do I look as old as I feel?"

Hattie wrapped both arms around her and whispered in her ear. "Big sister, I've seen you through many dilemmas. This, too, will pass. You'll see."

Nathan stepped into the room and asked Hattie to show him where he could drop her luggage. As they climbed the stairs to the second floor, he whispered, "She hasn't improved since the last time I saw her. Mary says that her doctors have no idea about the causes of her illness. You'll likely be working on her care as much as on the sewing. On my way south, I will stop in Boston. Lottie's late father once introduced me to a physician who specializes in nervous disorders. He may have some thoughts on this case."

"I hate to say this because you will disagree that there may be some credibility to what Maeve and Janey have been saying all along. The cause may well be that she is under a spell cast by Aphia Stevens."

"No! How many times does this foolish idea have to bubble up before you realize that Stevens has no secret powers?"

"With each new difficulty that arises in this family, I begin to think it more and more possible that she is at least partially the cause. Maybe your contact in Boston will be able to scientifically explain what is ailing my sister, help to cure her. However, I've begun to doubt there is a rational cause."

"Do me a favor. Until I return, please do not get on board with the ridiculous idea of visiting the witch in prison. T'would be very dangerous for Liz at this point."

105

Nearly a month had passed since Eugene had returned from North Waterford. The memory of his final separation from Franny would not fade. He thought about it while working at the store, while eating, even in his dreams. A pervasive melancholy took hold of him, draining his life of interest and enjoyment. The store was open for shorter and shorter days. Often its door was closed for several days at a stretch. Deliveries piled up on the rear dock while disappointed regular customers turned away and sought other places to shop in nearby Westbrook Center.

At first, he hired Maeve's young son Owen to help. On two occasions, when the boy showed up for work, the owner was not there to let him in. He was also drinking more, as a way to forget his loss and enable him to sleep. After a while, he began to sip a beer or two in the morning, several tumblers of whiskey while preparing dinner, wine with the meal, and then another whiskey before bed. When he began to have headaches in the morning, he realized he had come to rely on the sedation, a habit which was not good for him.

One morning, Donald Pratt dropped by to collect payment on several overdue invoices. It was nearly noon, so he went first to the store. Not finding anyone there, he went to the house and walked straight into the grand entryway without knocking. He carried a large manila envelope and a few pieces of mail he had found lying on the store porch. As the architect gloried in his grand curved staircase, a masterpiece of workmanship, Eugene shuffled in from the kitchen holding a coffee cup. The merchant was still in his pajamas. His hair was a mess, and he had obviously not shaved for a few days.

"Bailey, why is your store closed? You're missing out on some sales."

Surprised at seeing a stranger in the house, Eugene shouted, "Get out of my house! Why didn't you knock like everyone else? This is not your house. How dare you disturb me?"

"Bailey. Eugene Bailey, don't you recognize me? Donald Pratt, your architect."

Eugene squinted at the man for a moment before realizing that he knew the visitor.

"Sorry, Donald. I didn't know it was you. I'm feeling a little weak this morning. Haven't been able to get ready for work. Please forgive me."

"Please sit down somewhere. You look horrible. What's wrong with you?"

As Pratt stepped closer, he caught a whiff of brandy coming from the coffee cup. He knew that his client was drunk or hung over.

"I've come here to check on why you have not been keeping up with payments to me and my vendors. You haven't remitted a penny to me for two months. Our friend at Back Cove Antiques has been complaining. He says he expects me to pay if you do not. When can we expect you to catch up?"

Eugene didn't know what to say. He knew that he had missed a couple of months to Pratt and was behind on monthly payments to Portland's Casco National Bank. Several letters had come from the bank. They lay unopened among the mess of mail on his kitchen table. He turned his back on the architect and walked back to the kitchen.

"Bailey, you must tell me your plan for bringing your accounts current. I'm sure you don't want to lose the house."

Taking his seat again and pouring another cup of strong coffee, Eugene took a deep breath before speaking.

"I have decided to put this goddamned castle on the market. It is too large for me. It is made for a family, and I am unlikely to be able to fill it with one. Perhaps you might like to make an offer."

Pratt threw the manila envelope on the table.

"Damn you! I put my reputation on the line for you. These vendors need to be paid and paid quickly," he said, pointing to the envelope. "They may never want to do business with me again. You can't be thinking of paying with proceeds from selling this place. That will take months."

"I'm sure that with your help I may be able to sell very quickly. You know so many rich people. And it is quite a prize."

Pratt stood with his hands on his hips, as he considered what this pathetic man was offering. Yes, he did know people in Portland who might be interested in owning such a choice piece of real estate. Although not many of them would consider living in a backwater like Westbrook, so close to the muddy Presumpscot River. But it might be worth a try. He'd have to act before the bank could take it over and sell it for only what was left unpaid on the mortgage. He pulled out a chair and sat down facing his disheveled client.

"Yes, I will be willing to find a buyer for you, but there will be a very specific contract between us. You obviously have fallen on hard times and will not likely be able to sell the house yourself. If I'm going to assist you, you must agree to move out immediately, give me the keys, and only come to the place at my request."

"I will be glad to agree. This house is an albatross around my neck. I was happier back in my old apartment. If only I had stayed there and run my store the rest of my life, I would be happier than I am living in a mansion that has ruined me. What little furniture I have in the old place will suit me more than all this claptrap you have forced me to buy."

As he rose from his chair, he pointed to the door.

"Now, Mr. Pratt, if you don't mind, leave my house as quickly as you entered. I will prepare to leave later today. Until you present me with a contract, the house is still mine. I want you out of my sight."

As Pratt left, he glanced back at the sorry man and clenched his fists. He knew he would find a way to get back at him and make a profit.

106

Hattie immediately threw herself into the work at hand on Monday morning. She spent a couple of hours under Mary's tutelage reviewing how to use the larger Singer electric sewing machines, which were much faster than the treadle machine she had at home. The rest of the day, she sorted through unfinished designs with Janey, who would be leaving at the end of the next week. To her surprise, at the end of a very tiring day, Mary still had enough energy to cook a small supper. Bert joined them at the start of the meal, then went to bed earlier than usual. As tired as both Hattie and Mary were, they stayed up to chat with Lizzie. Soon Mary began to doze off and went up to bed, leaving the sisters in Liz's room, alone for the first time in months.

"Little sis, you are so kind to be staying here with us."

"I'm excited to be able to work with you all. To be able to be with you is a true blessing. It has been some time since I've seen Maeve. She looks so radiant. And her Janey is as sharp as a pin."

"The girl has been a big help. She reminds me a lot of your Francena."

"Somewhat. Janey is certainly a lot taller and stronger than Franny."

"Taller maybe, but you'd be hard-pressed to convince me your daughter is not as strong."

"I can't say that she doesn't have a strong character and constitution. I just can't forget that she was such a little thing at birth and in her early years."

"But she's so healthy now. I've watched her grow into such a beautiful and intelligent woman in the years she's been living with me."

"I agree. You've been a wonderful influence on her."

"Take some credit. You and Nate gave her a great start in life. Having two good parents is so important. Maeve has done a marvelous job raising her children, but Janey and the others have sorely missed the caring hand of a father."

"Yes indeed, a tragic death. When Will was killed, we all lost a family member."

It was getting late, so Hattie stood and excused herself, heading out the door toward the stairs. Lizzie, who was already in bed, asked her to wait for a minute.

"Hattie, you mentioned Janey before as being very intelligent. Do you think her idea of forgiving Aphia Stevens has any merit? Nathan certainly doesn't. Mary gets angry any time the idea of a visit is mentioned. I believe Maeve has begun to think that something good might come of it."

Hattie did not want to discuss the subject, but she realized her sick sister wanted to talk about it, so she returned and stood next to the bed.

"I'm not sure. The woman has caused serious harm to this family and our friends for many years. I see how sick you are, and for no good reason. Then there's Lottie going through such a hard pregnancy for the second time. Are these difficulties caused by the witch's curse? Nathan believes we ourselves give her some power over our lives by living in fear of her. I suppose he's correct. Still, I wonder."

"For the last few months, I've been unable to live a normal life. Lie here in bed most of the time for no cause that a brace of doctors has been able to diagnose. Sometimes it seems I might be under some sort of spell."

"Do you think it would be wise for you to participate in such a journey? I think it might prove very risky. And we can't expect Lottie to join in. Not in her condition."

"If I believed one hundred percent that forgiving Aphia would free us of continued problems, it would certainly be worth a try. I would have to go because, in her mind, the anger and resentment toward us is because of me. Lottie wouldn't have to go."

"Nate or Franny might go in her place. You know Aphia blames both Lottie and Clarence for the loss of her house. Lottie thinks that Aphia may have cursed Clarence to his death."

Lizzie shuddered as she breathed deeply.

"I didn't know that. If that were true, then the visit would have to take place as soon as possible, before Lottie has any more problems. She might lose the baby if there really is a curse."

"Or she might lose the baby and die."

Once more Liz took a very deep breath. She sat upright and reached for her sister's hand.

"I know my dear Mary is against Janey's idea. I must speak with her tomorrow and explain how important it is to make the visit to the State Prison right away."

107

Eugene received Pratt's contract in the mail at the end of the week. He reviewed it, saw nothing in it that he couldn't accept, signed it, and sent it back by return mail. He felt relieved that by turning the house over to the architect, all his debts would be forgiven when the place was sold. He immediately vacated and moved back into the small apartment behind the store as he had agreed. He was sure his life had been improved.

The store was once again open on its regular schedule. Customers who had been inconvenienced by having to travel a longer distance were happy to have him as their main merchant once more. Several of his local vendors, angry at the loss of business and not having been paid for old deliveries, required him to pay cash until the debts were settled.

Pratt showed up at the store one day accompanied by two brawny young men whom he introduced as his nephews. They stood blocking the doors while the architect explained he had a demand not originally included in their original agreement.

"We have cleaned the house from your slothful neglect so that it is now a castle once again, not a pigsty. I am planning a big open house next Thursday evening and, as the original owner, you must attend. If you refuse, I will make sure you are arrested for violating our agreement."

"There was no such stipulation that I remember. You asked me to stay away, and I accepted. You can have your big party without me."

Pratt gestured to his two companions to close and bolt the door. One of the men, the taller of the two, approached Eugene and grabbed him by the collar. He had a small goatee and a handle-bar mustache that was waxed into points. By the smell of the man, Eugene guessed the wax used came from some wild animal.

"Mr. Bailey," the ruffian began, "Mr. Pratt is an honorable man. More honorable than either Billy or me, to say the least. You best go along with his request or we two shall have to negotiate on his behalf."

"Jimbo, don't mess the man's nice white shirt," said the other thug. "I'm sure he understands how important it is that he cooperate with our uncle."

Pratt smiled and walked up to Eugene until they were face to face.

"Well, my good man, I'm sure you see the advantage of being at the open house on Thursday. It starts at six p.m. I expect you to be a few minutes early to welcome any locals whom I do not know."

Once the door was unlocked and the three men had departed, Eugene retreated into the apartment and took a flask out of a kitchen cabinet. He gulped down two mouthfuls of brandy, then put his hands flat on the table and leaned over them, shaking his head. What had he gotten himself into?

108

Eugene rose early on Thursday morning, opened the store, and took a seat behind the counter. When Mrs. Holt delivered fresh-baked bread, he asked her what she had heard about that evening's open house.

"Me and the husband received an invitation in the mail yesterday. Don't think we will be goin', though. We already have a nice house. I didn't even know your place was for sale. 'Tis a pity after all that work."

"Yes, Mildred, indeed. Such a pity. Sometimes you must admit that you made a mistake—take your medicine and move on."

"There'll be some music and dancing at the open house— Billy Bay and his friends. They're very good at a barn dance."

"Really? I would have expected a more refined type of entertainment from Mr. Pratt. Round dancing is popular with folks in the neighborhood, but I'm not sure his urban friends will appreciate the straw and sawdust on the barn floor—might dirty their polished boots."

All day, he surveyed customers on whether they would be attending the party, and most said no. Mrs. Choate, whose husband was a lawyer with many Portland contacts, said they wouldn't miss it. She revealed that several of Mr. Chaote's clients had expressed an interest in purchasing the house.

"We aren't interested. The place is not the type of place we'd want to live in. Too big for our small family. It really is a castle," she said.

He concluded that the party might turn out to be an interesting place to spend a couple of hours. Closing the store an hour early, he made a small dinner for himself. It included two glasses of lager and finished with a large tumbler of brandy. At five thirty, when he walked toward the mansion, he was ready to have a good time. After all, if the party resulted in a sale, the future would look much brighter.

One of Pratt's nephews was stationed at the door as both greeter and bouncer. As Eugene neared the front door the thug pulled at the points of his mustache and called out to him.

"Oh, Mr. Bailey. So glad you decided to attend tonight's party. You're a smart man. You must enjoy yourself."

Eugene recognized the man as Jimbo, the one who smelled like a raccoon. What a disgusting stink. Did other people not find this man obnoxious?

"Whether I enjoy myself or not is none of your damned business. The sooner this monstrosity of a castle is sold, the faster you and Pratt will be out of my life."

"Hold on there, buddy," said Jimbo. "No need to be so unfriendly. One might think you're here to cause trouble, and that just won't do. You're here to help people have a good time. My uncle would be terribly unhappy if you were to cause any sort of trouble. Understand?"

When the man stepped aside, Eugene entered the large entry-way. He laughed out loud at the scene before him. Two young women in checkered dresses were tying strings of multicolored helium balloons on the bannister of the floating stairway, from the top landing all the way down to the first floor. There must have been at least fifty balloons. Another woman stood behind a long table near the parlor door. She had posted a large sign on the wall behind her which said BARN DANCE TICKETS. Pratt was flitting around from place to place. He was dressed in a blue serge suit and a pair of polished shoes which were a shiny blue. He flew to his client's side.

"Eugene, so good of you to join us. I want you to stay in the barn all night. The people who will be dancing are most likely to be your neighbors or people of that type."

"Why did you bother with the dance if you didn't want the neighbors to come?"

"I want to show the world that my lovely house is perfect for a large party. What better way than to fill it with all sorts of people? Here, make your way back to the barn. The band will start very soon. There's plenty of hard cider out there. Serve yourself."

Walking through the kitchen, Eugene laughed again as he saw a sign above the rear door which said BARN DANCE and had a big arrow pointing the way. Billy Bay was tuning his fiddle and gave him a nod as he entered. A man he didn't know sat strumming a guitar, and another stranger with a large stand-up base viol rubbed rosin on his hands. Three women, perhaps the musicians' wives, were already at the large cider barrel drawing drinks. In the back of the barn, standing in shadows cast by the hay loft, the architect's second nephew, the shorter one, sat on a high stool smoking a pipe. He wore a sharp new fedora.

As the band warmed up, a few couples gathered around the barrel. He didn't recognize anyone as being from Prides Corner, but several people nodded at him as if they knew who he was. Not feeling a bit friendly, he exited through a small door that led to Francena's garden, now overgrown with weeds and meadow grass. The sun was going down behind a stand of tall pines, and the sky was awash with stunning red and pink. Someone called his name, and when he turned, he saw the nephew wave the fedora at him.

"Mr. Bailey, please return to the dance. It is your job tonight to help keep the crowd happy. Uncle Don has told everyone that you have thrown this party. Now, get back in there and do your job. Have a cider or two; it will help. I insist."

The young man walked up to his side, grabbed a sleeve of his jacket, led him back inside to the barrel, and drew a glass for him.

"I don't like hard cider."

"Don't care. You drink that or I'll force it down your throat."

"Idiot! Go to hell!"

He walked back to the garden mumbling under his breath. In a moment, both men were on him, throwing him to the ground. The bigger one held him down while the other pried open his mouth and was about to pour the cider into it.

"Let go of me! You can't do this! I'll scream so loud everyone inside will come running!"

Pratt ran from the house.

"Boys! Stop this! You'll make a ruin of the evening. Let him stand."

Eugene stood up and brushed dirt off his pants. Pratt pulled at his arm and helped clean grass from his jacket.

"Forgive these boys. They're only following my orders. You have offended them. If you'll go back inside and act the host, I'll make sure no further trouble happens. Have a couple of drinks. Perhaps you might dance with a lady or two. Don't forget that I can have you arrested if you continue to disobey. Don't you want to sell this house as soon as possible?"

Disregarding the glares from the two thugs, Eugene walked back toward the party.

"Pratt, I'll go along with you for the moment. Keep your attack dogs off me or there will be trouble."

As the night went on, the crowd of dancers grew. One man, a local farmer, stood in front of the trio and called out round-dance steps for the couples. Soon so many people were dancing that their feet raised a cloud of dust from the sawdust and straw spread on the floor. When Eugene's throat became dry, he filled a tumbler with cider and sipped until it was empty. Soon he was so drunk that he danced by himself in front of the band. Several times, people clapped at his steps and laughed. He actually was having fun.

The musicians took several breaks to have a drink and smoke. During one break, Eugene sat right down on the floor and fell asleep. When the music began again, Pratt entered from the house and helped him to his feet. He gestured to the nephew in the fedora to help lead his drunken ex-client outside for a breath of fresh air. Once outside, the two men walked slowly around the lawn until the other nephew joined them. Then the two rogues grabbed hold of his shoulders and began to lead him down the driveway toward Forest Avenue. Darkness had now fallen, and although there were several streetlights along the usually busy road, no vehicles passed them by as they headed toward the river.

Every few steps, Eugene would stumble and fall, and the men would pull him back up. The first time this happened, they ripped the jacket right off his back, leaving it in two pieces on the ground. When one of his shoes came off, they removed the other before picking him up again. At a dark, narrow woods road that ran down to the Presumpscot, the thugs dragged him into the shadows, removed his shirt and left him prostrate in mud from recent heavy rains.

He lay there unconscious until the chill of fog forming along the river woke him. Not knowing where he was, he rose and began walking away from the main road in the direction of the river. Barefoot and shirtless, he kept stumbling on branches and stumps. Soon he cleared the heavy woods. In the foggy moonlight he thought he was approaching the Brook Street Bridge, which crossed the Minnow Brook near his store.

"What is happening to me?" he mumbled. "How did I get out here half naked? There was music and I was dancing. When the music stopped, I sat down. That's the last thing I remember. Where am I? Is that the brook? My store must be right around here."

The fog was so thick that he could hardly see his feet. In the darkness, he found it difficult to stay on the pathway and kept bumping into trees along its edge. He suddenly found himself at the stream bank just above where it fed into the river. Recent storms had brought the water level to freshet stage so that he was standing in water up to his ankles. Thinking that he was north of the bridge, he turned to the south in error and fell into the stronger turbulence of the Presumpscot. Such cold water rushing toward the sea shocked him into understanding his error. It was too late. The current pulled him under.

109

On Friday, the CLOSED, OPENING AT 9 A.M. TOMORROW sign greeted every customer. On the Saturday, Owen Cain, who had been sent by his mother for some groceries, read the sign and wondered. He went to the rear and knocked on the apartment door. When no one answered, he returned to the dress shop to report that something might have happened to Mr. Bailey. Soon the sheriff was summoned. He was able to climb into the apartment through an unlocked window. Seeing no sign that the man had been there recently, he decided to investigate. He began by making a phone call to Mr. Pratt, who he knew had hosted a barn dance at the missing man's house.

"Hello, I'm trying to reach Mr. Donald Pratt."

"You have reached him. Who's calling?"

BARRING THE WAY TO THE SEA
IN SEARCH FOR BAILEY'S BODY

1905

Boom To Be Stretched Across Presumpscot River So That It
Will Not Be Allowed To Float Away in the Darkness---Diver
May Be Sent Down To Search the Bottom of the River.

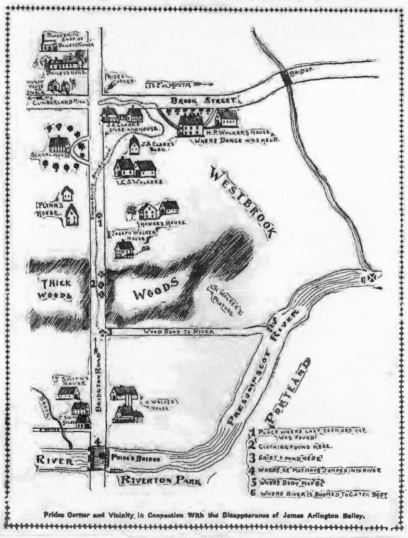

Illustrative map clipped from a Portland newspaper in 1905

"Mr. Pratt, this is Cumberland County Sheriff Tamminen. Do you have a moment?"

"Sir, please be quick. I have a meeting going on."

"Yes, this will take only a moment. It's about a client of yours, Mr. Eugene Bailey of Prides Corner."

"Yes, I know the man, but he is no longer my client."

Tamminen took note of the critical tone in the man's voice.

"Well, Mr. Bailey is a missing person. May I ask a couple of questions about the last time you saw him?

"Sheriff, the last time I saw Bailey was Thursday during a party at his new house. He was there that evening until about nine, I'd guess. He was quite inebriated when he left and headed home."

"Did he leave alone?"

After a slight hesitation, noted by the sheriff, he answered. "Why yes, he did leave alone. A friend of his tried to revive him by walking him around in the cool air. The drunk pushed him aside and staggered away."

"Which way did he go?"

"I assume he went toward home, but I was occupied at the time. Sheriff, are there any more questions? I am with a client."

"Just one more. What is the name of the friend who tried to help Choate?"

"I have no idea. Never saw him before. Sir, I was very busy that night. There wasn't time to get everyone's name. Now, may I go?"

"Yes. Thank you very much for being so helpful. But I may need to contact you again."

"Please do not call me during the day. I have a very full schedule. Goodbye."

Tamminen sensed that the man knew more than he was telling. He deputized a search party of local men to look for evidence in an area running from the new house down to Prides Bridge over the river. The searchers quickly found clues. A man's jacket, torn in half, lay in the drainage ditch along the highway. Shoes and a torn white dress shirt were found in a puddle where a farm path left the paved road. Prints of bare feet marked the way down to the merge of Minnow Brook and the Presumpscot, where the flooded banking had fallen away. There was no question in anyone's mind on what had happened to the missing man.

The drowning of an upstanding member of the community brought a call from local authorities to drag the river bottom for a body. Pleasure craft were borrowed from Riverton Trolley Park on the opposite riverbank, but the wild current had turned the stream so cloudy with mud that nothing on the bottom could be seen. One man, who had served as a diver in the Army, volunteered to drop into the river at three areas where snags of fallen trees and roots might have caught the body and kept it under. Again, visibility was so clouded that the diver was not able see a thing through the helmet of his diving suit. Several men suggested that the snags could be dynamited to release the body. The sheriff thought such an extreme tactic would destroy any remains.

A boom was spread across the river a hundred yards downstream from the supposed drowning site. Operators of the mill dam upstream at Sacarrapa Falls were asked to draw down the water level for a day so that the remains might be caught in the boom. This was done, but like all the other attempts, it fell to naught.

110

Mary let the rear door slam behind her as she entered the shop. She had heard from Maeve about the drowning and wanted to let Liz know as soon as possible. When she ran up the stairs and down the hall to Lizzie's room, she almost ran into her friend, who was dressed for work and on her way to the shop.

"Whoa, Mary. Slow down. You might have knocked this patient over. What has you so excited?"

"Do I ever have some news for you! Our customer Eugene Bailey has drowned. Sheriff Tamminen is sure he fell into the Presumpscot on Thursday night."

Shocked by the news, Liz returned to the room to sit on her bed. "Does anyone know how it happened? No one ever goes down to that muddy river in the dark. It's always dangerous, even in daylight."

"Apparently he had been drinking hard cider at the barn dance at his place. A few pieces of his clothing were found on Farmer Walker's woods road next to the river. Theory is that he was going swimming and got pulled in by the current. The water's been running at freshet for a few days."

"Doesn't the body need to be found before he's ruled dead? Has there been a search?"

"Oh, yes. A party was organized by the sheriff on Friday morning, but other than clothing and a few footprints, nothing else was found. A diver went down into the water to have a search. It was too muddy. A log boom has been stretched across the river below Minnow Brook. A selectman has suggested that we dynamite some dead tree snags where the body might be trapped."

"Dynamite? What? Oh, my God! Franny will be beside herself. They were such good friends. She hinted to me that he might ask for her hand. How unfortunate."

"Hattie told me he did pop the question right before Franny left for Lottie's. I'd hate to be the one to tell the girl what has happened."

"Better that she doesn't know about it."

For a moment Liz stared in silence at Mary, then turned away to look at a maple just outside her window and lay back on the pillow. Mary thought she was going to sleep and walked toward the door. As she was closing it behind her, she heard Liz begin to cry and went back in.

"My love, what is so wrong as to make you cry? The merchant's death, though a tragedy, is no personal loss to you."

"I weep for Franny. Her plans for the future may be crushed by the man's death. It reminds me of my pain when my fiancé was lost to Aphia Stevens."

"Liz, dear, please don't grieve again over your own loss. And don't manufacture the same level of pain for Francena. Eugene's death may not be blamed on anyone but himself. There is no parallel in your and Franny's experiences."

"If what Janey and Maeve say about Stevens is correct, she may have had some part in this man's death."

Mary stepped back and pointed her finger at Liz.

"I don't believe that even *you* are beginning to subscribe to that damned misconception. How can you? It harms you all to fear the woman has any continuing unnatural powers to affect our lives. Bad things happen to good people all the time. Stop blaming a madwoman for our calamities."

"I'm not as sure as you are that Aphia is not capable of cursing us. She's been convicted of three murders. She may have had something to do with Clarence's mining accident, Lottie's miscarriage, and her difficult pregnancy right now. Perhaps she cursed Bailey to punish Francena for helping her friend."

Liz saw that Mary was about to explode in anger. She held up her hand and continued. "Let me finish before you holler. She might even have something to do with my strange illness. There may be something I can do to check her powers."

At that, Mary waved her arms and shook her head in frustration.

"Botheration! You are as foolish as the others. If you decide to put your life at risk by making the long journey to visit that woman in prison, you can be sure I won't be living here when you return."

111

"Warden Johnston, I have done nothing to deserve being moved to solitary confinement. Those other prisoners are making a federal case out of my sleeping habits. Yes, I have dreams. But they're making it seem like I keep them from their own sweet dreams. I haven't complained when that tall one stays up all night singing. Or the colored girl bangs on her door with that damn cup."

Dorothy Johnston sat behind the same big desk that Warden Lewis had used. Aphia wondered if she also had a liquor bottle hidden in the bottom drawer. The woman was attractive in a severe sort of way, with gray hair cut very short. She wore a black jacket with no collar. Her only adornment was an American flag pin on the jacket pocket.

"Prisoner Stevens, it is not my choice to move you to solitary. It is my only option. We have too many women prisoners being held at this time. I know that you have been well-behaved of late, and I appreciate that. You appear to have your anger under control."

"Ma'am, does such good behavior deserve solitary confinement?"

"As I said, it doesn't. Perhaps we can make an arrangement of sorts."

"An arrangement?"

She thought back to Warden Lewis making the same type of proposal.

"Stevens. Or I will call you Aphia. It's such a pretty name." She rose from her seat and stood next to Aphia. "You seem to be in fine health and have a good head on your shoulders. I need someone who will assist in cleaning my apartment and helping with meal preparation. If you would be so kind as to take the position, I may be able to make your accommodations much more to your liking."

Aphia did not at all like the manner with which Johnston stood up close to her, touching her shoulder. What was this woman proposing? Was she to be her slave?

"Warden, under your proposal, would I be able to continue spending my free time in the library? I've been working on a legal appeal to one of my convictions and have put together what I think is a very strong case."

"Why yes, Aphia. You would likely have *more* free time. Also, my home office could offer you the use of a telephone and a much more comfortable environment for your study. Do you know how to use a typewriter?"

"No, but I certainly could learn to use one. It would make the appeal much more professional than my scribbling. Warden, when can I start working for you?"

"Please call me Dorothy. No need to stand on formality if we're going to be friends. I will speak to the head matron tomorrow and let her know my plan."

Johnston reached out her hand to shake Aphia's, took the offered hand between both of hers, and gently rubbed its back for several minutes while staring into her prisoner's eyes.

Aphia wondered how friendly the two would become.

112

Maeve arrived at work Monday morning in a gay mood. Her smile was so wide and her manner so joyful that Hattie and Mary asked what had happened. At first, she told them the lovely morning made her happy. When Janey showed up a few minutes later for her final week, the girl revealed her mother's secret.

"Mom, you're so fortunate. He is such a wonderful man."

"Hush, girl. I told you not to tell anyone until we're ready. Now everyone will know."

"Know what?" the other two women said in unison.

"What's happened? What man are you talking about?" said Mary. "Is it that handsome Charlie Van Dam?"

Janey waited for Maeve to respond, but after a couple of moments of silence, she said, "Yes, yes! He proposed to her last night and she accepted. Isn't that fantastic?"

"My dear sister, what wonderful news!" said Mary as she grabbed Maeve in a bear hug. "A welcome addition to the family. Have you set a date? Let's see the engagement ring."

Maeve, smiling and blushing at the same time, held out her bare left hand.

"He hasn't given me one yet. That's why I wanted to wait. It isn't official until you have a bright stone on your finger."

Everyone laughed so loudly that Lizzie came into the shop to see what was going on. Hearing the news from Maeve, she clapped her hands together and rushed to her old friend's side.

"So wonderful! He's such a lovely man! Are you planning a big wedding? When?"

"We were discussing an elopement. Now that Janey has let the news leak out, we'd have to invite all of you to elope with us."

As everyone chattered happily, Liz turned silent. The smile left her face, replaced with a sullen look. She gestured to Janey to join her in the former storage room where they could speak in private.

"Janey, I didn't want to pour water on the celebration in there, but I need to discuss your idea about forgiving Aphia. With your mother about to add a new husband to our family, we probably should make that journey sooner, rather than later."

Janey was surprised to hear that Lizzie was supporting her plan.

"Aunt Lizzie, do you really agree with me?"

"It took me a while to figure it out. There has recently been a lot of time for me to consider the plan, and there are just too many unexplained calamities in this family. Your mom has already lost one husband at Aphia's hands; no need for another good man to be lost."

"Not everyone agrees. I know Nathan thinks the idea is foolish. So does Mary. Not sure how Hattie feels about it."

"My sister agreed with her husband until recently. But she has confided in me that there may be something to it. She said it might be worth the effort, even if our forgiveness might not have the desired effect."

"Would you be able to go to the prison? Are you strong enough for that?"

"I think it is imperative that I go. I've always been the primary target of her wrath."

"When shall we go? I must go back to school next week. If mom thinks the journey of forgiveness is important, perhaps I can put school off a week or two."

"Janey, if you and I can make all the arrangements, let's plan to do it early next week. Don't say a word right now. It might ruin a happy time for all. I'll bring it up later today."

113

The women were cleaning their work area and getting ready to leave for the day when Lizzie entered the shop. She was walking with a cane yet stood tall and straight as she made her announcement.

"Ladies, I have something to say that may not be acceptable to all of you. For two days next week, I want to close the shop so that Janey, myself, and anyone else who is so moved may journey to the Maine State Prison in Thomaston to visit Aphia Stevens."

Janey said nothing and sat back down at her desk. Maeve and Hattie looked at each other in surprise and then stepped closer to Liz to hear her soft voice more clearly. Mary sat back in her chair and hung her head in her hands.

"You all know what we will be doing. Janey has explained the importance of forgiveness so many times. Looking into my own heart, I saw that I have never forgiven Aphia Stevens for the pain she caused me nearly thirty years ago. I've covered that hurt under many layers of regret until it has become an unrecognizable scar."

Everyone stared at Liz with intense interest. Mary raised her head and wiped tears from her eyes. Janey stepped forward and linked arms with her mother.

"Mary and Nathan may be correct," Liz continued. "We may be on a fool's errand. Perhaps she has no power over my life and the lives of my loved ones. However, I want to do whatever I can to rid myself of this hurt which gives that woman more influence on my life than she deserves."

At that, she burst into tears, dropping the cane to put her hands over her face. Mary rushed forward, grabbed her arm, and helped her sit at her desk. She spoke with great emotion.

"I don't want you to do this. It is an arduous undertaking which will drain your energy. You are so strong willed that you won't listen to me. I can't turn my back on you, so I will join in the journey. Know, however, that I will not spend one second in that witch's presence. She can just go to hell."

114

Janey found Bert asleep, wrapped in the hammock behind her house where he napped on warm days. It was nearly dusk, and she smiled, thinking that if no one woke him, he would likely sleep there for the night. She wanted him to know that the prison visitation was finally going to happen, and very soon. He would be the only man in the group and the one who knew Aphia the best. She poked his shoulder.

"Get up, Bert. You'll be catching pneumonia if you sleep out here with no covers."

He wouldn't budge, so she began to rock the hammock gently back and forth. Instead of waking, he began to snore. She poked him again, this time quite roughly.

Finally, he stirred. "Harrumph. Who in blazes—?"

When he saw it was his favorite girl, he smiled and whistled.

"Pneumonee, you say. I'll not hear of it. Had pneumonee years ago. Who says I have it again?"

"I didn't say you have it. But you might if you sleep out here in the open. Get up and come inside. I have some news for you."

"If it's bad news about that drowning, I don't want to hear another word. The storekeeper was a good man. Didn't deserve to die like that. And at such a young age."

"No, this is good news. Now come inside. Mom is making supper."

Climbing down from his perch, Bert stretched his arms above his head and then brushed off his overalls.

"So, what's the good news?"

"Aunt Lizzie has decided to make that visit to Aphia that we've been talking up forever. Mary's going, too. Auntie wants to go to Thomaston next week."

He stared at her in disbelief.

"You're joshin', ain't ya'? Just pullin' my leg?"

"No, Bert. This is for real. I've been asked to make all the arrangements. We need transportation, a place to stay. I imagine we'll have to stay overnight. Then we must make arrangements at the prison. I'm not sure I can do all this alone."

"I'd help, missy, but I'm not real good on the telephone. I bet your brother Owen would be able to help better than me. He's a talker. I'm saying that we would best travel by train from Portland. No good roads from here to Rockland and Thomaston."

Janey excused herself and ran off to find her young brother. After she left, Bert climbed back into the hammock, humming a tune with a smile so wide, all of his few remaining teeth showed.

This is gonna be one hell of a journey, he said to himself.

115

Nathan called home that night from Philadelphia. He wanted to make sure that Hattie knew he would be away for a few more days. She was both glad to hear his voice and disappointed in the delay of his return. She could barely restrain herself in announcing that Lizzie was going to visit Aphia. She knew he would be upset about it, but he would never forgive her if she didn't give him the news.

"Dear Nathan, I have something to tell you about Lizzie. I know you will be disappointed. By the time you return, she will have visited Aphia in jail."

"What? Are you sure? How can she do that in her condition? Not a very good idea, if you ask me. What does her doctor say?"

"I'm not at all surprised that you're upset. I have concerns myself and have expressed them to both Liz and Mary, who is going with her. I'm afraid there is nothing either of us can do to stop her. And, you know, there might be something to the idea that Aphia does have some manner of influence on our family. Not any sort of *magical* power, of course."

"Hattie, the only curse that Stevens woman has on our family is one that some people make up in their minds, like a child's fantasy of demons in the closet. Did you say Mary was going with her? I thought she was as much opposed to the idea as I am."

"Oh, she still is. Once she realized that Liz was determined to go, she decided to go along to take care of her. She really doesn't give a damn about the purpose of the visit."

"Who else is going? Not Lottie?"

"No, not Lottie. Bert is going along because he knows the woman best, though I wonder that he will be much help. And Janey because she's organizing the whole trip. It was her idea, after all."

"I hope they're going by rail. It would take forever to go by coach or wagon. Where are they staying overnight? God! Now I wish I was home to help with the details."

"Now you're making me sorry that I told you. Don't be such a worrywart. Janey and Owen seem to be doing a thorough job making arrangements."

"Hopefully they've made an appointment with the prison warden. It wouldn't do to have them travel all the way to Thomaston and then wait days to get an appointment. Especially with a *group* of visitors. I should be there to help make the arrangements."

"Please don't return from your trip because of this. You must accept the fact that it will all be happening without you. And I believe only two people, Bert and Liz, will be meeting with Stevens, not a big group."

"Hattie, you were good to let me know. I will worry, no matter what you say. I pray all will go well."

"Lizzie will be fine. She is such a strong woman. Oh, I almost forgot to tell you some other news. Franny's friend Eugene Bailey has died, drowned in the Presumpscot this week."

"The storekeeper? Drowned? How did that happen?"

"The sheriff has yet to find the body, so it's still speculation. Isn't that tragic?"

"Does Franny know yet?"

"I've not told her, and given that news travels slowly out to Oxford County, I doubt anyone else has either."

"I'm sure she will take this as a personal loss. You know how she is, especially with a man who has proposed marriage to her."

"Looks like you've missed a lot during this trip. That will teach you to go away for too long."

"Hopefully no more momentous things will happen before I get back. I'll pray for Lizzie's safety and our daughter's happiness."

116

The two boys ran around the kitchen playing tag. Francis was "it," and no matter how fast he moved his short legs, he was unable to catch up with his older brother. When Con raced through the screen door to the rear porch, he plowed into Franny, who was carrying dry laundry. Trying to avoid a collision, he fell to the ground and his brother jumped on him.

"You it now! You it!" shouted the little boy. He was so excited that instead of touching Con's arm, he slapped him hard across the cheek.

"Ouch! No fair! You hit too hard."

Con jumped up, pushing his brother to the ground. Francis hit his head on the edge of the low wooden porch. He burst into tears. Franny grabbed them and pulled them apart.

"Stop right now. Stop hurting each other. It's time for both of you to stop running roughshod around the house and go read for a while."

When Francis turned to her, blood was running down his face from a small cut over his eye. She wiped the blood away with her handkerchief and looked closely at the wound.

"You'll be okay. It's just a small cut. Come inside so I can clean it and put on a bandage."

Suddenly Con, who was standing behind her, wailed and threw himself back on the ground. He lay on his stomach and began to bang his forehead on the dirt. Franny released the little one's hand and rushed to help the other.

"Con! Conny! What is it?"

"I hurt my brother! He might have died because of me! I'm a bad person!"

Tears streamed down his face, and when he wiped them away, dirt from his hands turned to streaks of mud across his cheeks.

"No, dear. It was an accident. You didn't mean to hurt him. Don't think of yourself as a bad person. You both are good boys."

"No, I'm bad. I think bad thoughts. Bad dreams."

She was considering whether to bandage Francis's wound first or calm his distraught brother when Nate, who had heard the crying, came through the door. He pulled Con up from the ground and led him toward the pasture.

"Franny, I'll take care of this one. He's been like this before. I know how to deal with it."

In the middle of the field where tall grass waved in the breeze, Nate knelt before his seven-year-old son.

"Con, your dreams are not real. They're imaginary, just like your thoughts. They're made up by your mind—like stories in the books you read. Nothing more. And your brother is all right. Take a deep breath and stop crying."

The boy grew silent and stepped back from his dad.

"That's what you told me before, but the dreams are so real. And I can't forget them when I'm awake. Last night, I saw a man fall into some deep water. It was that man who visited Aunt Franny a few weeks ago. There was thick fog all around him. He fell into the water and his head went under. I think he drowned."

Again, he began to cry and rub his face with dirty hands. Nate held his son's arms to his sides and said, "Son, it was only a dream. Please try to forget what you saw. Come, give me a big hug and I'll get you a slice of that chocolate cake Franny made for you."

"No, I don't want any cake. I want that dream to go away. All the others, too. Why do they happen to me?"

"Con, you are both blessed and cursed with a sensitivity most other people never know. It's a sixth sense—you know, like seeing, hearing, smelling, touching, tasting. You know those regular senses, don't you?" When Con shook his head, Nate continued. "Well, the sixth sense you have is the ability to feel what others feel. When you meet someone who is sad or troubled, you feel what they feel. And that feeds your dreams."

From the look on his son's face, Nate knew that the boy was putting great effort into understanding what he said. After a moment of silence, Con spoke softly.

"So, you think the friend of Aunt Franny's didn't drown. That he was sad about something, and I became sad, too?"

"Yes, that's pretty much what I'm saying. It is a mighty powerful ability to know how other people feel. You're lucky to have that power, but it *can* make you very unhappy. You must realize that another's sadness and problems are not yours."

Con smiled. "Okay. I think I understand. I'll keep last night's dream to myself. No need for Franny to worry about her friend."

"Yes. That's a great idea. Now, let's go have that cake."

Later that night, after the boys were in bed, Franny sat at the kitchen table reading her latest issue of *Western Home Journal* magazine, while Nate split firewood in the barn. Tiring of the work after a busy day, he returned to the house and looked in at his sister on his way to bed. She looked up from her reading.

"Nate, please tell me how you were able to calm that boy down this afternoon. He worries me sometimes. His imagination is so powerful."

"Sure is," he answered. "He allows his dreams and thoughts to get hold of him. I told him he's blessed with a sixth sense making him very sensitive to the feelings of others. He just needs to control it, or he will be unhappy. That's why he has such power-ful dreams. They are so vivid, he believes them to be real."

"I'm not sure I would call that a blessing. It must be hard for a little boy to separate dream from reality."

"Last night he had a dream about your friend Eugene. He has only met the man once, and then only for a few minutes, yet he felt that the man was troubled about something."

"Well, he's right about that. Eugene came here to get me to marry him. When I asked for more time to decide, he gave up on the idea. He knew I wouldn't leave Lottie even before he got here. He was sorely troubled."

"That may be what Con sensed. Anyway, in his dream he saw the man drown. That was what made the boy so distraught. It wasn't only about hurting his brother at all."

Franny closed the magazine and threw it on the sofa. "What an imagination. Eugene drowned? Not likely. He wouldn't go near a body of water. I doubt he ever went swimming in is life. Perhaps I should make light of his visit in the morning to calm Con's worry about the man."

"No. Best to let it pass."

117

Two days later, Franny sat in the warm early-morning sun on the front porch. She was enjoying an article about efforts by President Roosevelt to designate the Grand Canyon in Arizona Territory as a new national park. The magazine cover was a map of what the President called "a wonder unlike anything in the world." Included were two photographs of men riding mules along the river surrounded by majestic canyon walls rising to block out the sky. These pictures and the description of the canyon took her breath away.

Looking northward across the valley, she tried to visualize how such cliffs would dwarf Albany Mountain in the hazy distance. She thought the Grand Canyon would be a magical place to visit someday. As she put the journal down on the bench, a cloud of dust appeared far down the road. Soon she could make out a man on horseback approaching from the direction of North Waterford village, and she knew it was Ethan. No one else she knew would be riding with such abandon. As he neared, she left her seat and walked toward the road, wanting to greet him at the gate. She hadn't seen him since their outing to Waterford Flat a month before.

"Ethan Blaine, why to do drive that horse so hard? You'll wear her out."

"She loves to race, as do I. We were made for each other," he said as he dismounted. After walking the sweaty horse around to cool it, he tied it to the fence and stepped to her side.

"You're out quite early today. Are you off on an adventure?"

"Just wanted to visit you before Nason opens the store. How've you been keeping? How's the patient?"

"Thanks for asking. Some days she may be doing a little better than me, but we both are doing pretty well."

"I didn't know if you might have already left. It's been a while since we've seen each other."

"I'll be here for another month or so, according to what Dr. Stimpson tells me. Lottie's time is coming close, so she's on her back in bed most of the time."

"And you—why are you up so early?"

"Couldn't sleep very well last night. It's all right, though. Gives me more time to read before Con and Francis want their breakfast."

"Your brother is so fortunate to have you as his helper with those boys. You're such a good mother."

Not knowing whether to take that comment as a compliment or a bit of sarcasm, she said nothing and took a seat on the top fence rail. He removed his hat, used it to knock the dust off his clothes and then leaned on the rail close to her. Each of them turned their faces away from the bright sun as it rose above the pines.

"Francena, I've missed you these past few weeks. Our parting was none too friendly, and I wanted to apologize for offending you. It wasn't on purpose, you know."

"At the time, your comments hurt me deeply. Perhaps I was oversensitive. I still feel that my private life is not really any of your business."

"Yes, I realize that now and will try to do better in the future."
She smiled and placed her hand on his shoulder.

"Oh, good. So, we have a future as friends? I *would* like to
have you show me some more of your hidden places, like that
wooded lane to the top of Beech Hill. I enjoyed that so much."

"Yes, let's do that. I did have some news to bring to you, and it
will not be to your liking. It's about your friend Mr. Bailey. Please
don't blame me for what has happened to him or for telling you.
I felt you needed to know."

She stared at him for a moment and then jumped from the
fence. "What has happened to him? Tell me at once."

"One of Nason's vendors, a Gorham farmer who makes
cheese, made his delivery yesterday. While we were chatting,
he told me of a rumor he had heard in Westbrook that your
friend had drowned. When I asked him for details, he said he
wasn't sure how it happened. When he left, I made a phone call
to a friend of mine who works at the Haskell Silk Mill on the
Presumpscot. He verified that the sheriff has indeed confirmed
Bailey drowned in the river. A body has yet to be recovered, but
they continue to search."

She reached for the rail to steady herself. How could that
happen? She remembered how sullen he had been when they
parted. For several minutes she could find nothing to say. Yet she
didn't cry.

"No, Ethan, I'm not angry with you for telling me such tragic
news, as sad as it makes me. I would have heard it from Nate or
some neighbor, if not from you. I must ask you to leave. Please
forgive me. I must be alone for a while."

"You've no need to ask my pardon. May I return in a few
days to take you out on another excursion?"

"I'll come to the village on Tuesday to visit you at the store,
and we can plan a time together then."

Once he was gone, she walked back to the porch. Inside, she
heard noises from the boys, who were already in the kitchen.
How could she ever see Con as a normal boy again?

118

Lottie sat up in bed, shocked at the words Franny had just said. "Your fault? What? That's crazy! I don't believe that for a minute."

"It could be true, couldn't it? He came to show me his love, and I refused to accept him. He was downtrodden and depressed when he rode away. I am at least partially responsible for his drowning."

"I have never heard anything so preposterous. Girl, you did nothing to drive a man to suicide. And you don't even know if it *was* suicide. How did you reach that conclusion?"

"Well, I'm *not* sure he did himself in. Just my speculation, that's all."

Lottie moved to the side of the bed next to where her best friend was sitting. She put her arms around Franny and spoke slowly, as if searching for the right words.

"You are the dearest woman on earth. You're so caring that you are willing to sacrifice your own life for another. Look what you've done for me. I'm sure he wanted you in his life because he saw that in you. It must have been a shock when you told him you wanted to wait, but you didn't mean to hurt the man."

Franny sighed and moved her head from side to side. "I know you're right, but his death makes me so sad. My heart is broken, and I'm confused. What if he was the best man for me? I drove him away. Now he's gone, and I am left alone."

"You know there are others," said Lottie. "Look how much Ethan Blaine thinks of you. People *like* you, Francena Hallett. How could they not? You are an angel." Then she stood up and began flapping her arms like wings and singing the Christmas carol "Angels We Have Heard on High."

Franny cleared her throat. "Mrs. Hallett," she said through her giggling, "you must stop making fun of me. You may think me a kind angel, but as your *guardian* angel, I must demand that you stop making a fool of yourself and get back into bed before you get hurt."

Lottie stopped dancing, looked at herself in the mirror that hung on the closet door, and smiled.

"My angel, I'm as surprised as you that I'm making such a performance. Where did such energy come from? I haven't felt this frisky in many months."

119

The train ride from Portland to Rockland was uneventful. Bert fell asleep in their cabin before Union Station disappeared in the distance. Liz and Mary chatted in the opposite seat for several hours, until Liz dozed off. Mary then read her novel and stared out the window at the passing scenery. The weather was so warm and the breeze coming off the Gulf of Maine so cooling, that Janey stood outside on the gangway breathing deeply and reviewing her notes on plans for the jail visit. She was so happy with how well everything had gone to that point. They had boarded an open trolley at Riverton Trolley Park so early in the morning that the sun was only beginning to brighten the sky. Only one hour later, they boarded the B&M Coastal Express, catching the first coach of the day to mid-coast.

The train pulled into Rockland Station at eleven, right on schedule. Getting the party out of the coach cabin took a bit of work. Bert was so deeply asleep that, when she finally was able to get him out of his seat, he kept dozing off on his feet. He dropped his duffel several times, so that she finally took it away from him and carried it herself. Lizzie was also slow to fully wake. Fortunately, Mary was able to both hold her partner erect and carry both bags. By the time everyone reached the platform, Janey had made arrangements with a coachman to transport them to the Thomaston Prison, four miles distant.

The driver was inquisitive about their destination. "Missy, I don' want ta seem too nosy, but you got quite the group of prison visitors here wit' ya. Mostly the folks I deliver there in Thomaston are lawyers or prisoners' wives."

She didn't want to give him too much information, so she met his question with her own. "Sir, do you drive to the prison very often?"

"Oh, not often, but enough to know the way and back. My passengers usually asks me to wait for 'em. Make sure they has a wagon ready for the return trip. Do ya want me to wait?"

"That is a smart idea, but we're staying the night in Thomaston."

"Stayin' at the Black Dragon?"

"Yes, do you know it? Perhaps you might wait and take us there after our appointment."

"You got an appointment? Are you all goin' in for the visit?"

"Just two of us will go in."

"Visitin' anyone I might know?"

"Mister, that really isn't any of your business, now, is it?"

The teamster glared at her and said nothing. She felt his anger but didn't care how he felt. Their plan had nothing to do with him. So what if he was offended.

"You sure in hell won't need me to wait. The inn is almost next door to the prison. It's th' only hotel in town."

"Will you come back for us in the morning?"

"Ma'am, there are a couple of guys with rigs in town. You won't be needin' me."

She looked back at her party. All three of them appeared to be sleeping. The wide-open pastures that lined the County Road between Rockland and Thomaston gave way to clusters of neat white houses, each with a barn or series of outbuildings. As they entered the town center, the road abruptly became paved with granite cobbles. The horses' hooves began to loudly ring as their shoes struck the stone. The noise caused the three to wake as they neared the prison.

It was by far the largest building in town, a long, two-story wooden structure with small windows and numerous turrets protruding from the roof peak. As they neared the building, it was clear that there were two wings, each several hundred feet long, attached to a two-and-a-half-story house-like structure set between them. This section displayed a copper-topped cupola in the center of its roof and odd canvas coverings extended on frames outside its barred windows.

"If that's not the strangest buildin' I've ever seen," said Bert, "it's damn close."

Janey, who had been sent a drawing of the building layout by the warden, pointed to the part of the structure with the cupola.

"That center section is where the women prisoners are housed. Look at those heavy shades on the windows. Not much light can get through those. According to this drawing, the warden's office is on the first floor. That's where we must go to gain admittance."

They made an odd procession: a fair young woman followed by two middle-aged women walking arm in arm, and a tall, thin old man in coveralls bringing up the rear. Janey grasped a large metal knocker on the double arched door and banged as hard as she could. When no one answered, she knocked again. A rotund woman in a blue uniform opened the door and stood with legs spread wide to block the way.

"Yes, miss. May I help you?" The woman was at least six feet tall and must have weighed nearly two hundred pounds. Her arms were folded on her ample bosom, a monumental obstacle to entry.

"Ma'am, I am Janey Cain. My friends and I have an appointment to visit a prisoner."

"All of you? That's very unusual. It is standard policy to allow only one visitor at a time. For security reasons, you know."

"I made the appointment last week with your Warden Johnston. She told me that two people would be able to visit prisoner Aphia Stevens." She pointed to Lizzie and Bert. "Miss Millett and Mr. Learned here are to visit. We others will wait outside the visiting room."

"Please, Miss Cain, you and your friends may step inside. I will check with Warden Johnston. She's in her apartment today, not here in the office. It's Prisoner Stevens you've come to visit?"

When the matron returned from a call to the warden, she looked more calmly at the foursome. She carried a canvas sack under her arm.

"This is highly unusual. Stevens is working in the warden's home today, and you are to visit with her there rather than in the visiting room. As is standard procedure, I must ask you to leave any personal items—handbags, wallets, purses—in this bag. Please empty every pocket."

When all four had complied with her request, she asked each to turn around in front of her so that she might inspect for any items that might be hidden. "I'm sorry to be so thorough, but you would be surprised the things visitors try to smuggle into the prisoners. Knives, bottles of booze, that sort of thing."

She then directed them to exit the door and turn to the left. They were to walk along one of the wings which held the male prisoners, then across a ball field to a white two-story raised cape house with black shutters. When they reached the house an attractive woman with gray hair stood in the open door.

"Which one of you is Jane Cain?" the warden asked.

"I am she. These are the people I mentioned to you who wish to visit Miss Stevens."

"I believe I was quite clear, Miss Cain, that only two people might be admitted. Prisoner Stevens is most insistent that she only see people whom she knows. In fact, she was reluctant to speak with any of you. She is my cook and housekeeper, and I explained that, as such, I expect her to accept a friendly visit with friends who have come to wish her well. She has agreed to spend only thirty minutes with Mr. Learned and Miss Millett. I must ask you other ladies to wait outside."

Hat in hand, Bert moved to the front of the group. After smoothing his thinning hair, he bowed to Johnston.

"Miss Warden, at your service. I am Bert Learned. I wouldn't lie and say that Aphia Stevens and me are best of friends, but we have known each other right well for many years."

Johnston smiled at him. "Yes, I checked her court records and find that it was on your testimony that she was convicted for murdering her husband. I'm surprised she would see you."

"Well, that testimony was righteous. She knows that as well as me. We go back a lot further than that. We were nearly married, you know."

Janey took Lizzie's hand and pulled her forward.

"Warden Johnston, Miss Millett has known Aphia since they both were teenagers. There have been some rough times between them. My aunt now wishes to settle things with her."

Lizzie shook the woman's hand.

"Warden Johnston, Janey has also been offended by Aphia. Her father was killed by your prisoner. I would like to have her come in with us."

"I'm sorry. Our prisoners do have a right to refuse visitors. Stevens tells me she doesn't know Miss Cain. You must accept her decision. You may wait over there on that garden bench."

Admitted to the apartment, Liz and Bert were asked to wait in the entry. A male guard, wearing a pistol in the holster strapped around the waist of his blue uniform and armed with a long nightstick, entered without a word to them and went into a room to their left, closing the door behind him. The two heard a discussion coming from the room.

"Bert, from the sound of those voices, I think we may not be getting a warm welcome," said Lizzie.

When the door opened, the guard, now with pistol drawn, reentered and gestured for them to come into the room. Aphia sat on a comfortable-looking stuffed chair. She glared at her visitors as she rose to greet them. No longer was she wearing a prisoner's jumpsuit. Instead, she had on a floral print dress nearly covered by a dark green apron. As was standard for all prisoners, her hair was cropped very short. The guard stood directly behind her while Warden Johnston sat behind a huge mahogany desk at the opposite end of the room.

Aphia was the first to speak.

"Bert Learned, I'm surprised to see you still alive. And Miss Lizzie, you've lost so much weight since the last I saw you. Been ailing?" Her grin sent a chill down Lizzie's spine.

Bert smiled at his former lover, said nothing, but turned to address the warden.

"Ma'am, would you kindly have a seat for Miss Millett? I can stand for a while, but this lady has been sick and could use a chair."

"No, Mr. Learned. You both will stand for the duration of this visit. Guard James has requested that for security reasons he be able to watch your movements very closely."

Liz spoke. "Bert, I'll be fine. No need to worry."

Aphia smiled at the conversation and began to giggle.

"So sorry you are feeling ill, Miss Millett—or is it Mrs. Webber? I thought you were married, but perhaps I'm mistaken."

"Aphia, I don't really care which name you use. Bert and I have come for a friendly visit."

"Friendly visit? Neither of you is a friend to me. It's because of you and your clan that I'm here. You've been bothering me throughout my entire life. Meeting you was my downfall."

When Bert stepped forward to see the woman more clearly, the guard raised his pistol and pointed it at him. Johnston quickly stood and displayed a small Derringer which had been concealed below the desk.

Squinting at Stevens, Bert noticed the guard's movement and raised his hands above his belt. "No need to shoot me, mister. My old voice is a bit weak. Want to make sure my old friend hears me. Aphia, we have come in peace. It ain't good for any of us to hold a grudge. I loved you once. Remember?"

"What in blazes are you mumbling about, old man? You ran out on me, you coward. And it is your fault I'm in prison for life. Hold a grudge? *I'm* the one who's entitled to hate you for as long as I live."

Lizzie pulled Bert back.

"Aphia Stevens," she said, "we have had confrontations ever since you married Henry Greene. Our problems have spilled over to affect many of my family. People have died because of our animosity. Hardships have befallen people who have nothing to do with our disagreements. I have come to apologize for any harm I have caused you and to forgive you for any you have caused me and others."

Aphia laughed. "Forgive me? Are you making a joke? It's a bit late for that, isn't it, missy. The pain you and your assistants have inflicted on me are like steel pellets lodged in my soul that will last forever. You'll regret our paths ever crossed."

Bert became agitated. Aphia was now standing, shaking her fist at the visitors. The guard grabbed her shoulder and pushed her back into the chair. Warden Johnston, rushing from behind her desk, moved between her prisoner and Lizzie, bumping into Bert and knocking him to the floor. On his knees, he reached into his worn boot and pulled out a pocket pistol. He pointed the gun directly at Aphia's chest and pulled the trigger twice.

"I won't allow you to ruin any more lives!" he shouted as the guard discharged his revolver into Bert's arm and then his chest.

Lizzie fell to the floor and rolled her old friend onto his back. Blood was squirting from a small wound just below his shoulder.

"Bert, why? Why did you do this?"

He looked up at her and smiled. "It was for the love you've always shown me, Miss Liz. She has always been so cruel to us all." Those were his last words.

Warden Johnston was aghast. She stood over the dead woman's body which slumped forward in the stuffed easy chair marked with blood spatter. "Guard, help me move the prisoner's body out of my good chair before it's ruined. She looks to be dead. We will both lose our jobs for this, mark my words."

Janey and Mary burst into the parlor and rushed to Lizzie's side. Mary moved her partner away from Bert's body while Janey accosted the warden.

"How could you let this happen?"

"Guard, take these women to the cell block and hold them in an empty cell. They are accessories to murder."

120

When Guard James led the three women into the cell block, the only vacancy was the cell where Aphia had been staying since she'd started working for the warden. The cell contained a comfortable single bed with mattress, blankets, and a clean quilt. On a small table sat a white porcelain wash basin and matching ewer. Canvas tarps had been draped to cover all bars except the door. A tan carpet covered most of the bare concrete floor.

Lizzie was beside herself. She rubbed her hands together and looked around the cell with a blank stare, as if she couldn't make sense of where they were.

"Mary, I can't believe what just happened," she said between breaths, "Bert shot dead before our eyes. Aphia gone, too. Are we okay?"

Janey sat down next to her and took hold of her nervous hands.

"Lizzie, please forgive me. I never thought anything like this would happen. I can't believe Bert had a gun. He told me he wanted to make peace with her, not kill her."

She then turned to Mary and pleaded. "I am so very, very sorry. I never paid attention to what you said about the dangers involved in coming here. You were so correct."

"My concern was with Lizzie's well-being. Who could think that anything like this would ever happen? It certainly isn't any fault of yours."

After a few minutes, Lizzie lay down on the bed, pulled the quilt over herself, and appeared to sleep. Janey and Mary were so shocked that they paced back and forth without looking at each other.

"This prison cell looks more comfortable than my dorm room," said Janey after a while.

"It can't be typical for the other cells," said Mary. "Solitary confinement must be very popular in this prison."

The overweight matron who had originally greeted them appeared at the door carrying several more blankets.

"Ladies, you'll likely be needing more covers. It gets cold in here at night, even when it's warm outside. I'm sorry to say that we have no extra beds available. With these blankets you may be able to make the floor more comfortable."

"Ma'am," asked Janey, "are we to stay in here overnight? The three of us did nothing wrong."

"Mr. James told me what happened. You're probably correct, but Warden Johnston is in charge. What happens to you is up to her until the sheriff arrives. Sorry for your discomfort. I must follow orders. You understand?" She slid the blankets through the bars of the locked door and walked away.

"You can't hold us!" Janey shouted to the matron. She gripped two bars tightly. "We did nothing wrong!"

Mary laid one of the blankets on top of Lizzie, who was still asleep. She pulled a chair up to the bedside and stroked her partner's hair. Janey finally let go of the bars, laid a second blanket on the floor, sat down, and began to cry.

As daylight was fading, the matron returned accompanied by Warden Johnston and a tall man dressed in a tan uniform. Assuming that the man was the sheriff who would free them, Janey sprang from the floor and dried her eyes.

"Miss Cain," said the warden, "Sheriff Shaw has asked me to release you in order that he may interview you. I've told him that you were the one who organized this tragic crime. The others will be held pending your interrogation."

Shaw removed his hat as the matron unlocked the door.

"Miss, I assure you that I am not arresting you at this time, but you must be treated as a suspect in a major crime."

He then handcuffed Janey and led her out of the block. Shocked that she was being treated as a criminal, the young woman clenched her jaw.

Mary remained in her seat and continued to watch over Lizzie who hadn't moved since going to sleep. The matron stepped up to the bed and took Lizzie's hand to feel for a pulse.

"This one is okay. Her pulse is strong. Just sleeping, that's all."

Warden Johnston opened her office door to admit the

sheriff and his witness. When she went to sit at her desk, Shaw stopped her.

"Ma'am, I must ask you to leave the two of us alone so that the young lady will be free to answer my questions."

"Sir, this is my office, and this crime was committed in my prison, in my own home, for God's sake. I believe I have every right to participate in the questioning."

"Warden, if you do not leave immediately, I will release this woman and the others under their own recognizance and speak with them at a later date. From what I've observed to this point, the only person clearly guilty of a crime is the dead man who shot your prisoner. The Maine Department of Corrections will surely take an interest in why an armed man was allowed to be in your jurisdiction in the first place."

"Don't try to threaten me. These women were allowed to enter the prison only after being thoroughly searched. However, they brought the murderer with them, and for that they must be accomplices."

Shaw, who remained standing at the doorway with Janey, turned to the girl and removed the cuffs.

"Miss Cain, I believe that you and your friends are now free to go. I ask that you leave me with your names, addresses, and phone numbers, if you have phones, so that I may follow up with you in the future. Warden Johnston has made it clear to me that the three of you were unarmed, and therefore innocent of any crime."

"Sir, we'll be staying here in town at The Black Dragon Inn for the night if you need to contact us. I can provide you the information you request. Here is a business card for the dress shop where we three all work. May I go now?"

When she walked back to the cell, the door was already open and both Mary and Lizzie were chatting with the matron in charge. The woman shook hands with all three of them.

"I'm sorry for the loss of your friend," she said. "From what I know of Prisoner Stevens, he may have done us all a good deed. His body will be disposed of when it is released by the coroner tomorrow. Shall the State bury him for you?"

"Dear God!" cried Lizzie. "No. He is a lifelong friend. We will carry him back to Westbrook for a proper burial."

121

The following morning, Janey, Mary, and Liz sat at breakfast in the inn dining room discussing how to get Bert's body back to Westbrook. Sheriff Shaw arrived and explained that he had handled many of the details. A teamster had been hired to carry the body, already in a wooden coffin, to Rockland's train station. There, the ladies would have to make further arrangements. They would be able to travel on the same wagon—if two of them didn't mind sitting atop the box. As the three women boarded the big two-horse buckboard, the driver explained that he would help them transfer the box to a train when they arrived in Rockland.

"I volunteer to sit up front next to the driver," said Janey as she threw her satchel onto the wagon.

Mary grabbed the girl's arm and whispered, "Oh, no you won't. Let Lizzie sit up front. At least she will have a more comfortable seat. We don't want her being tossed around back here on every rut and bump. Besides, your mother might not approve of having you sit so close to a handsome young man."

"Okay. Best for Lizzie to be a bit more comfortable. I thought you two would like to sit together."

The driver helped Lizzie climb to the high seat and wrap herself in a heavy woolen blanket. Mary expected her to doze off as soon as they departed. To her and Janey's surprise, however, she appeared to be more energetic than she had for many months, talking with the man about all manner of things. When they reached the station, she continued to amaze her friends by climbing down off the seat unassisted.

Mary stretched to rid herself of kinks in her back from the rough ride. Then she reached for Liz's duffel only to have her partner snatch it away.

"No, Mary. I can carry my own luggage. After all, it is very light. I'm wearing most of the clothes I brought."

Janey went directly to the station manager's office and arranged for the additional transport of the coffin, while the others made their way to a bench on the platform. When she returned, she assisted their driver in sliding the coffin onto a pallet which would be loaded by freight handlers when the train arrived.

Waiting for their train, the three women spoke of their dead friend.

"Lizzie, do you think Bert has always looked for a way to work his revenge since she drove him out so many years ago?" asked Janey.

"Mind you, I don't know for sure, but that would surprise me. I believe he had settled matters between them at the murder trial when his testimony put her away for life. In all the years I've known him, he never struck me as a vengeful man."

"So, why did he do it?"

Mary answered her question. "In his mind, he killed her to protect our family and friends. When he learned that Will had been killed, leaving Maeve to raise five children on her own, he began to believe Aphia was truly evil."

"Yes, you have a point there," said Janey.

"You know," Lizzie commented, "following Clarence's death, he must have realized that her being in jail was not sufficient to end the harm she was able to do. That was when he left the cabin and came to live with us. He was trying to protect all of us."

Janey sighed. "Oh my. I always thought he was a doddering old man, just waiting to die. He was actually a hero."

"Perhaps. You would have to believe Aphia was truly a dark witch with magical powers to call him a hero. Most would think him a murderer."

"Mary dear, what do you think?" asked Liz.

"I think he was a dear person seeking to do good for the people who respected and loved him. Whether he was correct about Aphia's bewitching powers has yet to be determined. You, my love, are showing vitality and energy you've been missing for months. Our return trip has thus far gone very smoothly. But time will tell what these things have to do with her death."

Seeing the train approaching, Janey jumped up to lend the baggage handler help with Bert's coffin.

"When we get home, we must check with Hattie for news of Lottie. If her condition is improved, that could be more proof of dear Bert's beliefs," she said.

122

B ack in Waterford, Nate sat in a chair he had moved to the side of his wife's bed. The two of them held hands as he told her about all the things he had done during the day. It was a ritual she had come to rely on for the two of them to keep connected. He was quite tired and leaned to kiss her face before going to bed himself. As he rose from the chair, Con came to the bedroom door rubbing his eyes and weeping.

"Conny, what is wrong?" asked Lottie. "Come over here and sit next to me."

Nate took the boy's hand and led him to the chair. "Here, son, tell us both what's wrong."

"Daddy, I've had another one of those dreams. Like the other ones you told me not to tell anyone about."

"Con, I've told your mother about your dreams. It's okay to talk with both of us."

The boy took a deep breath and began. His eyes were closed and his voice so quiet that the two cupped hands behind their ears.

"It's the bald eagle again. The same one that attacked Francis and me in the pasture. It's flying again high over the barn and landing on our chimney. Bert is standing in the barn door with a rifle in his hands. He aims it at the eagle and shoots it. The bird is hit and falls from the roof onto the garden. Bert walks to the bird, ready to shoot it again. It rises from the ground. Its wings are all bloody. It attacks him with its talons and kills him as it dies."

Con's eyes were red and puffy, but he didn't cry. Instead, he bowed his head to his chest and went to sleep. Lottie swung her legs out from under the covers and stood at his side.

"Conny, are you sleeping?"

He didn't answer and began to breathe heavily.

"Nate, he must have been walking in his sleep."

"He was dreaming while he was telling us about the dream."

"How sad. He worries me. When he wakes, he will think the dream was real."

"Remember the one about Eugene Bailey drowning? That dream turned out to *be* real."

"How can this one be real? Bert killing an eagle and then being killed himself? It makes no sense."

123

When Lizzie returned to her home, the first thing she did was call Hattie to report what had happened at the prison. No one was at home, so she phoned Tim Nason's store in North Waterford in hopes that Franny and the Halletts would get the news. Ethan answered the phone.

"Hello. Nason's Market."

"Oh, Ethan Blaine, is that you? This is Franny's Aunt Lizzie."

"Oh, nice to speak with you. How are you today?"

"Just grand, thank you. I was wondering if you might give Franny, Nate, and Lottie a message next time you see them."

"Yes, of course."

"This is a shocking story. I'm sorry to make you the messenger."

"That's okay. I'm used to telling them shocking news."

"Please let them know that Mary, Jane Cain, and I have returned from Thomaston Prison and are all doing well."

"That sounds like good news to me."

"Yes, yes. But a horrible thing happened while we were there. Our friend Bert Learned and Aphia Stevens were shot dead during the visit."

"Did you say they were *both* shot dead?" He almost dropped the phone.

"Yes, it was so horrible. I won't give you all the gory details right now. I'm sure you will hear them later. Please just let the family know the two are dead and that everyone else is fine."

"Miss Millett, I don't need to know any more. What you've told me is plenty bad enough. Are you sure you're okay?"

"Oh, yes. And tell them that I have been sleeping like a baby and feeling my old self again."

"Okay. I'll tell that to them first, before the bad news."

"Good idea. Thanks so much for being my messenger."

"My pleasure. I hope to personally meet you someday."

"Oh, from what Franny tells me, I am sure we'll be seeing you here in Westbrook soon."

When Ethan hung up, his hands were shaking. His pulse raced. Tim Nason looked over at him and asked him to sit down.

"Ethan, what ails you? Must have been some rotten news."

"Tim, that was Franny's aunt in Westbrook. Another friend of the family has died. Been shot. And a woman shot dead, too. Such bad events are happening to that family."

"Some sort of curse, if you ask me," said Nason.

"If so, the curse may be over. Can I have the rest of the morning off to ride out to Beech Hill and deliver the message?"

"Take the rest of the *day* off. Sounds like it will take a while to deliver this message."

124

On the way to Beech Hill Farm, Ethan thought over several ways to handle his errand. He might tell Nate and let him pass it on. That would only work in the unlikely case that the man would be home on a workday. Telling Lottie, who was still so ill, might cause further medical problems. He would best meet with Franny alone and let her speak with the others. However, it had only been five days since he had brought her the news about

Mr. Bailey's demise. She could begin to think of him as a carrier of bad tidings and not want to see him again.

When he reached the farmhouse, Franny was reading on the front porch as usual. She ran up to him at the gate and took his hand.

"Oh, I'm so glad to see you, Ethan. Our last meeting ended so abruptly. I was planning on visiting you at the store, but on a day when I could get away for our next adventure."

"Maybe while I'm here we can pick a date. It would be great to spend more time with you."

"It might be easier for me to get away now that Lottie seems to be feeling better. She is still supposed to be on her back most of the time, but lately she's been able to play with the boys. Last night she even helped Nate wash the dishes."

"Wonderful. When is she due? It can't be long now."

"We're in the ninth month. Dr. Stimpson is with her now. He's beginning to think that she may be able to have this baby naturally."

Ethan felt glad that Lottie might soon return to health, but he knew that Franny would then be leaving, returning to her regular life. How could he be able to make her stay for a while? Thoughts about life without her nearly made him forget the reason he had come.

"Francena, I've come to bring a message from your aunt. She sends shocking news, so I ask you again not to dislike me for being the messenger."

"I didn't hold it against you last time, did I? And you have to admit that news was pretty shocking."

"Well, this is just as shocking. She, Mary, and Janey Cain have returned safely from the visit to Aphia Stevens in prison."

"Great! That's not at all bad news."

"I know, but the rest is horrible. Your friend Bert has been shot dead, as has the Stevens woman. Aunt Liz and the others apparently witnessed both killings."

"*What?* How did it happen?"

"Don't know. She said you'd get the details next time you saw her. That's all I know."

Franny sat down on the ground, leaning back against the gate post. She looked up at the barn and then the chimney. "Oh my God, Ethan. Lottie told me Con foresaw Bert's death in a dream last night. An eagle the man had shot killed him as it perished."

Ethan didn't quite understand what she was saying. "He saw the man's death in a dream? How strange."

"I never told you that the boy also dreamed about Eugene's death. I knew about it even before you told me."

"How can that happen? It's spooky."

"Nate says Con has a sixth sense about other people's problems. I think he's clairvoyant."

"That's a French word, isn't it? I've heard of that, but don't know much about it. Must be difficult for him."

125

The entire family gathered for Bert's burial at the family plot next to the graves of Lizzie and Hattie's grandparents. Nathan had made all the arrangements as soon as he returned home from his business trip. At first, he had been reluctant to treat Bert like family, but neither Hattie nor Lizzie would accept anything else. Maeve, too, was insistent because of the long relationship the dead man had with her dear Will. Mary attended out of respect for the sacrifice the departed had made for Lizzie. Lottie and Nate sent flowers but were unable to attend because she was recovering from the birth of their new baby boy.

At first, Franny wasn't sure she could make it until Ethan offered to drive her there and back in Tim Nason's surrey. They left immediately after the service to return to North Waterford before it got too dark. She still was needed to help the Halletts during the final days of her friend's recovery. As they rode along Bridgton Road, she thanked him kindly for accompanying her.

"You are so dear to drive me," she said. "It's good to have your company on such a long journey."

CHEYENNE (Shy Ann)
(Harry H. Williams/Egbert Van Alstyne)
Billy Murray—1906

(Indian War Whoops)

Way out in old Wyoming long ago
Where coyotes lurk while night winds howl and blow
A cowboy's lusty voice rang out "Hello"
And echoed through the valley down below
Then came back a maiden's answer sweet and clear
Cowboy tossed his hat up in the air
Said he, "I've come to take you right away from here
Cheyenne they say is miles away, but they've a preacher there"
Then she just drooped her eye, she was so very shy
So shy, oh my!, and then he made reply

Oooh-oooh-oooh
Shy Ann, shy Ann, hop on my pony
There's room here for two, Dear
But after the ceremony
We'll both ride back home, Dear, as one
On my pony from old Cheyenne

(Indian War Whoops)

They rode that night and nearly half the day
Cheyenne was sixty-seven miles away
But when at last they galloped up the street
The cowboy's pride was really hard to beat
On his arm, his future bride a-carrying
But beneath the little church's dome
Said she, "I feel like turning back, not marrying"
His face got red and then he said, "You will or you'll walk home
If you ride back today, you honour and obey"
"I will" she cried, then he was heard to say

Oooh-oooh-oooh
Shy Ann, shy Ann, hop on my pony
There's room here for two, Dear
But after the ceremony
We'll both ride back home, Dear, as one
On my pony from old Cheyenne

(Indian War Whoops)

(Transcribed by Mel Priddle—October 2007)

"These last couple of weeks have not been too easy on you. It was my pleasure to make your life a little easier."

She slipped her arm into his and put her head on his shoulder. He began to hum a funny tune that she didn't recognize.

"What is that snappy little tune?"

"Oh, that's a song I've been trying to memorize called 'Cheyenne.' They have one of those Edison machines at the Alpine Hotel. I've been playing this song over and over to learn the words. I like the melody. It's sung by an Irishman named Billy Murray."

"'Cheyenne'? Like the town in Wyoming? That's one of the locations in *The Virginian*, you know. Do you know enough of the lyrics to be able to sing it for me?"

"Probably, but you might not like my singing voice. I only sing for myself."

"Oh, go on. Give it a try. I won't judge you."

He hummed for a few more seconds, then cleared his throat. When he started to sing, she looked up at him with her mouth wide open. He had a splendid voice. When he finished, she applauded and patted him on the back.

"Great job, Ethan. You have a wonderful baritone. What a funny song. Could you sing it again? This time I'll write down the words so I can learn them also. We might sing together."

He laughed so loud that the horse kicked its front legs and lost the pace. To get the animal back on track, he pulled the reins and stopped for a moment. Tying the reins around the carriage's brake handle, he reached into his vest pocket and pulled out a sheet of paper.

"No need to write the words down, Franny. Here they are on this note paper. I carry it with me and read them whenever I have a chance. Here, I'll hold the page so we can sing together. Just follow me."

The tune was simple, and she picked it up quickly. Soon the two of them were singing their hearts out with no one to hear them but the horse and a flock of sparrows that pecked weeds at the roadside. His arms were spread wide. Her hands were clutched to her chest. A splendid duet.

At the conclusion, she laughed so hard that her bonnet came off, letting her long hair fall down her back. Without hesitation, he put his arm around her shoulders, pulled her close and kissed her cheek. She stopped laughing and returned his kiss with a more passionate one on his lips. Then she pulled back and touched her fingers to his mouth.

"Ethan, we have such fun together. I enjoy your company so. Those times when I've been short with you are not your fault, but mine. There are many complications in my life that I have been trying to work out."

"I, too, have such 'complications,' as you call them."

"Well, perhaps we can work on our difficulties together."

Again, she kissed him, then put her arms around his chest, nestling her head under his chin. His heartbeat was racing. She knew his passion had been aroused, as had her own.

"Would you go to Cheyenne with me, Ethan? And to Arizona to see the Grand Canyon? I've read so much about these places that they often appear in my dreams. I know you are not one for traveling and would be happy to stay in Waterford forever. But if we journeyed together, you might enjoy other adventurous sites."

He was silent for a moment, then began to hum the tune once again.

"Would we be able to go to these places on our honeymoon?" he asked.

"Perhaps we could. But you will have to make one promise to me before I accept your proposal."

Snatching the paper from his hand, she scanned down to a few lines in the second verse:

Said she, "I feel like turning back, not marrying."
His face got red and then he said, "You will, or you'll walk home.
If you ride back today, you honour and obey." *

"You must promise you will not make me walk all the way home from Cheyenne to Waterford, if I don't honor and obey you all the time."

"I do," he said.

Afterword

Why is Francena reading *The Virginian*? America's romance with the wild "Olde West" of cowboys and Indians, wide open spaces and skies that go on forever lasted only three decades, 1865-95. It was the era of Manifest Destiny when pursuit of continental expansion by a nascent society permitted all manner of lawlessness and cruelty in the name of progress. The naivety of our American spirit, personified by the unchecked escapades of the cowboy became deeply embedded in our country's psyche. In that rough and tumble fictional world the cowboy heroes protected weaker women characters, often saving a fair damsel from a wicked Simon Legree.

Following the War between the States, short stories by journalist Brett Harte popularized images of life in an unspoiled environment of cattle drives and gun slingers. In 1902 Owen Wister's *The Virginian*, recognized as the first novel of the American West, became so popular that it was reprinted ten times during the first year following its release. By 1903 a play based on the western opened first in Boston and then played to full houses in New York City for six months. In 1914 and again in 1923, two silent movie versions were released. A talkie followed in 1929, starring Cary Grant; then a second in 1946. While these movies were not true to Wister's storyline, they did succeed in cementing the myth of the valiant cowboys and their sweet damsels in the public mind.

Francena Hallett my protagonist, like tens of millions, sees in that novel a romantic world, appealing because it differs so much from her own. She wants to visit Cheyenne, Wyoming, setting of the western, to confirm that her visualizations of the Wild West are true. Reading about Teddy Roosevelt's journey into the Grand Canyon whets her appetite for travel.

She absorbs so much of the mythic romanticism that she is confused. It sets her to wondering about the men she meets. Would one offer her a stable life, but be unable to take her on exciting adventures? Would another fill her life with excitement and chivalry, like a cowboy, but bring her life to an impoverished ruin?

Francena is a more modern woman than Molly Stark Wood, Wister's heroine in *The Virginian*. Franny wants to live an independent life. Can she do so unencumbered by outdated gender roles? In the twenty first century, when we look back at the images of men and women in the rip-roaring rush of Manifest Destiny, is it at all surprisingly we find such ingrained myths so difficult to put aside?

Sources

An Early History of Pride's Corner by John R. Lewis. Published in 1968 by the Men's Club of The Pride's Corner Congregational Church. Permission to use Bailey drowning map from Mr. Lewis and the Westbrook Historical Society.

The Virginian, A Horseman of the Plains by Owen Wister. Published in 1902. In the public domain in the US.

Selected Stories of Bret Harte. 1940. Puritan Publishing, Boston. Source of short story *Mliss*

History of Waterford 1775-1875. Waterford, Maine Historical Society.

Waterford, Maine, 1875-1976. Waterford Historical Society. 1976.

This is Waterford, Written Reflections on Life in Maine 1803-2003. Waterford Historical Society. 2003.

Cheyenne. Popular song recorded by Billy Murray in 1906. Lyrics by Harry Williams, music by Egbert Van Alstyne. Published by Jerome H. Remick & Co., New York. In the public domain in the US and Europe.